FINDING felicity

ALSO BY STACEY KADE

Novels for Young Adults

For This Life Only

The Ghost and the Goth

Queen of the Dead

Body & Soul

Project Paper Doll: The Rules

Project Paper Doll: The Hunt

Project Paper Doll: The Trials

Novels for Adults

Bitter Pill

738 Days

Starlight Nights

FINDING felicity

STACEY KADE

SIMON & SCHUSTER BFYR
NEW YORK LONDON TORONTO SYDNEY NEW DELHI

An imprint of Simon & Schuster Children's Publishing Division
1230 Avenue of the Americas, New York, New York 10020

For information about special discounts for bulk purchases, please contact
Simon & Schuster Special Sales at 1-866-506-1949
or business@simonandschuster.com.
The Simon & Schuster Speakers Bureau can bring authors to your live event. For more information or to book an event, contact the Simon & Schuster Speakers Bureau at 1-866-248-3049 or visit our website at www.simonspeakers.com.
Also available in a SIMON & SCHUSTER BFYR hardcover edition
Cover design by Lucy Ruth Cummins
Interior design by Hilary Zarycky
The text for this book was set in New Caledonia.
Manufactured in the United States of America
First SIMON & SCHUSTER BFYR paperback edition March 2019
2 4 6 8 10 9 7 5 3 1
The Library of Congress has cataloged the hardcover edition as follows:
Names: Kade, Stacey, author.
Title: Finding Felicity / Stacey Kade.
Description: First edition.
| New York : Simon & Schuster Books for Young Readers, [2018] |
Summary: Caroline must leave behind her fantasy world inspired by a 1990s television show and create a real life at college, despite her mother's concerns and her own self-doubt.
Identifiers: LCCN 2017015756 | ISBN 9781481464253 (hardcover : alk. paper) | ISBN 9781481464260 (pbk) | ISBN 9781481464277 (eBook)
Subjects: | CYAC: Interpersonal relations—Fiction. | Honesty—Fiction. | Self-esteem—Fiction. | Universities and colleges—Fiction. | Mothers and daughters—Fiction.
Classification: LCC PZ7.K116463 Fin 2018 | DDC [Fic]—dc23
LC record available at https://lccn.loc.gov/2017015756

TO ALL THE RESIDENTS OF 4 NORTH, LANKENAU HALL,
VALPARAISO UNIVERSITY

BUT ESPECIALLY BECKY DOUTHITT, DEBBIE BROWN,
EDWARD BROWN*, AND JULIE OSBORNE.
SO VERY GRATEFUL FOR YOU.

(*Okay, you didn't *technically* live on the fourth floor with us, but I'm counting it. You were there almost as often as we were. And always with your impeccable timing!)

Chapter One

By the time graduation is over, I just want to go home. The bobby pins my mom used to attach my cap are digging into my scalp, my strapless bra is sinking slowly toward my waist, and a sticky sheen of perspiration clings to my skin, thanks to the polyester confines of my graduation gown.

I'm done.

Unfortunately, Mom has other ideas.

"We're celebrating," she says, turning the car away from the direction of our house. "Netflix will be there when you get back. You only graduate from high school once, and we're going out to mark the occasion."

I feel a lightning bolt of dread. "Really, it's okay," I say. "We don't have to—"

"I'm not taking no for an answer, Caroline! Besides, we

already have reservations at your favorite place." She gives me a hurt look.

So I guess that settles that.

A dull roar of conversation and laughter greets us as soon as I pull open the door to Lucci's. It's crowded tonight with other graduates and their families, and I'm caught between trying to avoid eye contact and studying the faces to see who's here. Sweat prickles on my upper lip.

Luckily, with a reservation we're not stuck in the waiting area long before a hostess is leading us to a booth. Hopefully, a very dark booth, waaaaay in the back.

But about halfway there, Mom stops abruptly. "Oh, look, there's Mrs. Davidson. I need to say hello," Mom says, changing direction and threading her way through the tables.

Even with my desperation to sit—to hide—eating at me, I know better than to protest. It won't help. My mom works at the Merriman Hospital Foundation, in fundraising. She recruits donors and makes sure that their family members receive VIP treatment if they're ever patients at the hospital. It's her job to make sure they feel taken care of, which means she's on call pretty much 24/7, especially when one of her "people" is admitted or comes in to rule out a heart attack at three in the morning. She spends a lot of time coordinating with her donor families and networking with doctors. "It's all about relationships," she always says.

"How are you, dear?" Mrs. Davidson asks me, once she and Mom have covered the basics of small talk.

I smile and try to say, "Great!" But my throat does that thing where it convulses midway through a word, and I end up choking on my own spit.

"Too much excitement," my mom says with a laugh, patting me on the back as I sputter.

Can we just go home now? That would be celebration enough.

"Get whatever you want, Caroline," Mom says, once we're finally seated with menus. "And no arguments—we're ordering dessert, too. One for each of us!"

Normally, I'm the last person who has to be talked into getting dessert. But right now I want to be in and out as fast as possible. One wrong person walking in, the wrong family choosing Lucci's to celebrate graduation, and I could still be totally screwed.

But Mom is looking at me, so hopeful that all I can do is nod and say, "Okay."

Dinner takes forever, mainly because Mom can't decide what she wants, which is odd. We've been here hundreds of times over the years.

And she's being . . . weird. Studying her menu, avoiding my gaze, except when I catch her staring at me, her eyes almost welling to tears.

Finally I have to ask: "Is everything okay?" My stomach is tight with dread, and every time the door chimes, signaling new arrivals, I have to fight the urge to look over my shoulder.

But if there's something wrong with Mom . . . My imagination shoots rapid-fire through various disastrous scenarios: cancer, laid off, marrying some guy who wishes I didn't exist.

She waves my words away. "I'm fine. A little emotional, that's all." She takes a deep breath. "My baby, graduating and going away to start college!"

I'm not sure I believe her, but she promptly dives into a one-sided discussion about the pros and cons of ricotta cheese, clearly signaling that *that* branch of conversation is over.

And then, after what feels like an eternity, we're finished eating, the dishes are gone, and the waiter—who vanished for, like, twenty minutes—has finally returned with the check.

It takes everything I have not to bolt for the door as soon as Mom signs the receipt. I feel like I'm escaping my doom by a narrow margin, somehow. Which is ridiculous, because *nothing* happened. I've made it. I graduated. I'm done. Safe.

Mom is quiet on the drive home. Too quiet.

"Are you sure you're okay?" I press. "You know I'll come home on breaks. I'll only be gone for a couple of months at a time."

"I know, sweetie, I know." She reaches over and pats my hand with a laugh. "I'll be all right."

"If you don't have to work tomorrow, we could stay up tonight and watch one of your old movies. I'll let you pick a black-and-white one," I offer.

"Oh, such a sacrifice," she says, rolling her eyes. "You know the classics are the ones everybody else steals from."

"Yeah, yeah."

It's an old argument, comforting in its familiarity. But it doesn't seem to help much. The silence in the car is still too loud, and Mom seems nervous—anxious, almost—and I don't know why.

Once we're home, I start to head upstairs to change, but she stops me.

"Nope, not that way," she says with a wide smile, as she forcibly steers me toward the sliding glass door onto the patio.

And only then do I understand why the evening was so drawn out and why she seemed on edge.

Oh no.

Our backyard has been transformed into something out of a movie. A dozen tall tables—wrapped in white tablecloths and tied off with red ribbons to match our school colors—decorate the brick patio. White tea-light candles flicker on mirrored centerpieces. The band is setting up under a tent near the far end of the pool, which is full of red and white floating candles, bobbing gently with the motion of the filtration system. There's even an ice sculpture by the punch bowl in the shape of our graduation year, although the 2 and the 0 are already melting.

"I don't understand," I say, my voice coming out in a squeak. I face my mom. "What is this?"

"Surprise!" my mom says, beaming at me.

That is an understatement. It's absolutely perfect. And absolutely horrible.

"Sophie set it up while we were at dinner. I was so afraid I'd give it away!" She laughs. "I know you suspected something, but not this, right?"

"No," I agree weakly. Never, ever, this.

Mom steps forward to reach up and wrap an arm around my shoulders. Thanks to a late-breaking growth spurt, I'm now a few inches taller than she is. "You deserve it. It was rough starting over, but you dug in and made a life for yourself here. You kept your grades up and found your place with the yearbook committee and so many clubs." She shakes her head. "I'm not sure how you did it all."

Being on yearbook helps. If you're in charge of organizing the sign-ups for pictures, it's easy enough to slide into whatever photos you want. Boom. Instant proof of club membership.

"I'm so proud of you, Caroline." Her eyes sparkle with tears as she squeezes my shoulders.

"Thanks," I say past the lump in my throat.

"I know you said you and your friends weren't doing much for graduation night." Mom pokes me in my side.

I give a strangled laugh. "That . . . is what I said." *Because I'm an idiot.*

"So I thought it'd be the perfect opportunity to finally meet everyone. I've only been able to meet a few of them because my work schedule always seems to conflict," she says. "Actually, only Joanna, I guess." She frowns.

"Who did you invite?" I'm going to wake up at any second, right?

"We sent open-house invitations to the school, enough for everyone in your class," Mom says. Looking for confirmation, she glances toward Sophie, her personal assistant, who is waiting by the sliding glass doors into the house.

"Yes, Regina." Sophie gives a brisk nod, like a check mark on one of her endless lists.

"It said to keep it a surprise," my mom says. "I guess that must have worked, huh?"

"Mm-hmm." A sickening pit opens up in my stomach. So *this* is the source of those whispers and the sideways glances I received over the last couple of weeks at school.

"I know a lot of the kids will have their own family events tonight, but hopefully, they can stop by for a few minutes," Mom says, sounding so pleased with herself.

"I . . . that's great." I force the corners of my mouth up

into a smile and try hard not to pull at the sweaty fabric of my dress, growing damper by the second. My mind spins, rapidly casting up scenarios and dispensing with them just as swiftly.

If I tell Mom I feel sick, she'll blame it on excitement or eating too much rich food at dinner. She'll tell me to drink some ginger ale and lie down for a few minutes until my "friends" get here.

A hysterical laugh threatens to bubble up and out of my throat. A complete emotional breakdown, which would be both real and convenient, might distract her, but it wouldn't keep her from noticing the truth.

This is going to crush her. And it won't be great for me, either. If she finds out . . .

"I promise, I won't be in the way," Mom says, holding up her hand. "A few people from work have stopped by." She nods back toward the great room, where the now-lit-up windows reveal a handful of adults, mingling already with wine glasses in hand. "Keeping me company while I get used to the idea of being an empty nester." She flattens her palm against her chest with a dramatic sigh.

"Mom . . ."

"I'm teasing." Mom squeezes me once more. "Have a good time!" Then she disappears with Sophie into the house.

They reappear in the great room, visible through the windows. And the second my mom walks into the room, people make a beeline for her. Everyone loves her.

Seeing that sets off a pang of envy in me. I don't know how she does it, how anyone does. It seems that if you're going to form any real bond, people have to either really like you (my mom) or really need you (my dad).

But I've never been able to figure out what happens if you're not enough to make them feel anything.

I turn away from the house to walk along the edge of the pool, as if motion will somehow convey purpose and confidence to anyone watching. It really is perfect out here. Exactly the party I would have wanted. Under normal circumstances.

My eyes water, and I edge my finger carefully under them to keep my mascara from running. I don't want my mom to know that I've been crying when she comes back out to check on me, as she inevitably will when no one shows up.

What am I going to do?

I'm seriously contemplating whether a small fire—a few tea-light candles somehow tipped over by the "wind"—would be enough to get my mom to cancel this before it gets any worse, when the wrought-iron gate to the backyard clangs open loudly.

Ridiculous hope sparks inside me. Like somehow all the "friends" I've ever mentioned to my mother might suddenly parade into the yard.

But it's just Joanna. Her long dark hair is falling out of its braid, and she, unlike me, has been allowed to change her clothes. She's wearing leggings with a hole in the knee, and the thigh is covered in streaks of purple paint (used for shading on the dragon's wings in her mural project), and an oversized *Game of Thrones* T-shirt. Or, knowing Jo, maybe that's what she wore beneath her graduation robe.

"Nice spread," Joanna says as she steps onto the patio.

"You came," I blurt, rushing over as she moves to the food table.

"Yeah." Joanna drags a corn chip through the avocado dip. "My parents aren't big on the graduation-party thing. Not when you're the third kid. We're going to my grandparents' on Sunday for cake."

"Why didn't you tell me about this?" I hiss. True, Joanna and I aren't exactly close. We're friends by default. Lunch-room refugees who didn't have anywhere else to go. I was starting over in a new school and a new state (which might as well have been on another planet for all that Arizona had in common with New York), and horribly awkward. Still am. Joanna is just weird and doesn't care what anyone thinks. She once came to school dressed as her favorite character from *Game of Thrones*, with stuffed dragons on chains and everything. And it wasn't even Halloween. But despite our differences and our lack-of-other-options friendship, I still would have expected her to give me a heads-up about something of this magnitude.

"The invitation said it was a surprise." Joanna scoops the chip into her mouth, dribbling some of the dip down the front of her T-shirt, a green blob on Khaleesi's blond head. She wipes at it half-heartedly with a CONGRATULATIONS, CAROLINE! napkin. "What's wrong with you? It's not like anyone else is going to show up."

"Exactly!" I reach up to rake my hand through my hair, but stop in time, remembering the updo my mom insisted on. It is elegant and very Audrey Hepburn, not at all like me at the moment. Or ever.

"So what's the problem?" Joanna grabs a paper plate emblazoned with the words HAPPY GRADUATION! and piles on some shrimp rolls. "I think it's nice that your mom wanted to do it, even if we're the only ones here."

I take a deep breath and open my mouth to explain, but then I get a mental flash of Jo's reaction: nose wrinkled, her face scrunched up in disgust. She won't understand this. For someone who's obsessed with a show about medieval power structures, she has always been remarkably unconcerned with our position at the lonely end of the social ladder in high school.

"I need you to do me a favor," I say instead. Maybe this can still work out.

"Okay," Joanna says warily, around a mouthful of shrimp. "What?"

"When you go to say hi to my mom . . . ," I begin.

Joanna's perfectly groomed eyebrows—one of her older sisters tackled her and wouldn't let her up until there were two instead of one—go up.

"I need you to say something like, 'It's too bad Felicity couldn't be here because of the family emergency.' And that Julie and Elena are out of town." These new lies won't zero out the others that have come before them. Not even close. Mom will still have questions—and possibly, eventually, suspicions—but the story might get me through tonight, through this party. Hopefully. And it'll be way more effective coming from Joanna than me. My mom has never said, but I think she finds Joanna . . . disconcerting.

Jo is blunt and occasionally graceless in conversation, especially with adults. I tend to freeze up, but Joanna stomps right through, like a grimly determined soldier with the end of battle in sight. It won't occur to my mom that Joanna is lying, as it might if I tried it, because Joanna doesn't bother with—or is oblivious to the need for—polite social fibs. *The lasagna was cold and a little burned. Actually, no, your new haircut looks . . . lopsided.*

"I don't even know who you're talking about," Jo says. "Felicity? We don't even know anyone named . . ." She pauses. "Wait, like on that show you're always—"

"It doesn't matter," I say. "Can you just do this for me, please?" I squeeze my hands together in a plea.

She narrows her eyes at me, taking in my poorly disguised panic. Then her expression clears, and she sets her plate down on the table. "Is this about Liam?" Her tone is cool, deadly.

"No!" *Not exactly. Not at first, at least.*

"Bye, Caroline," she says with disgust, the exact reaction I was trying to avoid. She pivots away from the food table and starts toward the gate.

I chase after her. "Wait, Jo, it's not what you think!"

She pauses, shaking her head. "Seriously, Caroline? I have no idea what you're talking about, but it's always about him, one way or another. Isn't it."

I don't answer, because it's not a question. Also, because she wouldn't like the answer.

"It's pathetic," she says.

I flinch. She said "it's," but I know she means "you're."

"He's not that great. No one is. You build up these bizarre expectations and hopes around someone you don't even know."

But I do know him! As much as you can know someone you've talked to once—twice if you count the whole bake-sale incident. It doesn't matter, though.

He's my Ben.

"What about you?" Joanna continues. "Who are *you*? What do *you* want? What about, I don't know"—she puffs air up toward her forehead, making wisps of hair dance—"reality? What's wrong with reality?"

"Nothing," I say in a small voice. Unless your reality sucks. Then what's wrong with wanting something more or better?

Joanna sighs. "I'll see you around, Caroline. Good luck with . . . everything." She moves toward the gate with weary steps, her shoulders rounded, as if talking to me has exhausted her.

"Was that Joanna?" My mom emerges from the house, Sophie trailing after.

"She . . . had to go. Family stuff," I say. The words taste bitter. Was it so much to ask of our friendship that she help me out with this one thing?

"Really?" Mom asks, doubt filling her voice. She hesitates. "Caroline, is there something you want to tell me?"

"Like what?" I ask, stalling for time.

"Like why Joanna didn't stay? And where everyone else is?" she asks, and the gentleness in her voice makes me feel even worse. "Did something happen?" She reaches out to smooth my hair. Her dark hair is only a shade or two lighter than mine, and she's talked for years about dyeing it to match my "gorgeous color." "I know it gets complicated with college looming. It changes the dynamic. Especially when *someone* is insisting on attending a school so far away." She levels a pointed look at me.

"It's fine," I say quickly. I don't want college to come up anywhere in this conversation. It's a pristine box of untouched future, untainted by everything in my present. I have a plan. I'm going to have the life I'm supposed to have; I just need to survive tonight. "You know . . . the usual drama. A dumb fight. Joanna will get over it."

"And Felicity?" my mom prompts gently.

Oh God. "She's probably over it already," I say.

"Baby." Mom reaches out and pulls me closer. "Change is always hard. But never doubt yourself. You are absolutely perfect, just as you are. And your friends will realize that eventually."

The backyard blurs as tears fill my eyes. *If only that were true, Mom. Any of it.*

I take a deep breath and pull away once my emotions are back under control. "Mom, your guests," I say, giving her a gentle push toward the house. "You know, there's that new wine bar downtown. Maybe you guys could take this party on the road."

Could I eat enough appetizers to make it look like twenty people have come and gone by the time she's back? If not, that's what the neighbors' trash cans are for.

Sorry, Mom, you just missed my friends!

She pats me on the shoulder with a fond smile. "No, we're fine." Then she turns to stare at the empty party area. "I still think it's rude of them not to show up, fight or no fight. They can't all be that busy tonight." She bites her lip. "Maybe I should call Liam's mom to see if he's coming."

"No!" The word explodes out of me.

My mother gives me a strange look. "Honey, I'm sure she wouldn't mind. I don't know Dr. Fanshaw that well." She pauses. "Pediatrician," she says to Sophie.

Sophie nods immediately. "I have her number."

"But I think she would understand—"

"Please, let me handle it my way," I say, sweat trickling down my back to collect at the base of my spine. If she calls Dr. Fanshaw, it's over.

After a beat, my mother nods. "All right, if that's what you want." But her mouth is pulled up in a sympathetic grimace.

"It is."

She touches my cheek. "Okay."

"Good." Relief rushes through me like a dam has broken. I'm still going to have to answer questions later tonight, but at least there's this mythical falling-out to help explain things. And she can't expect me to talk about something that's obviously painful.

As soon as my mom returns to the house, I make my way to the other side of the patio, out of sight of the windows, as if that will convince her that guests have arrived and I must be off talking to them somewhere.

The band sounds more than decent, and the food smells delicious, making my mouth water, despite the fact that I've already eaten a full dinner.

For a moment I allow myself to imagine what it *would* be like. People chatting at the food table, possibly shoving around one another to get at the shrimp rolls. Someone would have spiked the bowl of punch by the ice sculpture by now, I'm sure.

I would be moving easily around the party, speaking to this group or that one, without stammering or freezing up. Maybe flirting a little with Liam, who would take me under his wing, including me in the conversations I would normally miss.

I can see it so clearly that it makes my heart lift temporarily. I want that feeling of belonging, of being accepted. Confident in knowing that they're mine and I'm theirs.

But it's not real. I blink and the image in my head is gone, not even lingering like the flash from a camera. Just gone.

An all-too-familiar sadness, the kind that always comes from the bubble bursting, rises up in me. It happens a lot more now than it used to. Some of the stories I've created in my head or told to my mom are so real and so close to what I want, it feels like a loss when something breaks the spell.

But this time I straighten my shoulders and push that sadness away. It's different now. Because in three months, I'll have my fresh start at college. I'll have my friends. And none of it will be fictional. I just have to be patient for a little longer.

I head toward the food table to kill some more time and because the meatballs in particular smell amazing. But as I do, I catch a glimpse of my mom through the bay window in the kitchen. And she's on the house phone, her brow furrowed.

A hospital call, maybe. Especially with Sophie there at her side, reading something off her ever-present tablet. Though Mom usually gets calls from the hospital on her cell phone. . . .

The pieces click together a fraction of a second too late. She's already talking.

Oh no.

"Mom!" I run for the house and throw myself through the partially open sliding glass door, my hip colliding with the edge of the metal frame. Pain shoots through me like an electric shock, but I keep moving.

I burst into the kitchen. "Mom! Hang up!"

"At Stella's lake house. I see," my mother says into the phone, turning away from me.

Dread bubbles up in me, like the nasty slime that spreads through the pool when the chemicals are wrong.

I can't hear what Liam's mom is saying, but I can fill in the blanks, imagine her confusion at this call. I've never been to Liam's house, never met his mother, though I've seen her when I've driven by their home.

I knew the truth would eventually come out—I'm not stupid—but I always imagined it as something I'd tell my mom years from now, something we'd laugh about long after it lost the power to hurt either of us.

"I don't understand," my mom says, fidgeting with a wine cork left abandoned on the quartz counter of the island. She is steadfastly avoiding looking at me. "Does this have something to do with the girls? Their falling out?"

I freeze, a statue in a too-bright floral print. *The girls. Oh no, no, no.* "Mom, please," I try again, moving closer. "Hang up."

But she's frowning at something Dr. Fanshaw is saying.

And then time seems to grind to an excruciating halt. "I'm sure you know them. Joanna Duncan, Felicity Porter, Elena Tyler, and Julie—"

"They're fictional!" I shout. Anything to make her stop. "I made it all up!"

My mom's head snaps around to face me, her mouth hanging open in shock.

"Not Joanna," I say slowly. "But Felicity, Julie, Elena, they're television characters. I borrowed them. I . . . needed them."

Mom stares at me, the color draining from her cheeks.

Liam's mother says something, tinny and faint in the phone, but I can't hear what.

Oh God. I turn away and sink to the floor in front of the island, the cool tiles burning through my dress to my skin.

"I'm going to have to call you back," my mom says into the phone finally. "Yes, I'll be sure to clarify with Caroline." Her words, thin with anger and confusion, sound like the end of everything.

Chapter Two

It's not as bad as it sounds.

Okay, maybe it is. But it's not like I always intended to lie.

It's just . . . I've never really connected with anyone. You know, having that one person—or maybe even a couple of people—who is a true friend, someone you can text when your life is turning to utter crap, and they know exactly what to say. How to help. And you're that person for them, too. It's like your own version of family, you know? Framily, like in that stupid commercial.

I had friends in New York. But my yearbook was always filled with messages like, *Carolyn, it was great sitting next to you in geometry! Have an awesome summer!* Or, *Stay sweet, Caroline!* But once class or book club or whatever was over, the friendship went with it. My two closest friends, if you could call them that, were Aurelia and Madison: a pair of best friends who preferred to have a third as a backup, in case of an argument or scheduling conflict.

If it sounds like I'm feeling sorry for myself, let me be clear—Madison told me as much one day when we were eleven. "I wanted Aurelia to come over, but she's at her cousin's birthday party," Madison said with a dramatic sigh. "So my mom said I should invite you. But we're *not* playing with the stupid Barbies this time."

Looking back, maybe Barbies *were* babyish at that point, but Madison had piles of them, including a Ken with a beard that you could shave. And the Barbie pool! At my house, the Barbies had the bathroom sink for a pool—usually filled with globs of toothpaste and hair from my dad.

So I guess what I'm trying to say is that I've always been out of sync with everyone else. Like they received an e-mail on what to say and do, how to talk to people, what to be interested in. But my version of that e-mail never reached me. (Maybe because my mom refused to let me have my own e-mail account until I was in high school, and she still thinks AOL is a thing.)

And all of that was *before* we moved across the country to Arizona. My dad took off with his girlfriend, and then suddenly Mom and I were packing boxes. New job for Mom, one that would support us without Dad, and a new town. When I walked into Merriman High South on the first day of sophomore year, it was like landing on Mars. Literally. It was hot and dry and dusty. The buildings were white, flat, and low to the ground. No public transportation; everyone drove. Even their clothes were different. The girls wore short shorts and strappy tops that would have gotten you sent home the second you crossed the doorway at Saint Agnes.

Plus, it was a small school; everyone already knew each other. They had established friendships, inside jokes, and lunch tables. It was completely overwhelming. I didn't even know where to begin.

So I did what anyone would: I hid. Behind books, shows, movies, and music. Whatever I could buy/download/stream on my phone, the savior of shy and awkward people everywhere. You aren't alone and unwanted; you're reading, watching, listening to something on your phone. *Do not disturb.*

And it worked, for a while. That's how I found Joanna. She was pretty much doing the same thing, only she'd lived here her whole life.

But then two things happened. My mom emerged from her work coma—eat, sleep, work, but mostly work—to start questioning me about school. Who was I talking to, what clubs had I joined, was I doing okay? Apparently, homecoming, both the game and the dance, was a big deal in Merriman, enough that the other parents at the hospital were talking about it. Buying dresses, scheduling hair appointments, ordering corsages, etc. I hadn't said anything about it—because I wasn't going, obviously—and that had raised a red flag with her.

I'm honestly not sure why. It wasn't like I would have gone to homecoming in New York. We didn't even do that at Saint Agnes, not in the same way. It was more like a career day, with alums coming back to talk to our classes.

The second thing that happened was, around that same time, I discovered the wonder and majesty that is Felicity Porter. Okay, she's not actually majestic, but that's kind of the point.

Felicity is a show from the late nineties. It started before I was even born. But that doesn't matter, because Felicity and I? Total soul mates.

She is possibly the most awkward person on the planet—besides me, I mean—and there's a whole show about her, where she's the main character, *not* the comic relief.

Basically, it's a show about a girl who, at high school graduation, talks to this guy she's had a crush on for years. She's never had the courage to speak to him before, and when she does—asking him to sign her yearbook—he, Ben, writes the most amazing message. A message that convinces her that (a) she's in love with him and (b) she should throw away her very carefully outlined future (Stanford, med school, doctor) to follow him to New York for college.

That one moment changes her life. *He* changes her life.

Of course, it's not just about Ben, but also about Felicity figuring out who she is, who she wants to be. And in the process she finds people who love and accept her, even with her awkwardness showing like granny panties over the top of those awesome nineties jeans.

That show was the first time I'd ever watched anything and seen myself in it. My hair is not glossy and sleek. My complexion is iffy on its best day. I'm not good with witty retorts, I don't have more than one immortal male fighting over me (or any at all, for that matter), and I'm not gifted with a special destiny. But a girl who speaks before she thinks, hesitates and stammers her way through conversations, and feels like there's something missing or wrong with her life, even if she doesn't know what it is or how to get it? Yeah.

Felicity is my hero. And watching her stumble her way through figuring stuff out (friendships, parental drama, jealousy, plagiarism, pregnancy tests, college parties, sex, a crazy alt universe version of her life) made me feel less alone. Like we would be friends, if we knew each other. And, you know, if she were real.

So, one night over really horrible Chinese takeout, not long after the homecoming inquisition, when my mom started pushing with the questions again, the lies sort of . . . popped out.

"So tell me about school. How is it going? Have you made any new friends? Did you try the activities board, like I said?" My mom's expression brightened. "I'm telling you, that's how I met some of my best friends in high school. Signing up for anything that sounded interesting, even if I wasn't sure what it was." Her laugh sounded forced. "Always good to try new things."

"Mom, it's not . . . it doesn't work like that anymore," I said. "They don't have a board like that."

"Oh, how about dance?" she asked, leaning forward in encouragement. Or desperation. "You used to love going to your dance classes when you were a little girl. I'm sure there's a cheer squad or a pep team or something here!"

I went to ballet classes when I was eight because Aurelia and Madison were into it, and I wanted to be wherever they were. "No, I don't think that's for me, Mom."

She stayed quiet for a long moment. "I know this is hard for you. And you have no idea how sorry I am for that," she said, her voice breaking. "But I'm trying, I'm really trying, and we're doing okay, aren't we?" Tears spilled down her cheeks to drip off her chin, where she tried to catch them with one of the rough brown napkins.

It freaked me out, seeing her cry. I nodded quickly. "Yes, we're okay!"

"It's going to take some more time, that's all," she said,

trying to sound positive even as tears dripped onto the table below. "Moving. The divorce. New town. It's a lot to adjust to. But you're going to be okay. We both are." I wasn't sure if she was trying to convince herself or me, and something about her uncertainty made me feel all panicky inside.

"There is . . . I did meet someone new today," I blurted. Anything to make her stop crying.

Her face lit up. "You did?" she asked, sniffling.

"I . . . yeah. Her name is Felicity. She's new too. From California." The words spilled out as easily as the truth.

"Felicity? That's an unusual name. You don't hear that one very often." She took a bite of noodle and chewed, with a contemplative expression. "You know," she said, "I think there used to be a show called that. *Felicity.*"

I couldn't breathe for a second.

"I never watched it, though." She wrinkled up her nose. "Too melodramatic."

Melodramatic? *Melodramatic?* Try emotionally fraught and delicious with angsty tension.

I forced the edges of my mouth up in a smile. "Oh, yeah, I think she's, uh, named for that. The show."

"So, she's new to Merriman; that's good. You'll have that in common."

"Uh-huh."

"What else? Do you like any of the same shows?"

You could say that. "Yeah, but she's dealing with some stuff right now. She's kind of in love with this guy who doesn't know she exists. For now, at least."

"So, Felicity has a plan, then," my mom said, amusement flickering in her expression. I hadn't seen her that happy in a while.

Yes, yes, she does. Maybe not a good plan, but one that would do for the moment.

And that was that. I never meant for it to go on this long. I thought of it more like a placeholder. Something to keep my mom at bay until I had a chance to make real friends. Only that never happened, and I found I liked making up the stories. The crazy things Felicity and her friends—and therefore my friends—would get themselves into. Auditioning for the play and failing horribly because *someone* confused *Hamlet* and *Macbeth*. Going to the basketball games but sitting in the visitor section to cheer for our team and unnerve the opposing players. Driving by a crush's house until a neighbor freaked out about potential robbers and called the cops. I took the things I heard people talking about at school, the things they were doing, and reinvented them for myself, using versions of the characters from the show. It was like fan fiction . . . on crack. It was way easier than showing up places alone and putting myself out there, only to be ignored or rejected.

And it was harmless, mostly. Until tonight.

"Sophie, can you give us a minute, please?" my mom asks quietly.

My mom's assistant bobs her head in a nod and backs through the swinging door into the living room.

"Caroline, I don't think I understand," Mom says. But it sounds more like she's afraid that she does. "Can you explain, please?"

I take a deep breath. No matter what I say, it's not going to come off sounding good. But I have to try.

So I tell her everything. The move, how different it was here, how I wasn't particularly good at making friends to begin with, why Felicity was—and still is—important to me. Then I brace myself for the yelling to begin.

But she's silent instead, and that's worse. So much worse.

"You . . . borrowed them?" Mom says finally, her shaking voice lifting in question. "You made up stories about them? Made me think that they were real people? For *years*?" She sounds genuinely baffled, like I've told her I want to coat myself in honey and roll around on a nest of fire ants.

I wince. "I'm sorry. I didn't mean to—"

"I know maybe I wasn't handling everything very well, especially not during our first few months here but—"

"Mom, it's not that," I say.

She hesitates for a long moment. "Was this . . . honey, did this have anything to do with your dad leaving? I know you must have felt abandoned. But his leaving has nothing to do with you. He loves you, I'm sure of it."

A pain like poking at a bruise rises up. Sure, he does. That's why he cut me off as cleanly as a sixth finger, like those surgeries he performed on needy babies from other countries. People get divorced all the time and still stay in contact with their kids. But not my dad. His girlfriend and Guatemala—or wherever they're saving lives this week—are more of a draw than I am, apparently.

"No," I say. "I . . . I'm over that." I peel my sticky self from the kitchen tiles and stand to face my mom. Her arms are folded tightly across her middle, as if she's holding herself together.

"It's only . . . when we moved here, it was so different," I try again.

In the backyard, the band strikes up the first chords of a familiar song. "Brown-Eyed Girl." Murmurs of conversation and laughter from the adults drift through the closed door to the living room.

"Everyone here has been friends practically since birth. And they don't have to wear uniforms . . ."

"This is about school dress code?" Mom asks in disbelief.

"No! It was . . ." My words fail me.

She rubs her forehead wearily. "This is my fault," she says, more to herself than to me. "I knew I shouldn't have moved you once you'd started high school, but I couldn't—"

"No!" This is veering way too close to the arguments she and Dad had before he left, the ones they thought I couldn't hear. The blaming, the recriminations, Dad raining down the verbal blows—"too needy and way too damn emotional"—and Mom simply taking them. "You were so happy when I had something to report. When I told you about Felicity that first time. And I liked feeling like I fit in better than I did, better than I ever could," I add in a small voice. "It just got out of hand."

"But you went to the art show at school for Joanna and Felicity last year," she says, still trying to process. "To support them."

"The art show was real," I volunteer. "And Joanna had a couple of drawings in it. But . . ."

"But not Felicity. Because she's fictional." She gives a strangled, disbelieving laugh. "Her sweet-sixteen party, though—I saw pictures. I've *seen* pictures."

I squirm inwardly. "I . . . it's not that hard to borrow someone else's stuff on Instagram. I found a party that looked like it could be the right one. And some of the pictures were from Stella's sweet sixteen." To make it seem more real. None of the birthday girl herself, in a tiara, of course. But the partygoers had familiar faces, people my mom might recognize from town. Like Liam.

"You went to Stella's—"

I snort before I can stop myself. Stella Weaver is Liam's

girlfriend, probably the most popular girl in school, and kind of a bitch. "Like she would invite me anywhere." I bite my lip. "I went to the movies. When I was supposed to be at Felicity's party."

Mom's hand flutters at her neck, like the words are lodged in her throat. "I think maybe you need to see someone," she says.

It takes me a second to process what she means. "Like a psychiatrist?" I ask. "No, Mom."

The thought of talking to a stranger about my feelings or whatever—and seeing judgment, or worse, pity, in return—makes my chest hurt. And then what if I can't convince them that I'm okay—what if they think there's something really wrong with me?

What if there is?

I shove that thought down. "I'm fine," I say.

"I don't think you are," my mom says. "You know I tell my colleagues about you, about what you're up to." Mom takes a deep breath. "If they recognized the names from that television show—"

"I'm sorry," I whisper.

"This is serious, Caroline. I've worked hard to rebuild the foundation. People at the hospital and in town, they need to trust me. With their money, with their important patients. And I've been talking to them for years about these girls who don't exist. Do you realize what kind of damage that could do?"

I shift miserably. The truth is, I hadn't thought about it that way. I was just trying to make life here . . . livable.

She sighs. "I'm assuming that you're not really friends with Liam Fanshaw, either?"

Liam. Immediately I get a flash of him standing over me in the hall at school, helping me off the floor with that smile that makes his dimples show, those deep divots high on both sides of his mouth. I wanted to touch them, smooth them out.

I hesitate. "Not exactly."

"I can understand, sort of, why you might make up friends," she says, though her tone suggests otherwise. "But why would you lie about real people?"

"He was nice to me," I mumble.

"So why not actually be friends with him?" she demands, incredulous. "Why make up these stories and—"

"Because I can't!" I burst out. "It doesn't work like that. I don't know, maybe back when you were in high school, you could just walk up to people and start talking to them. But you can't do that now. Or . . . I can't." And maybe that was the real problem: *I* couldn't. Not here.

"I work with his mother," my mom says. "Not directly, but still. I've spoken to her about you in passing, in the cafeteria, in the coffee shop." Her fingers worry the jet beads of her necklace, before she forces herself to stop. "She must think I'm crazy after that phone call."

"I'm sure she doesn't," I say. "There's no way she knows all of Liam's friends. He knows everybody." He was the student council president, varsity basketball team captain, and homecoming king, twice.

Mom blanches. "So that makes it okay to lie about him? Because you can get away with it?"

"No, of course not! It wasn't like that," I say, curling my fingers over the edge of the counter in desperation. I can feel this conversation slipping away from me—if it was ever in my grasp to begin with. "But look, it doesn't even matter anymore." I fling my hand toward the window and the empty graduation party outside, the band still playing away. "High school is over. In three months, I'll be starting over somewhere else. At Ashmore. And this time I'll handle it better. I'm ready for it. I have a plan." College is about reinventing yourself, right? That's what Felicity did.

"Caroline, how am I supposed to send you off to a college halfway across the country after this?" she asks in disbelief. "I'm not even sure you can distinguish between reality and fiction."

I can't breathe for a second. "Mom, that's ridiculous! I know the difference, okay?" *I just choose to ignore it. Most of the time.* I blink back a sudden wash of tears. "Besides, Ashmore is expecting me. I have a roommate and everything." Lexi Chandler, from Iowa, a nursing major. From her profile picture, she looks just like what I imagined people from Iowa should—pretty, with wheat-colored hair and a big, open smile. She's local, too; she lives in Ashmore (the town), so she'll have a handle on what we need to know, good places to eat, cool things to do.

Mom ignores me. "You could still register for classes here and—"

"No, Mom, you don't understand. I need the chance to start over. I can't do that here." The thought of two or four more years of what would essentially be high school in a different location makes me shudder.

"But why Ashmore? It's a small liberal arts school in the middle of a bunch of cornfields."

This is a conversation we had multiple times in the spring.

"It has to be Ashmore," I say firmly. "It's the right place for me. They've accepted me and I'm *going*."

"Caroline . . ."

"So it's okay for you and Dad to pick up and leave, to split up and start over somewhere else, but not me?"

My mom stiffens. "You know that's not fair."

It isn't. It's not fair that she got stuck with me, that my dad got to take off and forget that we existed. Nothing about this situation is fair. Fair is no longer a guideline. For anything, it seems.

Her expression softens, revealing weariness beneath.

"Caroline, you know I want you to have every opportunity in the world, no matter what you choose."

Relieved, I nod. "Thank you. I'm telling you, once I'm at Ashmore—"

"That's why I have to make sure you're okay."

I straighten up, opening my mouth to protest.

She holds up her hand to stop me. "You need to talk to someone. Maybe this is some kind of phase or coping mechanism"—her forehead furrows at the idea—"but I want to hear that from a professional."

And there it is. My future, my fresh start, hangs in the balance, on the opinion of a stranger. What chance do I have of convincing a stranger of my reasons for doing what I did, when the person closest to me can't even understand?

My stomach hurts already.

"I don't want to mess you up any more than I already have," she says in a choked voice, before her hand flies up to cover her mouth, tears shining in her eyes.

Guilt sears through me. "Mom, you didn't," I say, moving forward to hug her awkwardly. "I'm okay, I really am."

She opens her arms, pulling me close. Maybe everything is going to be all right.

Then she steps back and squeezes my shoulders. "I'll call in a favor and make an appointment for tomorrow."

I need a plan. And fast.

Chapter Three

Dr. Wegman's office is not what I was expecting. Unlike what I've seen on various shows, it's not a rented space with cool gray walls and black-and-chrome furniture in a high-rise somewhere. Instead Dr. Wegman works out of a sunny room in the lower level of his house. It smells like peppermint and, vaguely, wet dog. But in a comforting, homey way.

The wood blinds are dusty and partially closed; I can see a sliver of bright turquoise water in his backyard. Every once in a while, a splash or shriek of laughter penetrates the glass of the window—the doctor's kids are playing in the pool.

"I'm not crazy," I say again, shifting uncomfortably on the soft, worn leather sofa. In my pocket, the edges of the talking-point index cards I prepared last night dig into my hip. It wasn't a *great* plan, but I managed to make it through my prepared speech without fumbling or stammering too much.

Dr. Wegman nods. "So you've said."

He isn't what I was expecting either. He's older than my mom by like a decade. Going bald and trying to make up for it with a beard. But as I shared my story over the last forty minutes, he really listened—and without the judgmental, narrow-eyed expressions I was anticipating.

"Your ability to distinguish between reality and the fiction you've created for yourself was, I believe, your mother's primary concern," he says. "But from what you've told me, I see no reason to be worried in that regard."

I try not to show my relief.

He leans back in his chair, crossing his feet on the ottoman. "You clearly understand that your 'friends' aren't real. I'm seeing no evidence of delusion."

Would he still think that if he knew my real reason for choosing Ashmore? Probably not.

"It seems to be a coping mechanism," he says. "Albeit an elaborate one. I suspect you felt powerless in a new environment, and taking the risk of rejection, after your father's abrupt departure, felt too overwhelming."

I sag against the cushions. Yes, yes. That sounds good. Well, not *good*, but not a diagnosis that will panic my mother. She even mentioned the coping mechanism thing last night.

"If you're looking for a specific name or condition . . . ," he begins.

I'm not, but I bet my mom is.

"You should know I try to avoid using labels, as I don't think it aids in the healing process," he continues. "That being said, I think we're dealing with a combination of several things, including anxious introversion, some abandonment issues, and low self-esteem."

My mouth falls open.

"All of which we can work on. But I want to loop back to something you said earlier," Dr. Wegman says.

Uh-oh. Please let it be something covered on my cards.

"You mentioned that you're excited to start college because you're ready now, you're going to 'get it right' this time," he says.

I nod cautiously.

"Talk to me about that."

Great. I hate open-ended questions, no simple "yes" or "no" to move things along. How much is enough of an answer? How much is too much? I have no idea.

I open my mouth, and he holds up his hand to stop me.

"It's okay to take your time, if you need to gather your thoughts," he says, not unkindly.

"I just . . . I mean, it's a chance. For me to make friends. Real ones, like the ones I . . ." My words dry up.

"Like the friends you made up for yourself here," he says.

I nod.

"By getting it right?"

"Yes," I say, relieved.

"That's what I want to know. What does that mean, 'getting it right'?" Dr. Wegman studies me intently.

"I mean, I didn't . . . know before," I say, squirming.

"Didn't know what?" he asks.

"It was like . . ." I shut my eyes. Sometimes that helps me find the words. "When I moved here, the merry-go-round was already spinning, right? So I couldn't figure out how to get it to slow down to let me on."

He doesn't respond right away.

I open my eyes. "*That* probably sounds crazy," I mutter.

"No," he says. "I think it sounds lonely."

My eyes fill with tears. It *was* lonely, and talking to someone who understands, without judging me, is a relief.

I take a deep breath, trying to will the tears away. "But at Ashmore . . . the merry-go-round isn't moving yet, you know? We're all getting on together."

"And what do you think that being on the merry-go-round—your metaphor for being included—will give you?"

Friends. A place to belong. Home.

"Caroline?" Dr. Wegman prompts.

I clamp my mouth shut against the thoughts running loose in my head, afraid of what I'll see in his expression if I say them aloud. "Something better."

He lets the silence hang for a few seconds, trying to get me to elaborate, but I've said everything I'm going to say on that.

"You think Ashmore will give you the opportunity for a clean slate," he finally says.

I nod rapidly, swiping under my eyes with the backs of my fingers.

"Which is a valid point. But what I don't understand is what you expect to happen. What do you plan to do differently there that you couldn't do here? Changing locations isn't going to make some magical difference. You're still you, just in a different place."

"No," I say.

"No, what?"

"No, I don't have to be me. I can be anybody." Someone outgoing. Friendly. Popular. Not weird.

I sit forward on the couch, the leather cushions squeaking behind me. "I have a plan."

His eyebrows go up, only a fraction of an inch, but enough that I know I've caught his attention. "All right. Let's talk more about that."

I hesitate. "Like I said, I wasn't ready when we moved here, but I'm prepared for Ashmore. I signed up for the 'social' freshman dorm. I'm working on an entirely new wardrobe, one that will fit in with everyone else's." Unlike when we moved here. "And I'm going to go out for . . . activities. Parties, maybe even, I don't know." Whatever it takes. "I'm going to say yes to stuff. Seek out new experiences."

"Do you think you'll enjoy those things?" he asks.

"Sure. I mean, some of them. Probably."

"Because I would think that some of those things might make you quite uncomfortable."

"Maybe at first. But not once—" I cut myself off.

"Once what?" he prompts.

"Once I get used to it," I finish lamely, avoiding his gaze.

Wegman sits up in his chair, as if this posture will convince me to take his words more seriously. "Caroline, college is certainly a common time for reinvention. However, most adolescents are using that space and newfound freedom to become more of who they perceive their true selves to be. My concern is that you seem to want a version of yourself that has little grounding in who you actually are."

But I don't have to be me. Not at Ashmore—that's the point.

"For example," he continues, "I could decide to quit my job and follow, I don't know, the Grateful Dead on tour around the country. Live in a tent or a van, drag my family with me."

"I think they're dead," I say. "The band. Aren't they? Like, *dead* dead. Not just the name."

"I don't know, actually," he says after a beat. "I'm not really a fan. That's what I'm trying to say. I can reinvent myself into someone who has no connection to my current self, but do you think I'll be happy? Camping out all the time, using porta-potties?" He shudders.

I don't think anyone is happy using porta-potties. Though I might be slightly happier if he never uses that word again.

"What I'm saying is that growth and exploration are very important to your development, of course. But using those things to try to become someone else is a no-win scenario. Because even if you succeed at convincing others and gaining acceptance, it's still not *you*."

"But it could be," I say. "If I'm better that way."

He sighs. "Better as defined by whom?"

I shrug, the only answer I'm willing to give him.

"Caroline, you have to learn to be comfortable with who you are. Some people will like you and others won't. You can't control that. Even wider acceptance doesn't make you rejection-proof." He pauses. "Look at Felicity. You admire the character—idolize her, even. But part of what you admire is that she is herself: flawed, imperfect. 'The queen of awkward,' as I believe you phrased it. And yet she manages to find a place for herself, acceptance. Why do you think that approach won't work for you?"

Because I can't take that chance. And besides, that was TV and this is real life, and contrary to what everyone thinks, I do know the difference. You have to help real life along a little sometimes.

I yank a tissue out of the box on the coffee table and wipe under my eyes. "So that's it—you're going to tell my mom that I can't go to Ashmore?" Why doesn't anyone understand the idea of wanting more? What's wrong with that?

"I'm afraid you're missing my point," he says.

I tense, waiting.

"I think you should go," Dr. Wegman says, after a long moment.

I look up from the crumpled tissue in my fist, startled. "To Ashmore? Or . . . you want me to leave your—"

"To Ashmore," he confirms, and relief washes over me, leaving me dizzy. "Though I have some conditions."

Wariness sets in. "Conditions?"

He holds up a finger. "First, you have to stay there for at least one semester."

A semester? I'm planning on staying forever.

"Second"—he lifts another finger—"we meet once a week until you leave for school, and then you agree to maintain regular sessions with me via Skype or phone."

That shouldn't be a problem. I could time it when Lexi, my roommate, isn't around. Needing a psychiatrist on a regular basis is definitely *not* part of my plan to reinvent myself.

"Third, you do your best to avoid reverting to your former pattern."

I frown, confused.

"Retreating to fantasy, inventing friends and situations. Creating a false life," he clarifies.

Oh. That.

"I want you to work on living in the moment and accepting it for what it is, good or bad," he says. "Making up stories about yourself or others is an understandable response to rejection or fear of rejection. But it's getting in the way of you accepting yourself for who you are. And if you can't do that, how can you expect others to?"

Well, obviously, because I plan to *be* someone better. A version of me that I can accept and others will too. Besides, I only started making stuff up because I didn't have a choice; I wasn't prepared. In my new life at Ashmore, it'll be different. I won't need Felicity, Elena, or Julie. Well, I'll always need Felicity, but the TV version, not the one I made for myself.

Wegman lowers his hand, his requirements complete.

"That's all?" I ask, to be sure.

"I need to speak to your mother, but assuming she agrees with my thoughts on the matter, yes." And yet he doesn't seem pleased about the pronouncement.

I want to be excited. But something about this is too easy. I should let it go and take the win, but suspicion is eating at me. "Why?" I ask, unable to stop myself.

"There are some things in life that you can't tell someone else." He folds his hands in his lap. "Some things, Caroline, you'll have to experience for yourself, for better or worse."

I don't like the way that sounds. So fatalistic. Like somehow I'm already doomed and don't realize it. What does Wegman know that I don't?

I study him, searching for the answer in his face and finding nothing.

Then I realize how ridiculous I'm being. He doesn't know me, only what I've told him. He's making a guess based on what might happen to *other* people, not to me.

It'll be fine. No, more than fine. It'll be awesome. It has to be. I repeat the words over and over in my head until the clenched-tight knot in my gut eases.

"Caroline?" Dr. Wegman asks, startling me. His head is cocked to one side, his gaze evaluating.

"What . . . yes?" I've been quiet for too long. I can see the concern in the wrinkle between his eyes.

"Are we agreed?" Dr. Wegman asks.

Maybe it's me, but I sense a challenge in those words, in the tone of his question. And that lights a fire in me.

Sticking my chin out in defiance, I scoot forward on the couch and offer my hand for him to shake. "Agreed."

I'll show him. Because I've got this. I'm going to reboot my life, and Ashmore Caroline is going to have everything I've ever wanted.

Chapter Four

Pulling at my seat belt in the backseat of the cab, I edge closer to the window for a better look. "It's so green here," I say, surprised. Four hours ago I was in the desert, and now . . . *Iowa*.

In my head the word sounds dreamy, exciting, full of potential. It's a little out of sync with the stench of manure drifting through the vents and the very slow tractory thing on the road ahead of us, making the cabdriver curse under his breath, but even those things seem vaguely exotic.

"It's corn, Caroline. Nothing to get excited about," my mom says, sounding worried. Then she tugs on my sleeve to urge me back.

Except it *is* something to get excited about. It's the first real sign that I've done it. Even with the acceptance letter, the various forms and e-mails from the university registrar and the housing office, a generic welcome e-mail from my freshman advisor, and the quick roommate-business messages with Lexi over the last few months, nothing felt real until *this* second when I looked out the window and saw corn.

Almost there. I made it this far, only a little more to go. According to the app on my phone, campus should only be fifteen minutes away now.

Flutters of excitement make me shift in my seat with impatience and eagerness.

"I want you to know, no matter what Dr. Wegman said, you can come home any time," Mom says quietly, watching me with concern. "You don't have to feel bad if this doesn't end up being the place for you. If you're not ready."

"I know," I say. It's easier to agree with her than to try to explain why her worry is unnecessary.

I watch as Ashmore emerges from the cornfields slowly at first, a scattering of buildings on the highway that grow closer and closer together until it resembles a small college town. Not that different from Merriman, back at home.

As we turn at the end of a downtown strip of shops and restaurants, I catch my first glimpse of Ashmore University in real life. In the distance, the white-domed science building, Kleppe Hall and Observatory, hovers on the crest of a hill.

So close now.

I lean forward, straining against my seat belt for a first

glimpse of Brekken, my dorm. The social dorm, where my life will likely change forever.

But the angle is weird, and I can't see much more of campus with the trees in the way.

As the cab winds up the road, though—the oh-so-creatively named College Street—suddenly students are everywhere. Laughing and talking with one another, clustered in groups on the sidewalk, or striding with purpose across the quad with backpacks slung over their shoulders. They project an ease and sense of belonging to this community, and I envy them so strongly that my teeth ache with it.

That can be you. That will be you. Soon. Maybe even tomorrow.

"You want the student union or the dorms?" our cabdriver asks when he reaches a four-way stop.

"Brekken, definitely," I say. I'm ready to be there, living my new life.

"You got it."

He turns right, and then, after a few seconds, I see it looming ahead: Brekken. The silver lettering attached to the outside wall has tarnished slightly, but it is still readable. The building is bigger than I expected and its brick darker, more like something out of the movie version of Gotham rather than bright and sunny Iowa. And now that I'm seeing it in person, it looks more run-down than I thought. The bike rack to the left of the doors is bent and mangled; the painted window frames are peeling at the corners.

The turnaround in front of the building is jammed with cars. People, many of them red-faced and sweating, in a variety of blue-and-gold T-shirts with either ADMISSIONS on the back or Greek letters on the front are weaving their way through, seemingly trying to help. Belongings are everywhere: boxes, plastic crates, pillows, and suitcases, all in teetering piles on the paved driveway. Like semiorganized wreckage from a very specific college-bound plane. Or the world's largest yard sale—something I never experienced in any size until we moved to Arizona, because in New York you put stuff you don't want out on the corner and someone takes it—only this has way more flat-screen TVs and Xboxes.

As our cab carefully noses into the drive, waved on by a guy in a blue shirt, my nerves kick in without warning.

We're here. *I'm* here.

There are so many people. So many *strangers*.

Feeling slightly dizzy, I search the crowd, hoping to see a face—*the* face—I recognize. No luck.

I can feel myself pulling back, like my insides are retreating, abandoning my outer shell to make themselves smaller beneath my skin.

"Caroline?" My mom squeezes my shoulder. "Are you

ready?" There's a gentle, knowing tone in her voice, like she's aware of what I'm thinking.

That's enough to snap me to attention. I can do this. I *need* to do this. I just have to think about it the right way.

What would Felicity do?

Exactly what she did do. She got out of the cab at her dorm, with her bags and a smile, prepared to start her new life on the right foot.

I can do that.

The lobby area of the dorm is more of the chaos outside but jammed into a smaller space. It's hot in here and smells of deodorant, body wash, and people who opted out of both. The furniture has been shoved back against the far wall, every inch of the place given over to luggage, boxes, and sweaty, frustrated, and overexcited humans, like a subway platform at five on a Friday afternoon before a long weekend. Music, tinny and undefinable, plays from several sources—different songs, adding to the general din. Several guys are shouting at one another while throwing a football overhead.

Brekken, in addition to being the social dorm, might be the athlete dorm as well.

Mom flinches when the football veers a little too close to our heads before thudding into a meaty hand behind us. "Got it," someone bellows.

"Do you see the check-in?" my mom asks, her mouth twisted in distaste. "Or the stairs?"

Even with my few additional inches of height, all I see are backs and elbows.

It reminds me so much of that scene at the beginning of *Felicity*, where she runs into Ben while getting her photo ID, that I push myself up to my tiptoes . . . looking.

"Any luck?" my mom asks.

"No."

"Maybe we should ask someone," she says.

That's a great idea. But before either of us can move, a woman suddenly appears above the crowd. She must be standing on a chair.

"If I can have your attention," the woman—Diane, according to her name tag—shouts, "the line for check-in starts over there." She points to the other side of the crowded room.

Everyone around me groans, and we start shuffling that way. I keep an eye out the whole time.

After about twenty minutes, we reach the front. My mother puffs out a breath of exasperation—and possibly exhaustion—as she drops my duffel bag, a suitcase, and a spare backpack on the ground. I keep a sweaty grip on the rest of my stuff.

This is it. I can feel the return of my nervousness, closing off my throat. But I can do this. I've practiced this. I can't get what I want by being who I was.

"Name?" a girl in a blue T-shirt with RA printed on the left side asks, her fingertips poised over an iPad. Her dark hair is cut short in a gorgeous glossy bob that I would never be able to attain, even with a truckload of product.

"Caroline," I blurt, pitching my voice up in a cheery tone. My goal is a nicer version of Stella. She was, after all, the most popular girl at Merriman South . . . despite screaming at me once for getting in her way on the volleyball court during gym. *Something* was working for her.

I try again. "Caroline Sands. Oh my gosh, hi! I'm a freshman, so excited to be here!" Not as smooth as I practiced, but I got the words out there.

My mom makes a tiny distressed noise.

My face burns, but I ignore it and her.

The girl looks up from her iPad with a smile. "Caroline, yes, I've got you. You're one of my residents. I'm Ayana, your RA. It's nice to meet you." Her words roll out in a melodic cadence that sounds warm and welcoming.

"Nice to meet you, too," I say, with relief. It's working. My script. My plan.

"So you're on the fourth floor," Ayana says, consulting her screen. "Room 412."

"Okay, great! That's awesome!" I lower my voice then,

conscious of my mom next to me. "Um, is there a way to tell if someone else has already checked in?"

"No, sorry," Ayana says. "We've already got a lot going on. But—"

"Heads up!" someone shouts, and then a large male body plows into the line behind us, scattering people like bowling pins.

Ayana grimaces. "Enough with the ball!" she calls. Then she turns her attention back to me. "You'll have plenty of time to get to know everyone over the next couple of days. There are lots of fun meet-and-greet activities scheduled."

"Great! Of course!" I can't seem to shake the exclamation points from everything I say.

"Kiley has your orientation packet and your key." Ayana gestures to a girl sitting at a small table behind her.

"Oh." I struggle, readjusting my bags, switching my attention to Kiley, who is also wearing a name tag. "Hi, Kiley! I'm—"

"Welcome," she says, handing me a folder and a tiny white envelope marked 412.

I lean forward to take it, one of my bags sliding off my shoulder to slam into the edge of the table. "Sorry!" I try to force a lighthearted giggle, but it comes out more like a gurgle.

Kiley steadies the table and immediately returns to sorting through a box full of identical little envelopes, like I'm not even there. I try not to feel hurt by that.

"She shipped boxes ahead of time," my mom says to Kiley, consulting her phone and, presumably, the list of details assembled by Sophie. "Where do we pick those up?"

Without looking up, Kiley jerks her thumb toward the set of glass doors at the opposite end of the lobby. "The caf. Talk to Chris."

Okay. It's not like I was expecting anyone to throw their arms around me and squeal that we must become besties. Except, possibly, my roommate, Lexi, though she's been hard to read in our limited text/chat interactions.

Still. I'm counting this as a win.

"Caroline?" my mother prompts, gathering the bags she dropped, with a grunt.

"You ladies look like you could use some help." A guy in one of the blue shirts with Greek letters appears in front of us, as if from nowhere. He's cute, with close-cropped hair, light brown skin, and gorgeous sea-colored eyes. And he's smiling at me.

My voice immediately curls up and dies, words fleeing like a flock of startled birds.

His smile fades as he looks from me to my mom in confusion.

"Yes, please," my mom says quickly, eyeing me sideways. "She has boxes to pick up."

"Right this way," he says, extending an arm to direct us

as he takes some of my bags from my mom. "I'm Jordan."

"I'm Caroline," I manage.

"So it's kind of overwhelming, I know, on the first day," Jordan says as we shuffle through the crowd toward the cafeteria. "But you'll get the hang of it."

All I can do is nod. His niceness feels more like pity, which is exactly what I don't want. Not here, not now.

I take a deep breath and try to recover. But everything feels too loud, and I can't focus with all the noise. It's like being jabbed by a hundred pins at once, while trying to solve a math problem. Dr. Wegman, during our conversations this summer, said that's part of the whole highly sensitive–introvert thing. Too much stimulation at once and I feel the need to withdraw.

Jordan recruits one of his fraternity brothers to help with the boxes. Once we have everything, I follow the three of them up the jam-packed stairs to the fourth floor. It's slightly quieter here, which helps. Jordan and my mom are chatting like old friends. He's premed, and she's telling him what she does for the foundation.

How does she do it? How is it so easy for her and everyone else? I don't remember worrying about it when I was little, but somewhere along the line, talking to people became this . . . thing for me. Something I had to think about, something I worried about instead of just *doing* it the way everyone else seemed to.

My dad understood. Or, at least, I thought he did. When my mom was out at various fundraising functions, we used to sit in silence for hours, watching the Discovery Channel or those bizarre conspiracy-theory documentaries on Netflix.

"See?" he'd say to me, ruffling my hair as he got up to get us more ice cream. "Time-traveling assassins sent by Hitler. That explains everything."

I had thought that silence was mutual, both of us drained and tired of talking to people. Now I think maybe it was my dad killing time until he could leave us, while I happened to be in the room.

At the entrance to the fourth floor, laughter echoes from girls already inside. Sweat trickles down my spine, dampening the waistband of my cute wool skirt. I have blisters on my heels and on the front of my shins from my new ankle boots.

"Caroline," my mom says. "Jordan asked you which room?"

I find my voice. "412."

Jordan turns right and we're winding our way down a hallway that seems much darker and narrower than the online campus videos made it seem. It smells like Bath & Body Works and stale, old carpeting with a hint of beer. Music fills the air: A song with a folky-sounding guitar competes with the thumping bass of EDM from the other end of our wing.

Most of the doors are open, with my floormates

unpacking or lounging on their beds. A couple of them are hovering outside in the hall, greeting people as they walk by. Including me.

"Hey, I'm Anna," one of them says with a wave as we walk by. She has bright blue hair that hangs halfway down her back.

I try to smile, but it feels too big or lopsided or something. "Hi! I'm Caroline!"

"Oh my God, I love your skirt." This is from the dark-haired girl next to Anna, her words curled with a Southern accent of some variety.

"Thanks!" I say before it dawns on me that she might have meant it sarcastically. I'm not sure.

"Don't you put the rest of us to shame!" she says with a laugh, and Anna joins her. They are, like everyone else, dressed for the weather and the task—in shorts and tanks, flip-flops or sandals.

I cringe. I'm wearing the wrong thing. Again. My smile wobbles and falls apart.

I should probably stop and try to talk to them, sarcasm or not. This is my chance—people are actually acknowledging my existence—but right now all I can think about is getting into my room and having some privacy. Just for a minute.

I tuck my head down and keep moving.

At the door marked 412, Jordan stops, studying it for

a long second. My name is written on a red cutout of an autumn leaf, as is Lexi's. He glances back at me with a frown, as if seeking confirmation that this is the right place despite the construction-paper proof hanging right in front of him.

"Is everything okay?" Mom asks, while I fumble to get my key out of the little envelope.

"Oh yeah." Jordan waves his hand dismissively, but his perplexed expression remains. "It's nothing," he says.

Once I get the door open, Jordan and his friend stack my boxes just inside. Then his friend takes off with a nod at me.

Jordan hesitates, his gaze flicking between the door and me, like he wants to say something more. But then he doesn't. "See you, Caroline."

"That was odd," my mom says once he's out of earshot. "Maybe somebody has a crush." She nudges me, amused.

"Mom. No."

"What's wrong?" Mom asks, as I walk in and drop my bags in my room. I instantly feel better. I have a door now, one that can be closed behind me.

"Nothing," I say. "Just ready to get unpacked."

A bright, sunny square, the room is small, maybe slightly bigger than my bedroom when we lived in New York. Not much space to hold two desks, two chairs, and two people. The beds, which slide partially into the wall to provide seating, kind of like a sleeper sofa, take up most of the room.

When they're pulled out, Lexi and I will be sleeping practically nose-to-nose.

But it's so empty in here that it echoes, the sound of our steps ricocheting off the painted cinder-block walls.

It looks nothing like the cozy rooms in the Ashmore brochure and on their website—the movie and Monet posters on the wall, the color-coordinated comforters, the laughing roommates curled up on their individual beds. It feels more prisony than homey at the moment. Although some of those things can and will be rectified—I have a brightly colored comforter in a box somewhere—it's enough to make me miss my room at home. The pile of paperbacks stacked and falling off my nightstand. The bed I've had forever, with the divot in the center of the mattress in the exact shape of me. I've spent hours huddled there with my laptop.

"Well," my mom says with a sigh. "Here we are."

Yeah.

The sink in the far corner drip-drip-drips into the silence.

Get it together, Caroline. I drop and shrug off the various straps and handles of the bags I'm carrying and stumble over to the door to close it.

"Caroline," my mom begins.

"One second." I sift through the bags on the floor until I find my leather backpack, the cute one that doesn't hold much. I packed my backup outfit in there, along with the few possessions that I couldn't stand to let out of my sight. "I have to change. These clothes are wrong."

"Honey," she says in a softer voice, the one that makes my spine go stiff. It's the same voice she used when she told me we were leaving New York, a few months after my dad dropped his bombshell. "Your clothes are fine. Though maybe a little warm for the weather."

Ignoring her, I reach into my backpack and pull out the jean shorts that make my legs look long and the deliberately faded-looking T-shirt with the Ashmore logo that I ordered at the last minute. The tags are still on it. With more time and access to my whole wardrobe, I probably could have come up with something better, but right now I have to get out of this outfit before anyone else sees me in it.

"All right," Mom says after a moment. "What can I do to help? Where are your sheets? In one of the boxes? You did remember to pack sheets?"

I kick off my ankle boots, wincing as one of the blisters breaks and fluid trickles out. "The green suitcase, but I can do it, Mom." Now that we're here, it feels strange to have her at my side, trying to help me settle in. It's like being pulled between my past and my future, making it impossible to be in one place or the other completely.

I look over in time to see a wounded expression flash across her face.

"I may not agree with this," she says, "but I am still your mother." She rearranges my suitcases and bags, lining them up for a more efficient deployment of their contents.

I unbutton and shrug out of my white camp shirt before throwing the Ashmore T-shirt over my head. Where is my deodorant?

Mom unzips the green suitcase and pulls out the sheets and mattress cover, shaking them free of any dust or lint they may have somehow accumulated on the trip to Iowa.

"You know, you don't have to do that," she says.

I shuck my skirt—a red band of heat rash now scores my waist—and pull on the shorts. "I told you—"

"Not just the clothes. I mean, pretending to be someone different."

"I'm not," I mutter.

"What was that voice downstairs? That's not you." She pulls the bed out and tugs the mattress cover into place.

"Mom—"

"I'm worried about you, Caroline," she says, reaching for the sheets. "I feel like you're trying too hard to be something you're not. You don't need to be anyone other than who you are."

The laugh that escapes me is too high-pitched. "I'm not sure anyone else agrees with you." *Dad. The entirety of Merriman South.*

"Caroline—"

"I'm not trying to be someone else," I say, frustrated. "I'm trying to be a better version of me, okay?"

Her hands, smoothing the bottom sheet, freeze in mid-motion, and she's quiet for a long minute. "I agreed to Ashmore on a trial basis for the semester because Daniel Wegman seemed to think it would be the best thing for you, but I want to be clear that I still have reservations. If it seems like this . . . experiment is not going the way we hoped, I will not hesitate to bring you home. Immediately."

"Mom, it's not an experiment! This is where I—" The doorknob rattles, interrupting me, and then the door swings open. I snap my mouth closed, and Lexi walks in.

At least, I think it's Lexi. She doesn't look much like her profile photo, her senior picture. People usually dress up a little for those, but this is more than that. Her long wheat-colored hair is bundled into a sloppy bun, revealing the freshly shaved sides underneath. The black sweater and pearls in her photo have been replaced with an old flannel, the sleeves torn out, and a white tank beneath it. Metal studs dot the outer rim of her ear with a hoop on the inner cartilage. Her cutoffs are paint-splattered—with actual paint, not as a design element. And she's wearing battered leather cowboy boots.

Shit kickers. The term floats through my head.

I try not to gape.

Lexi stops when she sees me. Something like resignation flickers across her face. "You must be Caroline."

Why does that not sound like a good thing coming from her?

It takes me a second, but I manage to nod.

The faded green duffel on her shoulder slides down, and she tosses it on her empty bed. A waft of stale cigarette smoke rises up in the wake of her movement. "Awesome," Lexi says, making it sound like anything but.

"Hi Lexi. I'm Regina, Caroline's mom." With a determined expression, my mom steps forward, holding out her hand.

Lexi looks at her hand, then shakes it, letting go as soon as possible.

She jerks a thumb over her shoulder. "This is my friend Erica."

I glance past Lexi and see for the first time the short girl behind her. Her thin dark hair has deep shades of magenta mixed throughout. Her eyeliner is thick and blue, and it matches the gem stud in her nose.

Erica looks us up and down with a faint sneer, snapping her gum. "Hey. What's up?" She gives a salute, an unlit cigarette caught between her index and middle fingers.

Glancing over her shoulder, Lexi smirks at Erica, like there's a joke we're somehow missing, and the ensuing silence is awkward and awful.

"So, I'll be back," Lexi says. "More stuff."

"Okay," I say faintly.

Then the two of them back out of the door, closing it behind them.

But the door only muffles their burst of laughter from the hallway.

"That was not what I was expecting," my mom says, her eyebrows arched in judgment.

Me neither, but I can't admit that, now can I?

"It's fine. I'm sure we're going to get along like . . . two peas in a pod." Mom looks at me but says nothing.

I move past her and grab the top sheet, spreading it across the bed. "You know," she says, stepping back. "Doug's been encouraging me to take more time off. I have all those vacation days saved up, and I'll lose them if I don't use them." She grabs the bottom end of the sheet and tucks it beneath the mattress.

Her too-casual tone is a warning, and my stomach clenches.

"Normally, it's too busy," she says. "But we have Sophie now, and she can manage things for a day or two. I'll come in a few weeks, spend some time with you, see campus, take you out to dinner. You and . . . your friends." Her tone is firm, not one of suggestion.

No! That will ruin everything.

"I don't need you to check on me," I say. Especially not that soon. The idea sets panic aflutter within me. That is not part of the plan.

"Maybe it's not for you," she says. "Maybe it's for me. I messed up, Caroline, and I know that. But I'm trying to fix it. So I need to know that you're all right. Really all right, not like—" She cuts herself off.

Not like before. Not like when I lied to her. For years. Not like now, when I'm still lying to her.

Guilt sits heavily on my chest. If I protest too much, that's only going to make her more determined.

"Okay," I say, trying to smile as my mind scrambles, trying to find a workaround that won't destroy everything. "Sure."

Chapter Five

It's not a crisis. I'm just going to have to step things up a notch, maybe switch things around a little. That's all.

That's what I keep telling myself in the hours after my mom leaves. But the truth is, I'm so screwed.

I have a plan. All right, more a set of guidelines than an actual plan, but still.

I'm going to:

Reinvent myself at Ashmore with:

- the correct clothing (epic fail already, Caroline) and attitude
- a more outgoing and bubbly personality (a.k.a. Stella)

. . . which will lead to making more socially

adept friends who then invite me to the right parties and cool events or whatever.

. . . which will then lead to Phase II.

But the plan or guidelines or whatever require *time*. Which I no longer have. My mom got weepy downstairs while we waited for the cab, but reiterated her promise to visit. Even pulled out her phone to block off a weekend . . . in three weeks. Three weeks!

How am I supposed to accomplish in three weeks what I couldn't master in three *years* at home? Granted, I'm more prepared this time, but that may not be enough.

Still. I'm here. At Ashmore. In Brekken. That sends a quiver of excitement through me.

I take a deep breath and hang the last of my clothes in the closet, straightening the hangers. I can make this work. I'll just have to make it work faster.

Laughter sounds in the hallway, making me jump.

I stare at the door as though it holds mystical wisdom, or at the very least suggestions on how to proceed. I should probably be out there. Talking to people. Or trying to. I could even take a tour around the other floors.

No. I'm not ready for that. Not yet.

Besides, I have so much to do in here. I haven't started organizing my desk or school supplies. And I'm pretty sure the *Felicity* poster—a rare find, thank you, eBay—hanging over my bed is crooked. I need to fix that.

Lexi's side of the room is bare, nothing but luggage, her striped mattress, and a laptop case on her desk. She and Erica came back to the room for about three seconds with another bag—an old-fashioned hard-sided suitcase in a deep harvest gold—while my mom was here. But I haven't seen them since.

The only thing remotely personal on her side is a shiny white WORLD'S BEST NURSE mug on her desk, next to the laptop case.

Lexi's different from what I pictured—different, literally, from even her own picture. I wonder if it's a recent change. Maybe I'm not the only one trying to reinvent myself.

It's easy to imagine, though, that she'll be someone who takes no shit. I've always wanted a friend like that. Someone who isn't afraid to stand up for herself or for those who can't do it for themselves.

Maybe once she's back from wherever she is, we can wander the hallways together.

The thought of not going out there alone makes the knot in my chest loosen. I could do that.

So I'll wait for Lexi. And conquer my desk while I'm waiting.

Twenty minutes later, I'm standing on the bolster above my bed, trying to straighten my poster, when someone gives a sharp knock on the door and shoves it open without waiting for me to respond.

"Wing meeting in the floor lounge in five," Ayana says, sticking her head in. She seems unfazed at finding me standing on the bolster.

"Oh. Okay." I try to keep my precarious balance.

"Great poster," Ayana says.

"Thanks. It's my favorite—"

"I hope you're using the nonstick stuff, or they'll get you for cleanup charges at the end of the year," she warns.

I nod.

"Tell your roommate," she says, as she vanishes from the doorway.

I assume she means I should tell Lexi about the meeting, not the poster stuff.

After finishing with the poster, I drop onto my bed to wait. Lexi and I are roommates—it would be weird to go to our first wing meeting without her, right? I think so.

My new comforter smells strongly of its plastic packaging and/or whatever finisher they used to make the fabric so stiff. Other girls walk by my door—*our* door—talking and laughing on their way to the lounge.

After a few minutes, the flow of people passing by my room dies down, and the chatter sounds more distant. The meeting is going to start, and I'm going to be late if I wait for

Lexi any longer. The only thing worse than walking in last is walking in *alone* and last. It screams, *I have no friends and no one wants to hang out with me.*

That is *not* going to be me. Not anymore.

I push myself off the bed. I'll have to catch up with Lexi at the meeting. Maybe Ayana caught her in the hall and sent her to the lounge already.

After one last check in the mirror—hair okay; makeup better after that last touch-up—I close the door and hurry down the hall.

The floor lounge is near the stairs, with a small kitchen area and a few upholstered chairs and a couch, all of which look like they escaped from a cheap motel in the show *Supernatural*.

When I walk in, the chairs are already occupied, plus half the couch, and most of the floor. And Lexi is . . . not here.

I hesitate at the threshold, not sure where to go.

There are twenty or thirty of us, and I am surprised by how quickly people seem to have formed pairs or small groups. Some of them are roommates, obviously, or sisters, in the case of the identical twins squeezed together on the couch. But others appear to be random. A few feet away, Anna with the blue hair is telling a story with a lot of enthusiastic hand gestures to her audience of three. On the opposite side of the room, another cluster of girls crowd together on the chairs, taking selfies and laughing.

The dark-haired girl, the one who teased me about my clothes earlier, slides past me. "Excuse me, darlin'." She perches with ease on the back of the couch, her tanned ankles crossed neatly on the ratty arm, like the princess of a rather poor kingdom, but one who still expects to marry well.

I look automatically to the far corner of the room, a place to hide and observe, but find it's already occupied by a girl with glasses and the end of her fuzzy braid tucked into her mouth like a pacifier. Her knees are pulled tight to her chest, like she's working to make herself as small and invisible as possible.

Exactly as I would have done. Except I'm not here to be *that* Caroline.

"All right, everyone!" Ayana raises her voice as she moves past me toward the center of the room, a clipboard in her hand. "Let's get settled. This should only take a few minutes."

I lift my chin, suck in a breath, and make my way across the lounge, carefully avoiding fingers and toes and phones on the floor, to the space remaining on the couch between the rightmost twin and the arm where the queen presumptive is resting her feet.

"Okay if I sit here?" I ask, the words running together in my haste.

"I'm sorry?" The princess looks up from her phone.

I can't repeat myself—the words are lodged somewhere in the depths behind my molars—so I point at the empty spot.

"Of course, of course." She pats the cushioned back of the couch with a beneficent smile.

I sit, careful not to knock into the twin next to me with my elbow or smash my cheek against the side of the princess's leg—awkward.

Ayana claps her hands to get our attention. "I think everyone's here now."

Everyone except Lexi. I flinch in empathy, imagining her walking in late.

"So, I'm Ayana Naqvi, your resident advisor. I met most of you when I was helping at check-in. We're meeting for a few minutes before we go downstairs. I want us to start getting to know one another."

Oh, please not icebreakers. I'm terrible at icebreakers.

"Introduce yourselves with your name and where you're from, and then share something about yourself."

At least we're not trust-falling or trying to play two truths and a lie. I can do this.

Silence hangs for a long moment, no one willing to go first.

"Okay, I'll start," Ayana says. "I'm a junior, and I'm from Lahore, Pakistan. This is my first year as an RA, and yes, I'm Muslim."

Technically, that's two things. I hope that doesn't establish a new standard.

"Who's next?" Ayana asks.

The princess raises her hand in a wave, her thin silver bangle bracelets clinking. "Hey, y'all. I'm Tory from Texas, and I'm so excited to be here, but I miss Major Neville. He's my horse. I have the single at the end of the hall. Come by and visit. My mama sent all kinds of goodies with me."

The twins stand up. They're pale with wide-set blue eyes and dark, curly hair that is exactly shoulder-length. One of them is in a red-striped shirt, the other in black stripes. "Hi, I'm Cara," says the one in black stripes.

"And I'm Lara."

"We're twins from Minnesota," they say together, and everyone laughs.

Lara holds up a photo on her cell phone. "And this is Max! My boyfriend." Her face is lit with obvious adoration. "You'll meet him in a couple weeks when he visits."

This announcement is greeted with whoops and *awwwws* that make her blush.

"We live in 409," Cara finishes, and they sit back down.

Gradually, the introductions work their way around the room. Anna with the blue hair—Tamika is her roommate. Jessica, Jaime, and Sari are the selfie girls.

Charlotte. Mimi. Demetria. Jen. So many names and faces,

they start to blur together. Plus, the imaginary mic is making its way back to me, and I'm going to have to say something.

My neck feels tight, like there's an invisible hand pressing against my throat.

Evie, the girl on the floor in front of me, finishes speaking, and all eyes are now on me.

The room feels like it's spinning, but I take a deep breath and make myself start. "Hi! I'm Caroline!" To my surprise, my voice comes out sounding almost normal. Well, the new, exclamation point-ridden normal. "I'm from Arizona. But I grew up in Manhattan!" That usually has a certain cachet to it.

A few heads bob in approval—I'll take it.

"Your fact about yourself," Ayana prompts.

Doesn't the Manhattan thing count? I don't know what else to say, and panic claws at me until my mouth opens and sounds emerge. "'Sometimes it's the smallest decisions that can change your life forever.'"

A sea of blank faces stares back at me.

"This is your motto?" Ayana asks.

My cheeks flush hot. "It's . . . a quote. From my favorite show, *Felicity*."

"Is that, like, that other show, *Dawson's Creek* or whatever?" Anna asks, twisting her blue hair into a loose knot on the top of her head.

No! *Dawson's Creek* was a teenage soap opera, not a

loving exploration about identity and finding yourself when you don't know who you are. Though they both featured love triangles.

But I nod. The shows were, theoretically, contemporaries, and the *Dawson's Creek* thing at least got some of the girls to "oh" in understanding.

Maybe I shouldn't have brought up *Felicity*. It is an old show, older than I am. Is it too weird to like something from that long ago?

Everyone's attention, thankfully, shifts then to the last girl in the corner, the one still chewing her hair.

"Sadie. Illinois. Premed," the girl mumbles around her braid.

"Great, thanks, everyone," Ayana says brightly. "So, the next couple of days are about getting to know one another and getting to know campus. Some of the events are required; some are not. The schedule is in the orientation packet you received at check-in. First day of classes for most of you will be Tuesday. Monday is freshman registration for classes. If you're transferring in with credits, you can still make changes to your schedule if you need to. Tonight, your agenda is pretty light. In fifteen minutes, we've got the residential director's hall-wide meeting outside on the lawn. And I'll warn you now: It's short, but required by the RD."

Everyone groans.

"If you don't go, you get vacuuming duty this week," Ayana says. "Please don't make me supervise that. You may not have a life here yet, but I do."

That gets a laugh.

"Then we'll meet in the caf for pizza, and after that, the Film Board is showing an outdoor movie at the union. It's hot now, but it will cool off, and we get a breeze up on the hill. So bring a blanket or whatever you want to sit on and a sweatshirt. No alcoholic beverages, please, unless you are of age."

Another groan mixed with giggling.

"Before you leave, make sure you grab one of these." She pulls a stack of pages from her clipboard. "It's a list of the floor rules, and you need to sign and return the bottom to me by the end of today, please." Everyone stands almost at once, and my wingmates start to filter past her slowly, taking the handout. "And don't forget, meet me at the door to the stairs in ten minutes, and we'll walk down to the lawn for the RD meeting."

I wait until Tory hops off the back of the couch and then follow her.

When I reach Ayana, I take my sheet and then hesitate. "Can I take an extra . . . for my roommate?" I jerk my chin toward her clipboard.

Ayana pauses, frowns at me. "Who is your . . . ?" Then her mouth goes tight. "Lexi."

What is that about?

"Uh-huh."

"Sure, yeah," she says, handing me a second sheet, but her tone is grim, the unspoken "good luck" louder than her actual words.

I take the pages and flee the lounge. We've been here less than seven hours; what did Lexi do?

When I get back to my room, I realize I might have at least a partial answer to that question, which is: deliberately skipped the wing meeting (a.k.a. flouted Ayana's authority).

Because Lexi is stretched out on her bare mattress, boots still on, texting with her phone above her face.

"Hey," I say, closing the door behind me.

"Hey," she says without looking away from her phone.

"So, I brought you . . . These are the rules for . . . You have to sign and return it." My voice grows softer, my Stella imitation fading until it's nonexistent. Lexi's refusal to make eye contact is making me feel more and more self-conscious, like I'm interrupting her during something important.

"Thanks."

I wait, but she doesn't move to take the paper, so I set it on her desk.

After that, I sit on the edge of my bed cautiously, not sure what to do with myself.

Should I tell her about the Ayana thing? How she reacted?

Probably not. I mean, if it's that bad, Lexi probably already knows.

Instead, for something to do, I read the floor rules—nothing too dramatic or unexpected, basically a regurgitation of the rules in the student handbook, which I perused when they sent it in the mail months ago.

Getting up to find a pen, I lean over my desk and sign the bottom of the sheet with a flourish, taking care to rip the page exactly along the dashes that indicate a tear line.

Lexi makes an impatient noise, and her bed squeaks as she gets up.

When I turn around, she's facing the mirror inside her closet, combing her fingers through the long portions of her hair, yanking it ruthlessly to the top of her head. The back of her head is shaved as well.

"So . . . we're supposed to go another meeting in a few minutes," I say. It's easier to talk to her back. "It's required. After that, there's pizza and a movie outside somewhere, and I thought maybe we could go to the . . ."

She faces me then. "Listen, Caroline, you seem nice," she says.

That falling feeling, the one I had when my mom left, returns.

"And I don't mean to be a bitch, but we're not going to be friends." She resumes her grooming in the mirror.

I can't breathe; air comes in my nose but won't go any farther.

"We're roommates. That's all. You do your thing, and I'll do mine." She winds an elastic band around her hair. Then her hands fall to her sides, leaving her to stare at her reflection in the mirror. "I didn't even want to be here," she says, more to herself, it seems, than to me. Whatever she sees in the mirror seems to strengthen her resolve, though, because she straightens her shoulders and walks out of our room.

Chapter Six

Standing there, frozen by the edge of my desk, I replay Lexi's words over and over in my head. We're not going to be *friends*. *We're* not going to be friends. We're *not* going to be friends. The meaning changes slightly, depending on where you put the emphasis. But none of the versions are good.

Felicity and her roommate, Meghan, didn't get along either. The look on Meghan's face when Felicity announced herself as her roommate was clearly one of disgust. When it wasn't happening to me, it was funny. Probably because I knew, even then, that Felicity was going to be okay. But with me, I'm not so sure. Felicity already had other friends by that point—Julie and Noel and Ben. I don't have that. Plus, it seems levels and degrees worse that Lexi felt compelled to make that pronouncement aloud. Even Meghan just rolled her eyes, letting the differences between them speak for themselves.

I'm not even sure what I did wrong. I go through the two encounters we've had, over and over—maybe it was that I took a side of the room without checking with her first?—until I realize that I have been sitting there for a while and the hall outside my room has gone quiet.

The RD meeting.

After grabbing my signed form, I hurry out the door and down the hall. The last of the girls from my wing are already disappearing through the doorway to the stairs by the time I arrive.

"There she is," Ayana greets me like I'm the pathetic puppy who keeps running into chairs and walls. I flush with embarrassment as she checks off my name. "No Lexi?" she asks.

I pause and then shake my head.

She makes a note on her clipboard, takes my form, and then waves me toward the stairs.

I end up behind the twins and Sadie. As we clatter down the steps, our group blends with others, including some from the guys' floors. The boys are louder, joking around and shoving at one another.

I suddenly feel light-headed. *I'm not ready.* And yet I can't stop myself from looking at the boys, searching for familiar features. But I don't know any of them.

Out on the lawn, everyone settles onto their own patch of grass between Brekken and Granland, the other freshman dorm.

I'm surrounded by strangers. That fledgling bit of early panic has now sprouted wings and grown into a full-size velociraptor, clawing at the inside of my chest.

To distract myself, I keep searching, my heart beating in a desperate rhythm, as Sadie and the twins claim a section of grass a few feet in front of me. People are scattered every which way now. Some are lying down, some have their backs to me, making my task that much harder.

In the distance, the doors to Granland open and a new crowd pours out, led by three guys hauling a sofa, of all things.

The Granland residents stick to their half of the lawn, some of them spreading out blankets and towels on the ground. The guys with the couch plunk it and themselves down toward the front.

Then the woman from check-in is up in front on the Brekken side, clapping her hands for our attention. "All right, Brekken Hall! Welcome, freshmen! I'm Diane Landry, your RD."

"Hey, are you going to sit down or what?" a girl behind me asks in an irritated voice.

I glance back and realize that (a) she's talking to me, and (b) I'm the only one still standing. Others are staring at me now too, including the twins and Sadie.

My cheeks burn. "Sorry. I was looking for my friend Felicity." The lie slips out without conscious thought. But then I catch the twins exchanging frowns and remember, too late, that I mentioned *Felicity, the show*, in our wing meeting.

I sink to the ground, hugging my knees to myself.

"I know you've signed and returned the acknowledgment of the Ashmore University code of conduct as part of the admissions process," Diane says, "and you'll be going over everything again during orientation, but to sum up—*respect* is the key word. Respect others. Respect yourself. Respect the boundaries we've established to keep you safe."

Behind Diane, a guy is standing up in front of the Granland crowd, likely giving the same speech.

But I'm barely paying attention to either, my ears buzzing. I've already starting lying and not even lying particularly well. And I don't see him anywhere. Did I mess this up? Is there, like, another Ashmore University somewhere? Or do people suddenly change their minds last-minute about where they're going?

Yes. Of course they do. That's exactly what Felicity did.

The thought makes me feel light-headed, and I consider putting my head between my knees to ward off fainting.

"Ashmore is a small community, and a safe learning environment is our top priority. Next year, when you're allowed to choose off-campus housing, you'll have more freedom, but this year, your first year, we want to keep an eye on you," she says, wagging her finger dramatically enough that it gets a small laugh. "I encourage you to talk to your resident advisor or me about any troubles you're having, especially this first week or so. That's what we're here for. The beginning is always a little rocky."

Tears burn my eyes, and I blink rapidly.

"My door is always open to you. Figuratively. If you knock at two a.m., you get what you deserve."

Another small laugh.

"In the spirit of that, let me share a few things I've learned in my fifteen years as director here." Diane holds up her first finger. "One, you're going to get locked out. Two, your roommate will do something that will make you want to switch rooms. Maybe not right away, but it will happen." She continues ticking items off on her fingers. "You will have at least one laundry mishap. Please try not to set the building on fire by forgetting about the lint trap. Gentlemen, I'm looking at you."

Diane pauses then and surveys us with a critical eye. "How many of you have hometown sweeties? Boyfriends or girlfriends you left at home or another school?"

Hands go up throughout the crowd. Lara bounces to her feet, waving her picture of Max over her head, like we're at a football game and it's a poster board supporting the local team.

"I'm sorry to tell you this, but the odds aren't good," Diane says crisply, not sounding sorry at all. "You're better off knowing that going in."

Lara sinks to the ground slowly, like her legs are dissolving beneath her. She's crying before her butt even hits the grass. Cara leans over, wrapping an arm around her sister's neck, pulling her close.

That temporarily jolts me out of my personal crisis. Is it Diane's job to crush our spirits? Plus, she doesn't know what she's talking about. Some couples are meant to be. Like Felicity and Ben.

Diane finishes her speech—I have no idea what I missed, something about ID cards—and there's a half-hearted smattering of applause as she wishes us luck and steps away. Then Ayana is up and waving us toward Brekken again, like we're geese.

I stand but let everyone—these people I *don't* know—pass me by. The longing for home in that moment is so intense, it immobilizes me. It's so easy to imagine curling up on my bed, under my worn comforter with the popcorn-grease stains, and tapping open my Netflix or Hulu app. In a room that I don't have to share with someone who would obviously prefer that I wasn't there.

Granland's meeting wraps up too, and the residents start to move toward their building. As I watch—trying to stifle the onset of sobs—the guys with the couch are struggling, mainly because the third guy who was in charge of cushion control has vanished.

Then a figure with sun-streaked hair and wearing a very familiar burgundy T-shirt darts forward to help.

Liam.

The electric shock of recognition is immediately followed by a warm rush of relief. *He's here.*

A ridiculous grin pulls at my mouth. I must look crazy, but right now I don't care. Because I was right. Because Liam is here. My *Ben* is here.

On my first day at Merriman South, I ran into him, literally, while on the verge of tears, trying to find a classroom that didn't seem to exist on the map I'd been given.

One minute I was hurrying along, checking once again the layout for this hall—A-22 and A-24, with no A-23 between them—and the next I was on the floor, notebooks and papers scattered everywhere.

The boy standing over me grimaced, shoving his blond hair off his forehead. "I'm so sorry," he said, bending to help me up. "Are you okay?"

I nodded, even though pain was shooting from my wrist to the tips of my fingers.

He helped me gather my scattered notebooks and pens, plucking the half sheet of paper containing my schedule from the floor. "You're trying to find your composition class," he said—a statement, not a question.

"Yeah."

"The odd numbers are in the side hallway, back there." He pointed in the direction from which I'd come. "It doesn't make any sense. Someone should have told you." He shook his head at the various someones who had failed me on this point, his mouth tightening to reveal dimples on either side.

And I fell in love with him in that exact second. No one in this school, or possibly the entire state, was on my side, but *he* was. Mr. Broad Shoulders, Blond Hair, and Dimples.

"Liam!" some impatient guy shouted from down the hall.

"I'm coming," Liam called before returning his attention to me. "Are you sure you're okay?" he asked.

I nodded again quickly.

He flashed a grin at me. "Then I'll see you around, Caroline," he said, moving past me with a wave.

Hearing my name sent a jolt of surprise through me until I realized he must have read it off my schedule.

For the first time that day, I'd felt like someone was *seeing* me, instead of navigating around me like I was annoyingly placed furniture, or whispering about me being the new girl.

I kept track of him after that, paying attention to his answers in the classes we shared, cheering him on at basketball games—the few I could talk Joanna into attending, anyway.

Joanna hated it. Hated him. She saw him only as the popular guy with the tight-knit group of popular friends. And he was that, yeah, but he was also more.

He always, *always* said hi and asked me how I was whenever he saw me, and then listened patiently, even to the point of holding up his friends, while I stammered out a lame response.

He made me feel good. Special. And that gave me hope that maybe I could matter. To him, to someone.

So when it came time to choose a college, a chance to reinvent myself, only one place truly made sense. I had this amazing opportunity to try to become the person I wanted to be, the person who would have those friends, that closeness with someone. Why not start with the guy who gave me the courage to think it was possible in the first place?

Across the lawn, Liam now laughs at something the guys say, tilting his head back in that unselfconscious way I recognize from years of observation. Then he grabs one end of the sofa, and the other guy scoops up the cushions that have fallen. The three of them make their way awkwardly toward the doors of Granland and then through them.

I guessed wrong on the dorm, that's all. Granland, though, is known as the "quiet" dorm, which is weird because I would never have expected Liam to choose it over Brekken. But at least the two buildings are right next to each other.

The impulse to run after him surges through me. I can see it playing out in my head. I would call his name, and he'd stop. It might take him a second to recognize me, but then he'd say hello and then . . .

And then he'd go back to his friends. Because Liam may be my Ben, but I am not his Felicity. Not yet, anyway.

I'm still too close to reverting back to the invisible Caroline I was in high school.

But seeing Liam helps. It feels like a sign. I am exactly where I'm supposed to be.

With that reminder, I take a deep breath and march back into Brekken. I'm ready now.

Chapter Seven

My first chance to put more of my plan into action presents itself at dinner. Our wing, Four East, minus Lexi, has gathered in the Brekken cafeteria for pizza and (wilted) salad, per Ayana's direction.

Two tables have been shoved together for us, and I've landed a seat across from Anna and Tory.

"I'm telling you the view will be way better," Anna says, twisting her berry-blue hair into a knot at the back of her head and securing it with an elastic from around her wrist. "Plus, my friend says no one even knows the astronomy kids have the key, so the roof will be ours."

"Eh." Tory lifts a shoulder as she dabs at the orange grease on her pizza, the white napkin turning translucent. "It's just a movie."

Anna stiffens. "You have something better in mind?"

"Hell yeah." Beaming, Tory drops her napkin onto her paper plate. "PBTs are having a party."

"PBTs?" Anna asks, echoing my internal question.

"Phi Beta Thetas, darlin'," Tory says. "It's upperclassmen only, but I can get us in." She winks. "My brother belongs to the Houston chapter."

"Awesome." Anna's mouth twists. "Celebrating the patriarchy *and* the potential for date rape. No thanks."

"Oh, come on," Tory says. "It's not like that."

Anna gives her a skeptical look.

"It isn't," Tory insists. "It'll be fun." She gives Anna a pouty look. "You're not going to make me go by myself, are you?"

"I'll go." The words surprise me as much as Tory and Anna. They glance across the table, as if noticing my existence for the first time.

"Really?" Tory asks as Anna makes a disgusted noise that I think, I hope, is directed at the idea of a fraternity party and not me.

"Yes," I say, even as my stomach shifts queasily. This is the opportunity I've been looking for. I never went to parties in high school. And Liam probably won't be there tonight, but it sounds exactly like his kind of thing. Which means it'll be a good start to meeting the right people, the ones who are better at the whole social thing than I am. I want my friends to be Liam's friends. *Our* friends. I need to be someone in his circle, or at least someone who could be. That's the only way he might one day—next year, next month—see me as *more*. That's ultimately the goal of Phase II: to become Liam's friend, and then, eventually, once he's broken up with Stella, to become his Felicity, just as he is my Ben.

I can picture it now: the slight tilt of his head, the happy bewilderment on his face. *I don't know when it happened, Caroline, but you're my best friend, and I think I might be in love with—*

Tory eyes me, considering. "Stand up."

"I'm sorry?"

"Up!" She flaps her hand in a summoning gesture.

I get to my feet reluctantly, and she sweeps an evaluating gaze over me, from head to toe. "Oh, definitely. I can work with this."

I resist the urge to cross my arms over my chest.

She taps her index finger against her lower lip in thought. "You have that skirt from earlier?" she asks.

"You want me to wear that?" I ask, confused. It's not the kind of outfit I pictured for a party.

"No, I want to borrow it." She grins slyly at me, revealing perfect white teeth, made even whiter by her tan.

"Okay, sure," I say. I'm missing something, but I'm not sure what.

"Perfect!" Tory claps her hands together. "I'll help you

find something to wear and do your makeup." But then she frowns at me. "Do you have base? Because I don't think I have anything that pale. Unless I use some of the contouring . . ." She squints at me. "We should go upstairs and get started," she says. "We don't have a lot of time."

"Come on," Tory urges, as she leads the way across campus. Greek Row is a couple of blocks of fraternity houses, just past the northwest edge—that much I know from our orientation packet.

She's wearing a white button-down shirt tied off right below bra level, and her hair is in two pigtail braids. Her skirt—*my* skirt—is rolled up at the waist so it flares out with every step, flashing the bright red cheerleader bloomers she has underneath. "The schoolgirl look," she told me earlier. "Always super hot."

So, it turns out there are a couple of pieces of information that Tory neglected to share at dinner.

First, it's a theme party.

Second, the theme is apparently Pimps and Whores. That's a thing, I guess?

The top of my maxi skirt is rolled down for that "exposed midriff look," according to Tory. My shirt, a blue button-down from my own closet, is tied below my bra like Tory's. The black lace bra, most of which is on display through the unbuttoned top half of the shirt, *is* Tory's. My makeup—smoky eyes, bright red lips, and false eyelashes—feels like an itchy mask. I'm also wearing fake glasses—another of Tory's accessories for some reason—and the scratched-up lenses make the world seem slightly foggy. But Tory nodded in approval, surveying her work with satisfaction. "PBTs are going to wish they spent more time in the library," she said with a wink. ("Library" in her accent comes out like "lah-brarry.")

I am, theoretically, a sexy librarian.

The thumping bass reaches us first, from conflicting sources in the distance. People ahead of us on the sidewalk are laughing and talking as they drift toward the party. Or parties, plural, it seems.

My palms are damp suddenly, and I'm longing for my yoga pants and T-shirt. I could be in my room, curled up in my bed and watching *Felicity* on my laptop. That's where I want to be.

But . . . that's a cop-out. I need to be someone who would go to a party without hesitation or fear.

Not only go, but *enjoy* it. Like Tory. Like Liam.

And the only way I'm going to become that person is to try. And staying in and watching the show pilot for the hundredth time—God, that scene when Felicity reads what Ben wrote for her!—isn't going to do it.

So I keep walking.

Tory leads us with confidence to the second house on

the left with big Greek letters attached to its siding. The images in my mental file marked FRATERNITY/SORORITY are influenced by old movies on Netflix like *The Skulls*, *Legally Blonde*, and *Accepted*. (I studied up this summer, watching every college-based movie I could find.) In other words, big, imposing houses that scream "wealth" and "exclusivity." With, like, pillars and stuff.

But this? This is not that.

With stone on the bottom and beige siding on the top half, this house looks more like the *Brady Bunch* home, except smaller and more run-down. The blinds hang at drunken angles in the front windows, the music pours out the propped-open front door, a dozen or so red cups are already strewn about the yard, and a cluster of smokers and vapers chill on the front porch. There are a few guys barbecuing on a small grill in the gravel drive next to the house, but it seems to be producing nothing more than an awful burning smell.

Oh . . . and there's a naked mannequin strapped to a mattress on the roof.

I hesitate at the bottom of the porch stairs. But Tory marches up to the front door and says something to a big blond guy wearing letters on his shirt. Seriously, he's at least three times her size, like Colossus, the solid-metal guy from the X-Men movies.

He frowns, confused, then he laughs and pats her on the

shoulder—almost knocking her over—and gestures for her to go inside.

Tory summons me with an urgent wave, and I hurry to catch up.

Once inside, we're stopped by the sheer force of collected bodies in the entryway. A girl in lingerie, like an actual red lace thing, slithers by me. Another girl has turned a dance leotard into a Playboy bunny outfit with ears on a headband.

I look like a real librarian—as in, fully clothed—by comparison. Which is a relief.

Some of the guys are wearing suits or suit jackets. One guy has a powder-blue tux that has to have come from an attic trunk somewhere—he even has a cane to go with it—but most of them have simply donned fedoras, both real ones and plastic. So, in other words, not that much different from what they might normally wear. It seems unfair.

"Come on, this way," Tory says, reaching back to grab my wrist and tug me along.

Wooden paddles bearing Greek letters hang on the left wall. And on the right, the wall opens up to another room, where two ancient sofas lean resignedly against each other. Large framed class pictures dominate the decorating scheme, if one can generously call it a "scheme."

A huge flat-screen TV is on, flashing too-bright scenes

from a video game, and three or four guys with controllers are shouting at one another. A dozen or so scantily clad girls cheer them on. They seem very comfortable here and with how they're dressed.

"Who are all these people?" I ask, having to shout to be heard. Guess I won't have to worry too much about making conversation.

"Upperclassmen, remember? Freshmen are invite only, darlin'," Tory says with a laugh.

Talk about starting in the deep end.

The hallway is darker than the entryway, and the smell of stale beer knocks me back a step. Every few feet there's another closed door on the right or left. Most of them have nicknames that sound Seven Dwarfs–like scrawled across them. *Patchy. Scratchy. Bounce. Pubes.*

Gross.

At the end of the hall, Tory twists sideways to fit through a doorway crowded by guys wearing fedoras. And one in a green Saint Patrick's Day hat.

"Hey, baby, wanna hit me one more time?" a fedora wearer asks as she scoots past.

It takes me a second to place the reference. I guess Tory does look like an old-school Britney. Before Vegas. Before the head shaving.

He makes a grab at the edge of Tory's skirt. She smacks

his hand away with a laugh. "Oh, no," she says, waving a finger at him. "Toxic."

That makes them laugh.

"What are you supposed to be?" the guy in the Saint Patrick's Day hat asks me.

I swallow hard, wanting to run from the attention. "I . . ."

"Librarian, obviously," the guy who talked to Tory says. "The glasses, duh." Then he turns his attention to me. "Want to charge me for my late fees?" he asks me with a leer.

"No," I say, the first thing that comes to mind.

That makes them laugh that much harder. "Burned, Jake!" the one in the green hat shouts.

"Bye, boys." Tory pulls me past them and into what turns out to be a stairwell. "Freshmen," she says to me with a delicate shudder of distaste as soon as they're out of hearing range.

At the bottom of the stairwell, the space opens up into a large basement. The music is even louder down here.

The room is divided into two sections by a flimsy wall that's been punched through with fist-shaped holes. On the side closest to the stairs, there's a keg in the corner, a small but actual disco ball spinning overhead, and people dancing, waving red cups in the air. Some of the girls are dancing on and around the metal support poles, to shouts and whistles from the guys.

On the other side, through the doorway and any number of holes, I can see three or four beer pong tables. As I watch, a player at the end of the table closest to me sinks a Ping Pong ball into a cup on the opposite end, and his side of the table explodes in cheers.

Tory spins around to face me. *Drinks?* she mouths exaggeratedly, tilting her head toward the keg in the corner, where some guy is handing out cups.

"Uh, sure." This is, like, breaking every rule established in every Lifetime movie I've ever seen. But none of the other girls here seem worried about taking beer from a complete stranger. Most of them have cups in their hands, and I seriously doubt they brought their own.

Tory leads the way, and I follow more slowly, dodging the flailing limbs of the dancers.

I can always take the beer and not drink it.

To my surprise, though, the guy operating the keg turns out to be someone I know. Jordan. The guy who helped me with the boxes.

Tory bumps up next to Jordan, touching his arm as he pumps the keg. "Thanks," she says, head cocked flirtatiously.

But his gaze is fixed on me. "I met you today, right?" he asks. "Fourth floor, Brekken?"

Tory answers for me. "Yeah, we're both fourth-floor Brekken," she says, moving even closer to him.

He gives a brief smile in her direction, but then shifts his focus back to me. "You're roommates with Lexi. How is . . . How is that going for you?" His expression seems too serious for the question, and I have no idea how to answer.

Tory's gaze flicks back and forth between us, and then, with an overly loud sigh, she takes her now-filled cup and flounces off toward the beer pong side of the room.

"Fine?" I say uncertainly. I'm not getting into the whole "we're not going to be friends" thing with him. And how does he know Lexi already?

"Good." He hands me a filled cup without asking anything else—though it *feels* like he wants to—and I take it and quickly tag along after Tory.

It's quieter by the beer pong tables, or maybe my hearing has adjusted.

Tory waves from the far corner; she's obtained seats in a roughly constructed wooden booth.

"Do you know that guy?" she asks after I sit down.

"Just from moving in. He helped me out."

"I bet," she says, winking.

"N-n-not like that," I stutter.

"I know. I'm teasing, sweetie." Tory pats my arm. "But nice eye—he's gorgeous. And at least a junior." She points to the cup clutched in my hands. "Drink up. You're stiffer than a dead armadillo."

I blink at her.

Then she straightens abruptly as the music shifts. "Oh, I love this song!" Tory shouts. She pushes me out of the booth ahead of her. "Come on, let's dance!" She tries to tug me along with her.

Dancing? Dressed like this? With actual people around to witness it? "Oh no." I pull free. "How about we stay here and—"

"Okay, see you in a bit!" she says.

"Wait, Tory!"

But she dances away, shaking her hips so her skirt—*my* skirt—flares out. Right up to Jordan, who has left his post at the keg to hit the dance floor.

She left me. She actually left me here, by myself. I wrap my arms around my middle and lean against the wall. I feel like a spotlight is shining on me, highlighting my left-behind status.

A couple, fiercely making out—hands up shirts and moaning loud enough that I can hear them over the music—stumbles into me and then half sits, half falls into the booth.

I shift away from them, closer to the corner of the room, hating the sense of vulnerability settling over me. Tory is out of sight now, and I'm trapped in a suffocatingly crowded room with a bunch of people I don't know, most of whom are very drunk or on their way to it. Why is this supposed to be fun again? I can't help but think of what Wegman said at our first meeting: *My concern is that you seem to want a version of yourself that has little grounding in who you actually are.*

"Hey, hey, librarian girl!" The guy in the green Saint Patrick's Day hat bounces up to me, the spring from the missing shamrock on the brim wiggling with his movements. "Come on, let's dance!"

He grabs my arm and starts pulling me toward the dance floor, his grip tight above my elbow.

"No, thanks," I say, trying to yank free.

But he keeps tugging. "Oh, come on, dance with me." The other guys from the stairway are clustered nearby, watching and shouting encouragement.

I can see it playing out like a movie in my head. Him dragging me onto the dance floor, rubbing against me while I stand there, while we're surrounded by his friends. I would be so easily lost in the crowd. It makes my mouth go dry with fear. I don't know them. I don't want this. But I don't know how to stop it without causing a scene.

In my head I hear Anna's voice at dinner: *Celebrating the patriarchy and the potential for date rape. No thanks.*

I plant my feet and jerk my arm back. "I said no!" My voice is too high, too shrill, too everything, and I feel people noticing, staring.

Green-hat guy swivels around, throwing his hands up

in the air. "Okay! Jesus. Loosen up. It's a fucking party." He stomps off.

I want to go home. Or at least back to my room. This is not what I thought it would be. But I can't leave, not without telling Tory. That's Girl Code 101, right? Plus, the thought of walking home alone in the dark, dressed this way . . . I shudder. I can easily picture the bright red flash of taillights, guys shouting out their car windows at me. Or worse, getting out to "talk."

I stand up on my tiptoes, with the safety of the wall behind me, and search for Tory's pigtails on the dance floor with no luck. I'm too far away. To really have a chance at finding her, I'll have to weave my way through the undulating crowd.

Or wait. I could wait, and I'm sure she'll eventually . . .

A guy bursts out of the crowd in front of me, lurching straight toward me, his gaze glassy and unfocused. But he veers off at the last second and stops a few feet away from me in the corner, his hand pressed against the painted cinder block. He coughs, and then vomit pours out of his mouth and splatters on the floor. A couple of nearby girls squeal.

I fling myself away from the wall and the guy.

I'm done. Tory will have to survive on her own. Clearly, she's not worried about being here by herself, or she wouldn't have freaking abandoned me.

Looking above the crowd, I find the nearest exit sign,

glowing red in the dimness, about twenty feet from me. Someone has painted over part of the *X* and *T* so it now reads "evil" in a mix of small and capital letters. It's not the same way we came in, but as long as it gets me out, I don't care anymore.

I shuffle between and around other partygoers, my heart beating extra hard as I anticipate another heavy hand landing on my shoulder or grabbing my arm. But I make it to the exit sign unmolested.

Shoving open the swinging door, painted a dingy white and decorated with Sharpie signatures and more punched holes, I find myself at the bottom of another darkened staircase, the twin of the one Tory and I descended.

Only this one has half a dozen guys, wearing the same Greek letters on their shirts, manfully wrestling several kegs down the steps.

I start up the steps with the full intention of following the advice my mom gave me when Mrs. Bukawksi's terrier, Sir Handsome, was terrorizing me in the lobby of our building every day after school in third grade: *Keep walking and ignore him.*

"Can't go this way!" one of the boys bellows at me as my foot touches the second step. "Brothers only!"

I freeze. "But I just want to leave—"

"Private staircase," the brother closest to me says, rolling one of the kegs down another step. "Off-limits. Go out through the front."

"Move, freshman!" one of them at the top shouts, and the rest of them crack up.

They might as well have shouted, "You don't belong here!" instead.

Stupid jerks. I didn't even want to be on their super-secret stairway. My eyes watering from the combination of humiliation and false eyelashes, I scurry down the few steps I've taken and plunge back through the swinging door and into the party, paying no attention to anyone or anything other than getting out of here.

Which works until I collide headfirst with someone in my path.

Hands reach out to steady me as I stumble back. "Whoa, whoa. You okay?"

I push away the hands before my brain registers the voice. I know that voice. I've listened to that voice answer questions about the quadratic equation and give speeches about the economics of ending world hunger.

Oh no. Please, no. Not like this. Maybe it's only someone who sounds *like him.*

But when I dare to lift my head, it is definitely Liam Fanshaw looking down at me with concern. He's wearing the same burgundy Merriman shirt I saw him in earlier, but now his blond hair is covered by one of those ridiculous fedoras. Wait. Does that mean he's here with those douchey guys?

"I'm fine. Thanks," I say, avoiding his gaze. This is not the meeting I've imagined. I've barely started Phase I of my plan, and Phase II is going to be completely ruined because of this one stupid party.

It's okay. He won't recognize me, and then I can—

"Wait. Do I know you?" he asks, his forehead wrinkling beneath the brim of his hat.

Seriously? Can I not catch a break tonight? "Oh, I, um—"

He snaps his fingers. "I do! Caroline, right? We went to high school together. Speech class."

And geometry, world history—both ancient and modern—and Brit lit, but who's keeping track?

In spite of myself, a burst of warmth spreads through me. He remembers me. He recognizes me even out of context. "Yeah."

"What are you doing here?" he asks in wonder.

I open my mouth to explain—I go here; I'm a student; I chose Ashmore because of the friendly campus and the small student-to-teacher ratio and *that's all*, nothing to do with you—but he keeps talking.

"And what are you wearing?" He gapes at me, stepping back to take in my outfit, his mouth curling up in amusement.

I want to die. Someone, please, kill me now.

I fumble to cover myself—the gap where my borrowed bra is showing, the expanse of skin across my middle. Oh. My. God. "It's a . . . my, uh, friend Tory, she . . ." I swallow hard. "I'm a librarian." The words barely come out.

"No! I didn't mean it like that. It's . . . you're . . ." He huffs out an exaggerated sigh. "Sorry, that was terrible."

It startles a laugh out of me, and he smiles again. And this time it doesn't feel like it's at my expense.

"This is crazy, huh?" he says, gesturing at the party around us with the cup in his hand.

"Definitely," I manage.

"I don't know about you, but this is not exactly what I was expecting," he says.

That makes the warmth return. This is my Ben. He's not one of the douchey fedora crew. He is the one who changed everything, the one who made me want more. And he's here. Talking to *me*. Maybe the plan didn't work quite the way I thought, but it is working. "Me either!"

Silence falls between us. "How is Stella?" I ask, in another bid to keep our "conversation" going.

He takes a swallow of his beer, staring at the wall over my head. "Good, I guess. We . . . uh, we broke up. Kind of. Seeing other people or whatever."

My mouth falls open in surprise. Even in my most detailed fantasies, I figured it would take weeks, if not months, for them to end things. A breakup was inevitable because . . . well, Liam is Liam and Stella is a bitch. But still.

"Oh," I manage. My brain is short-circuiting, trying to process this sudden gift. *Liam is available. Liam is single. Liam is* not *anyone's boyfriend for the first time in all the years I've known him.*

When the revelation finally sinks in, the elation that runs through me feels like a pure shot of adrenaline. My path is clear—there's nothing in the way now.

"Yeah, that sucked," he says flatly. "But it didn't make sense with me coming here. Four years is a long time. That's as long as we've been together. Better for both of us to give college a chance."

"That . . . does make sense," I say, working to keep any hint of inappropriate glee out of my voice.

"So, did you—" he begins.

"Fanshaw!" A guy shouts from across the room. "Time to wash the balls!" He holds up a Ping Pong ball. But that doesn't stop the snickers from spreading through the room.

Swiveling, Liam shouts, "Yeah, coming." Then he turns back to me. "I'm up," he says, but he doesn't leave right away. "It was good seeing you, Caroline." And he sounds a little surprised, but like he means it. "You'll be at the orientation stuff tomorrow?" he asks.

"Yeah."

"Cool. I'll catch up with you then." He shocks me by leaning down and wrapping an arm around me in a hug that presses the side of my face against his shoulder. He smells of beer and pine-scented deodorant.

I respond by reflex, letting go of my death grip on my cleavage and exposed middle to hug him back.

"I like librarians, by the way," he says with a wink, before he releases me to cross the room to his game.

I watch him go, stunned. Was he . . . was that flirting? What is even happening right now?

Tory, appearing out of nowhere, shimmies up to me, cheeks flushed with a sweaty glow. "Who was that?" she demands, her eyes sparkling with interest. She glances over her shoulder in Liam's direction. "I saw you when I was dancing . . . with Jordan, I might add." She smooths her hair with a dramatic gesture.

She's watching me, awaiting my answer with actual enthusiasm, and for the first time, I feel a flash of belonging. The relief is so intense it's almost a high.

"Oh! That's—" I start, but cut myself off. It takes me a second to figure out why: I don't want to share that information. I don't want to share Liam. Not with her.

"Just someone from back home," I finish.

"Really?" Tory asks. She turns to squint at him, where he's taken his place at a beer pong table. "Good eye. He's cute. Hang on. Is he wearing a T-shirt from high school?" she asks.

"Uh, yeah, I think so. What's . . . why is that bad?"

She scrunches up her nose. "It's like wearing your high school letterman's jacket on campus. Come on, we're in college now." She rolls her eyes, and I make a mental note to cull anything remotely high-schoolish from my wardrobe.

Before tomorrow. When I'll see Liam again. Because he said so. He wouldn't have mentioned it if he didn't mean it.

And he's not with Stella anymore.

Excitement zings through me.

Best. Night. Ever.

Chapter Eight

When I wake up the next morning, my grin is so wide that it makes my face hurt. I talked to Liam last night. And I'm going to see him again today.

Okay, so maybe I kind of completely skipped over Phase I. But that's okay, because Phase II—Liam—is the entire point of the plan. I'm going to be his friend, included in that shiny circle of warmth and happiness that seems to surround him. Plus, he's single now, after more than four years! It takes Ben and Felicity a few years to figure it out, but they are destined to be together. Maybe Liam and I have destiny working to our advantage too.

I giggle to myself before I realize how crazy that must sound.

I glance toward Lexi's bed. But there's only the bare, striped mattress, pushed in beneath the bolster. Exactly as it was when I came in last night at two a.m.

When I was ready to go home last night, Tory had insisted on hanging out on the porch first, so she could smoke.

But what became pretty clear as the night wore on was that Tory was less interested in having an actual friend at the party than in having someone to hold her drink or her hair as she puked—three times on the way home—or to come with her when she needed another beer or wanted to smoke.

Which sucked. But it's not like I was in the position to be choosy. Plus, without Tory, I never would have gone to the party, and I never would have spoken to Liam.

After we talked, I only saw him once more before we left the party—at a distance, talking to a couple of girls in short leather skirts, high heels, and garters. I'm not going to lie—I was jealous. But after he finished whatever he was saying, they laughed, loud enough that I could hear it over the music. They shook their heads in unison and walked past him, one of them patting him affectionately on the head as they went. They were rejecting him—Liam! Which made that the second strangest sight of the evening (the girl in the bunny outfit was really kind of disturbing).

In any case, Tory is fun. Sort of. She waved good night to me, once I helped her into her room and onto her bed. "So awesome, Claroline!" she said, garbling my name. "We hafta do it again."

Besides, when my mom comes to visit, it's not like I can

invite Liam to hang out and have dinner with us. Not yet. Which means I still need friends outside of Liam, and a social life here that I can share with my mom. Tory, with some heavy editing, might be the start of both those things.

With a sigh, I shove back the covers and get up, once more confronted with the sight of Lexi's empty bed.

Maybe I should tell someone? That Lexi's not here, I mean. But she's already plenty pissed at me. I don't want to make her hate me even more.

I decide instead to take advantage of her absence to check in with Dr. Wegman. I'm supposed to make contact as soon as I "get settled" so we can set up a schedule for weekly appointments. I guess I'm as settled as I'm going to be, for now.

Sitting on the edge of my bed, I pull open my laptop. Dr. Wegman answers my Skype call on the third ring.

His bearded face fills my screen from the nose down. "Caroline! Is everything okay?" He adjusts the camera on his end, and now I can see his whole face, including his ruffled hair. He's in his office. The pale morning light behind him reminds me it's barely eight in the morning in Arizona. Oops.

"Oh no, everything's fine. Great, actually!" I add, wincing slightly at the chirpiness of my voice. "I just have the room to myself. I'm sorry for calling so early."

"It's not a problem. Just give me a second." He speaks quietly to someone offscreen, and I hear brief, high-pitched sounds of protest. His daughters. And then a door shuts with a loud bang.

"I'm sorry," I say again. "I didn't mean to interrupt—"

"You're not. Go ahead. I want to hear how it's going."

"It's wonderful," I say, thinking of Liam. I can feel the goofy smile pulling at my mouth. "Made a couple new friends." I don't care, I'm counting Tory *and* Liam in that calculation.

"That's good to hear! I'm so pleased for you." Dr. Wegman genuinely sounds like he is, which makes me feel even guiltier for not telling him the truth about why I wanted to go to Ashmore. "Sometimes it can be rough starting over in a new place."

"Nope, not this time!" Except that's not exactly true. Yesterday was not awesome, especially at the beginning. Especially with Lexi. I hate to admit that not everything is perfect here, but if Wegman can help, it might be worth it. "My roommate . . . ," I begin.

Wegman's face gets slightly larger on the screen as he leans forward to listen. "What about her?"

"I think I did something to make her mad."

Wegman makes a thoughtful noise.

"But I don't know what," I say.

"Did you try talking to her about it?"

"She doesn't want to talk to me. She said we're not going to be friends."

"I'm sure that must have been painful for you," he says. "But you need to remember that not everything is about you and what you have or have not done. The first few days at college are stressful for everyone. Your roommate may be trying to deal with her own troubles, just as you are with yours."

I seriously doubt Lexi and I have that in common, given that she seems more angry than stressed, but whatever. "Uh-huh."

"Everyone has their issues, Caroline," Wegman says. "Even if it doesn't seem like they do."

By the time Wegman and I wrap up, setting a time for me to call next week, I have to hurry to get ready for a full day of welcome-to-campus activities. And Lexi still isn't back yet.

My brain whispers that this is exactly how every "missing college girl" story starts. Everyone thinks the girl is somewhere else—the library, a friend's house, her boyfriend's—when really she's, like, trapped in the back of some long-haul trucker's cargo area or whatever.

Before I can decide what I should do—if anything—the door opens, and Lexi walks in, unharmed and trucker-free. She's wearing the same clothes as yesterday, with a loaded backpack over her shoulder, three clear plastic containers of food balanced in one hand, and a silver travel mug in the other. "Hey," she says.

"Uh, hey," I say. I point at my shower bucket. "I'm going

to the . . ." I stop myself. She doesn't need to know. Doesn't want to know. I move toward the door.

"What time do we have to be at Knutsen this morning?" Lexi asks with a sigh.

I stop and turn to face her. "For the orientation thing?" I ask. It's a mandatory session with the president of Ashmore, a presentation of some kind from the Admissions Department, and then something ominously labeled on the schedule as FUN! But I didn't think Lexi cared about anything mandatory. She didn't yesterday.

She stares at me, like I'm the one who's behaving out of character. "Yeah," she says with a hint of impatience.

"It's at eleven. Do you want to—" I cut myself off. "I'm walking over at ten forty-five."

There. If she wants to walk over at the same time, fine. But I'm not being "friendly" or whatever.

"Okay," she says.

When I return from the shower, I half expect her to have vanished again, but instead her bed is made for the first time, with a brightly colored patchwork quilt and two fluffy pillows. That must have been what she brought in her backpack.

So she went home last night? I don't know exactly where her family lives in Ashmore, but evidently it's not far, or she has a car.

Lexi slings a towel over her shoulder and grabs a bar of

soap, a bottle of shampoo, and a disposable razor from inside her closet. "Give me ten minutes," she says, heading for the door.

I think that might count as a civil conversation. Wow.

What could have happened between yesterday and today to change that? Never mind—I don't care. Lack of open hostility is a low bar for a roommate relationship, but I'll take it.

"We have a ninety-two-percent job placement rating after graduation, so you have that to look forward to." The head of Admissions pauses, clearly waiting for cheers or shouts or even tepid applause.

But she's twenty minutes into a speech—with accompanying PowerPoint on a portable screen—about why Ashmore was a great choice. Something I think we all already know, because we've chosen to be here. There are a thousand of us crammed into two sets of floor-to-ceiling bleachers—no sign of Liam yet, as far as I can tell—and, for whatever reason, the air-conditioning isn't on.

So by conservative estimate it's approximately nine hundred degrees in here. A good percentage of my fellow freshmen are asleep, and it's starting to smell rank.

"It's hot!" someone calls from below us.

Flustered, the Admissions lady pushes up her glasses. "I know. I'm sorry. It's a little warm. We're working on fixing that." She looks nervously toward the troupe of student admissions counselors, dressed in Ashmore blue shirts, who are standing off to one side, waiting for her to finish her presentation to begin the "fun." As if she expects them to handle either the air-conditioning issue or the heat-induced riot that may be in the offing.

Next to me, Lexi exhales sharply in annoyance, shifting in her seat. Out of the corner of my eye, I can see that she's piled her still-wet hair on top of her head in a topknot, but she, like everyone else, is fanning herself. Only it has to be worse for her, because she's still wearing her boots instead of flip-flops like the rest of us.

On the way over, I kept expecting Lexi to break away without warning. Like, I'd look up and there she would be, cutting across the quad in the opposite direction, for reasons I couldn't discern. But she stuck with me the whole way, with most of our floormates clambering down the stairs at about the same time. Minus Tory, who was, presumably, passed out in her room or too hungover to get up.

"This is ridiculous," Lexi says under her breath.

Feeling fairly certain this was directed at me, I respond. "I know. I don't know why they didn't—"

Lexi stands up.

My mouth falls open. "What are you—"

Without a word of explanation, she squeezes past

everyone to the end of the row and then begins clomping down the stairs, with no attempt to quiet her footsteps. Heads turn in her direction, but it doesn't seem to faze her.

Is she leaving? If so, others might follow her. We were warned not to interrupt the presentation for bathroom breaks or phone calls, except in cases of "extreme emergency." No one said anything about leaving due to contempt. Or heat-stroke.

"We have . . . we, uh . . ." The Admissions lady stumbles over her words, her attention caught by Lexi, who has now reached the bottom of the bleachers. "We have a fully staffed career center with resources available to you, starting now if you want to get a jump on it." Her slide features a GIF of a girl jumping rope.

But I don't think anyone is fully appreciating the pun or the idea that we're supposed to start worrying about our career prospects *four years* before graduation, because they're too busy watching Lexi stroll across the gym floor.

She pushes through the doors leading deeper into the athletic center, and they slam shut after her, the noise echoing.

It sets off a wave of nervous giggling. Ayana is two rows below me, and I can sense her disapproval by the way her neck is craned in the direction Lexi went.

The head of Admissions labors on for another couple of slides, and then the door opens again and Lexi returns. Once more she casually walks across the gym floor in front of two thousand-plus eyes, like it's nothing.

When she's about halfway back to the bleachers, the huge air-conditioning units kick on with a roar, and everyone cheers like our team just scored the winning basket. Probably the reaction Admissions lady wanted for her 92-percent statistic.

And Lexi, in the face of Ayana's disapproval, is sporting a mocking, pleased-with-herself smirk as she climbs the stairs.

"Did you do that?" I ask when she sits again. "The air-conditioning?" I don't wait for her to answer, because it can't be a coincidence. "*How* did you do that?"

"It's Sunday; the air-conditioning isn't programmed to come on. When they realized it was off, they probably called the main physical plant office," she says.

I don't know what a physical plant is, but calling its office was clearly the wrong move.

"It's closed on Sundays," she adds. "Which Admissions would know if they actually paid attention. Plus, physical plant won't do anything without a signed requisition."

"So what did you do?" I can't imagine it's as simple as finding the thermostat on the wall somewhere in the building and flipping the switch.

"Used the building phone to call Jerry, the security guard. He has access to the environmental controls for the basketball team's weekend practices."

Around us, people are chattering and laughing like kids dancing in an open stream of water from a fire hydrant. The Admissions lady has virtually given up, racing through her last slides while no one pays attention.

I stare at Lexi.

"It's dumb. They should have been prepared if they were going to stuff us in here," she says.

"But how did you know to do that?" I'm still trying to remember where the *buildings* are on campus. Lexi seems to know that and a whole lot more.

She's silent for a long moment, rubbing the edge of her boot on the underside of the bench in front of her. "Because my dad works here. He's on the janitorial and grounds-keeping staff. Technically, a maintenance engineer." Her fingers move in sarcastic air quotes around the word "engineer." "My dad's been cleaning up Ashmore shit my whole life," she says tightly, staring at an undefined point in the distance.

Now I kind of see why she might not want to be here.

"It looks like they're breaking us up into groups." Lexi stands.

I glance down and, with a sinking heart, see that she is correct. Our classmates—still no Liam—are heading to the gym floor, where the blue-shirted student admissions counselors are divvying them up, like Best Buy salespeople diverting customers into cashier lines at Christmas.

This whole thing reeks of icebreakers.

Lexi starts down the stairs, only to pause. "Are you coming or what?" she asks.

"Yes!" I get up and follow her down the steps to the gym floor, relieved that if I have to do this, at least I'm not alone. The crowd is so loud, it's reached the point of sounding like nothing but white noise. No individual voices, no individual people, just a teeming mass of humanity. It makes me feel like I can't breathe. More of that highly sensitive–person stuff, Wegman would say, I'm sure.

Forcing myself to focus, I stand on my tiptoes, searching for the top of Liam's head.

"What are you looking for?" Lexi asks, leaning closer so I can hear her.

"I . . . a friend from high school," I say, raising my voice. "He goes here too. We promised we'd meet up today. . . ."

Okay, that's technically a lie, but he implied as much, didn't he?

Lexi arches her eyebrows in question.

"We weren't super close, but his friends were friends with my friends, and we used to hang out together." The words dribble out, and I can't seem to stop them. "Julie and Elena and Felicity and I—" I clamp my mouth shut. Lexi isn't stupid, and I have a giant *Felicity* poster hanging on one of our walls.

But she just shrugs. "Good luck."

I realize belatedly that her skepticism wasn't about me having friends—*duh, Caroline*—but about my ability to *find* someone in this crush. She's right; it's impossible with so many people milling around.

I try not to let my disappointment show. It's one day. So what? Liam and I are on campus together. We've spoken *and* made tentative plans to speak again. I'm way ahead of the game.

As soon as Lexi and I reach the front of the line, we're assigned numbers—she's a three and I'm a four—and then we're shuffled off to separate groups.

My group turns out to be three other girls and one guy. The guy, wearing plaid shorts and a pale pink polo shirt with the collar popped, insists on shaking my hand. "I'm Derek. We're going to win this thing." He squeezes my fingers too hard.

"Yes!" One of the other girls calls out, her fist pumping in agreement.

They are really into this. That is not a good sign.

The other girls introduce themselves as Beth, Hazel, and Dara. Beth and Hazel seem to know each other—they're whispering. Dara is the one who shouted in agreement with Derek. She's flipping her hair behind her shoulders repeatedly, and she and Derek are doing that thing where they're flirting by holding eye contact for a few seconds too long.

"It says here our first task is to name ourselves," Derek says, reading a half sheet of paper provided by one of the student admissions counselors.

Beth and Hazel immediately tilt their heads together and whisper—again—and Dara looks thoughtful.

"No, wait, guys, I've totally got this," Derek says. He waits until we're looking at him expectantly. Then he says, "Ash-holes." He puts the word out there, like he's handing us a giant gift. "Boom," he adds, in case it's not clear how world-shatteringly genius this idea is.

Dara nods immediately. "I love it!"

Beth and Sofie don't seem convinced, though, and neither am I.

"But we're calling ourselves assholes," I point out.

Derek makes an exasperated noise. "It's a play on words, Carolyn. Duh."

It's Caroline. "Yeah . . . I mean, I know, but it . . . it's a play on words that still—"

"Are we ready?" Derek asks. "Step two."

"—calls us assholes," I finish, and everyone ignores me. *Whatever.*

"We're supposed to find two other teams, introduce ourselves, and play Shoe Mingle," he says. He looks around, and then shoves the paper at Dara. "Here."

A few seconds later, he comes back triumphantly, leading

two other teams of five. They're the Molehills and the Sleepy Cardigans.

"We're the Ash-holes," Derek announces.

It gets a couple of snickers, but that's it.

I swallow a sigh. It's not like I was expecting this to be awesome, but the chance to meet people who *might* want to be friends would be nice.

Dara reads the instructions aloud. Everyone has to take one shoe off and put it in a pile with the others in the middle. Then we're supposed to grab a shoe from the pile—one that is *not* ours—and search for the match on its owner's foot.

That, at least, won't involve a lot of pressure or even small talk beyond "Hey, here's your shoe."

Except once we've got our shoes in the requisite pile, Derek, living up to our name, has to take it one step further. "First team with all their shoes back wins! Go!"

It's immediately chaos and people shrieking, throwing themselves at the shoe pile and running away with flip-flops in upraised hands.

I step back automatically, away from the wildly flailing limbs. No. Just no. I refuse to enter this version of the freaking Cornucopia from *The Hunger Games*.

When Beth slips and wipes out on the floor, several student counselors rush over to help her up. "Hey, hey, guys, we need to calm it down over here, okay?"

But Derek chucks my flip-flop at me from where he's apparently wrested it away from someone else's hands and lifts his fists in victory. "We win!"

I put my shoe on, and both the Molehills and the Sleepy Cardigans walk away hating the Ash-holes. I don't blame them.

The second game is even worse. Grandma's Root Cellar. According to the instructions, we're supposed to go around in a circle, each adding food items to "Grandma's root cellar" in alphabetical order, after reciting all the items that came before our turn and the name of the person who added them.

"So, like, Beth puts apples in Grandma's root cellar. Hazel puts bananas in Grandma's root cellar," Dara says. "Easy enough."

Despite the air-conditioning now blasting overhead, my palms are sweating. I wipe them on the sides of my shorts.

Derek returns with two new groups to play with us—the Pussy Bandits and the Delinquents, neither of which must have been close enough to see how the first icebreaker went down with the Ash-holes.

Lexi is on the Delinquents, and with her arms folded across her chest and her eyebrows drawn together in a scowl, she looks about as thrilled with this as I feel.

Which makes me feel slightly better.

Never trust anyone who likes icebreakers. If that's not on a bumper sticker or fridge magnet yet, it should be.

We arrange ourselves into a circle, and through either my bad luck or his conviction that I need more help, I end up right next to Derek.

The only positive is that I get *B* the first time through. But the alphabet is twenty-six letters long and there are only fifteen of us, so . . . this is coming back around again.

The problem is, I'm so busy trying to keep track of who is saying what that I don't have a chance to think ahead to what my letter will be the next time.

And it's *Q*, which I realize too late as Derek rattles off the whole list, adding "peppers."

Everyone looks to me, and my brain immediately goes blank. I can't think of anything except "quiet, queen, quite, quote." Nothing you can eat.

"Start with what you remember," Dara calls from across the circle, trying to be encouraging.

"Come on, come on," Derek urges me impatiently. It's not even like there's a timer or that the Ash-holes will win, as we're playing together. He just doesn't want "his" team to fall apart, apparently.

"I . . . um . . ." Under their scrutiny I can feel heat spreading up my neck. "D-D-Derek put apples in Grandma's root cellar; I put bananas in Grandma's root cellar."

By some miracle—and with some kind whispers from the other teams—I make it to *Q*. But I still don't have an answer.

To my horror, tears burn in my eyes. I'm not going to cry over this. I'm not.

"'Kumquat,'" Derek says, throwing his hands up in the air, his complexion blotchy with frustration. "Say 'kumquat.'"

At this point, though, it's too late. I can't say anything, my voice curling up in my throat like a small animal hiding.

"Hey, asshole." Lexi speaks up, taking care to emphasize her words. "Leave her alone. And 'kumquat' starts with a *k*."

I blink, my lashes damp with barely repressed tears. She's right, of course. A surge of gratitude washes over me.

"It does not," he retorts.

"It does," she says without hesitation. "Look it up."

A shadow of doubt crosses his face. "I don't have to. And it doesn't matter anyway," he says, turning his attention back to me. "Say something that starts with *q*, anything!"

"I said, leave her alone." Lexi stands and crosses the circle to stand near me.

"This is none of your business," he snaps, getting to his feet. "She's not even on your team!"

Lexi leans in, unintimidated. "I wouldn't want to be on your team. And she's my roommate."

He looks her up and down and makes a dismissive noise. "Right."

I don't even know what that means, but suddenly Lexi is shoving him. Actually *shoving* him.

The student counselors hurry over again, and this time, I recognize one of them: Jordan.

He steps between Lexi and Derek, his hands up to keep her from going after Derek again. "Stop. What's going on here?"

"She's a bitch," Derek snarls.

Jordan's gaze, though, never leaves Lexi. "Lex, are you okay?"

Oh. The softness in his voice says there's history of some kind between them—*that's* why he was asking about her—but Lexi can barely look at him.

"Do you need—" he begins.

Lexi pushes his hands away. "Don't call me that," she says in a low voice. "This guy is screaming at people." She points to Derek.

"I was not," Derek says, indignant.

"Take it down a notch, buddy," Jordan says sharply. He touches Lexi's arm, barely more than a graze, but Lexi stiffens like he made a grab for her chest.

"Don't." She spins away from him, marching across the circle and toward the double doors on the opposite side of the gym.

"Lexi!" he calls after her, sounding defeated.

"I said, don't!"

The rest of us stare at one another on the floor, not sure what to make of this unexpected drama.

Derek glares at Jordan. "She's just some trash charity case who—"

Jordan turns around and grabs his shirt collar. "Finish that sentence," he says. "I dare you."

Derek's face turns pink, but he snaps his mouth shut. Then Jordan pushes past him and walks away. In the opposite direction of Lexi.

After a brief hesitation, I get up and hurry after Lexi. We're not friends, but she got into the fight because of me, coming to my defense. Making sure she's okay is my responsibility.

When I push through the doors, I'm in a nondescript hallway—beige wall, beige tile floor—with closed offices lining both sides, and she's nowhere in sight.

But then I spot the bathroom a few doors down.

"Lexi? Are you in here?" My words echo off the acres of white tile when I step inside. This must be one of the bathrooms the crowd uses during games. It's huge.

"Go away, Caroline." She's in one of the closed stalls farther down. She sounds raw and close to tears.

I edge deeper into the room. "I wanted to make sure you were okay and to say thank you for—"

"Jesus Christ!" she shouts. "I said get out! It's bad enough that I have to live with you; I don't need you in my business, too."

I suck in a breath, then turn and bolt from the room.

Chapter Nine

I hurry through the back hallways of the athletic center, trying to find my way out without going through the gym. I can't go back in there. Derek and the Ash-holes will have to carry on without me. I'm sure they'll be horribly disappointed.

Pausing at a corridor intersection, I force myself to breathe and look up. The exits have to be marked.

I pick a direction that feels right, like it might lead to the front, and keep walking.

Okay, so clearly, there's something going on with Lexi and Jordan. Lexi's getting upset wasn't my fault.

At least that's what I try to tell myself.

But I know better. I should have left her alone. She was very clear about not wanting to be friends. I was only trying to help, but clearly, she saw that as me barging in where I definitely was not wanted.

Panic rises in me before I can squash it. Being here, reinventing myself, it's so much harder than I thought it was going to be. Ashmore was supposed to be my fresh start, all of us on level ground. Everyone figuring it together. Instead it feels like an intricate dance that everyone else knows the steps to, while I bob my head in the corner, jumping in every once in a while and completely floundering.

In other words, just like high school.

Finally the doors to the outside appear straight ahead of me, their windows glowing with the bright light of the sun. I feel a pulse of relief. Escape.

I know I should be trying harder. Going back into the gym with a smile and searching for Liam, like nothing ever happened. But right now my skin is too thin. I need to curl myself up in a protective ball and block out the world for a while.

On my right, a couple of the student counselors are standing at the entrance to the gym, talking to each other. And possibly keeping people from escaping. I don't care. I'm not going back in there, swimming in that sea of noise, and they can't make me.

I hurry down the hall and slam through the doors to the outside before the counselors can spot me and try to pull me back in.

Outside, my only focus is on getting back to my room to

bury myself under the covers with my laptop and *Felicity*.

Except it's not my room; it's *our* room. Lexi's probably not there yet, but she will be at some point.

How am I supposed to do this? If I'm there when she comes back, will she yell at me again? Does that mean even my room isn't a safe place?

The thought only makes me feel more panicky, and I walk even faster, and in the process I nearly plow down someone in my path.

"Sorry," I mumble, stepping to the side.

"Whoa." The person-shaped roadblock puts out his hand. "Caroline?"

It's Liam. Of course. It's always Liam when I'm sweaty and flustered and running away.

He's wearing another Merriman T-shirt—Tory would be so exasperated—this one with our bulldog mascot dribbling a basketball. He looks tired, his hair is rumpled, and he's holding a large water bottle.

"I overslept," he offers with a sheepish expression. But his gaze narrows in on me. "What are you doing out here? Are you okay?"

To my horror, my eyes well up at his kindness.

"Fine!" I say, trying to smile, like everything is normal. "Allergies!" I run a finger under each eye. *Please believe me. Please let it go.*

"Caroline." He reaches out hesitantly to touch my shoulder. "What's wrong?"

And that's all it takes for the tears to really start. Why is it always so much harder to keep yourself from crying when someone's being nice to you?

"I . . . It's nothing. Dumb, really." I wipe at my damp cheeks. "I thought it was going to be easier here. I thought it would feel like home, but it's just me in a different place." Exactly as Dr. Wegman had said. "My orientation group was awful, and I think my roommate hates me," I add, because that's somehow the worst thing, the final straw on the overloaded camel.

Liam regards me for a long moment. "I don't think my roommate has left the room since his parents dropped him off yesterday," Liam says. "And then this morning I woke up to what I hope is a water bottle filled with apple juice on his desk."

In spite of everything, that startles a laugh out of me. "Ew," I say, sniffling.

"Yeah." He chucks his empty bottle toward the wire-mesh trash can ten feet away, and it drops in neatly, the crinkle of the plastic liner the only sound.

"Nice shot."

He waves off my acknowledgment. "No buzzer, no pressure."

"You made the game-winning basket against Fiatville," I remind him. "From half-court."

His face lights up. "You remember that?"

"I was at the game." In the bleachers, near the top, away from everyone else in my class. After going to the first few, Joanna refused to attend any more sporting events unless they involved the phrase "to the death." But it was one of the last games of my senior year, and I felt the need to share in what everyone else was experiencing, even if I wasn't a part of it. "Are you on the team here?"

The light in his expression dims. "I tried out. But there are players with actual talent here, not high school talent, so . . ."

"I'm sorry," I say, stricken. I should never have asked.

Mouth tight, he shrugs. "No big deal."

Except it clearly is. Oh my God, I am *ruining* this.

He glances from me to the entrance of Knutsen behind me, as if calculating how soon he can make his getaway.

"You're already late. I'm keeping you from . . ." I choke, and my words die out.

But then he shakes his head as if coming to a decision. "Come on," he says.

I blink at him, unsure I heard him correctly. "What?"

He jerks his chin in the direction of across the street. Away from Knutsen, away from Brekken, too. "Let's go."

"Where?" Then it clicks. "I don't want to go to the dean or my advisor or—"

"No, not there," he says. "Somewhere else. Away from here." Then he starts across the street.

I should probably say no, pretend everything is great, and hope he forgets about my hysterical breakdown after a couple of days. I want him to like me, not feel sorry for me.

But it's Liam.

So I follow.

Liam leads me off campus to a Starbucks a few blocks away.

I hurry to catch up with him as he's holding the door open for me. "What are we doing here?"

"Almost everyone else goes to the union or the Broken Mug on the other end of campus," he says, as if that's an explanation.

The overpowering smell of coffee, immediately familiar and reassuring, washes over me as soon as I step inside. If I closed my eyes, I could be back at the Press, the hole-in-the-wall coffee shop that Joanna and I used to hang out in sometimes after school. A place that I, weirdly enough, miss at the moment. Things seemed simpler then, and there was still the prospect of college, like a fairy-tale land, where everything would be perfect.

Liam points me toward a table in the corner and then gets in line.

A few minutes later he's back. He sits across from me

with a paper coffee cup in one hand and an oversized plastic cup that seems to be mostly whipped cream and caramel drizzle in the other.

I never pictured him as a Caramel Macchiato Frap type of guy.

"Here." He offers me the napkin that's wrapped around the paper cup.

Suddenly I'm aware of the dampness on my cheeks and that my nose is on the verge of dripping. "Thanks. Sorry."

"Nothing to be sorry about. I have three sisters. Someone is always crying at my house," he says.

"Three? Wow," I say, though I already knew that. The newspaper wrote an article on him when the basketball team went to state. There are five kids in his family. He has one older sister and two younger. And a brother in there somewhere.

"Yeah," he says. "I'm the middle child. Only one brother. Mason, he's one of the twins."

Once I'm done drying my face and—ugh—blowing my nose, he pushes the big whipped-cream-and-caramel-striped thing toward me.

"It's what Stella drinks when she's upset. Well," he amends, rolling his eyes, "upset enough that she doesn't care about calories."

I frown. I'm not Stella's biggest fan, and she definitely

was paranoid about her looks and her weight—I witnessed it every day in the gym locker room, her studying her reflection in the mirror with an intensity that suggested there would be a test on it later—but I knew that part of that, at least, was about him. *Liam likes my hair like this. Liam hates this skirt.* Every other word was about him. I was jealous at the time.

Still, it was nice of him to get it for me. I take a cautious sip from the straw, and it's not, thankfully, as syrupy as I imagined.

"Do you think you made a mistake coming here?" he asks, fidgeting with the cardboard sleeve on his coffee.

I stare at him.

"I'm wondering if I did," he says, his mouth twisting in a grimace.

"H-how? Why?" I can't get out more than one word at a time, my shock is so great. He looked like he was having the time of his life last night. Fitting in way better than I was. Well, except for those girls laughing.

"No," he says. "You'll think it's lame."

"I won't," I say fiercely. Too fiercely.

Liam laughs, holding his hands up in surrender. "Okay, okay." He pauses. "I begged my parents for years to let me go here," he says. "My cousin Josh went to Ashmore."

I remember, suddenly, Liam wearing an Ashmore sweatshirt as early as sophomore year. That day that I tried to go up to him and his friends at the bake-sale table, in fact. (I wanted to ask for a lemon bar but couldn't get the words out with all of them looking at me. Liam was nice as always, but Stella made fun of me. And Donielle thought I was deaf and tried signing to me. It was a disaster.)

"Josh used to tell stories and show me the pictures on his phone at Christmas. He loved it. It looked awesome. And even then, when I was like thirteen, I was ready to be gone. There are five kids in my family, and my older sister is out of the house, and my parents are always working. Brynn has like a hundred activities every other day, and the twins have a bunch of health stuff because they were so premature, so it's like someone always needs something. A breathing treatment, a ride to ballet class, or shoes that need to be tied."

He grimaces. "I know that makes me sound like a selfish asshole. But I wanted a chance to get away, start somewhere new where I didn't have all these attachments and obligations. I mean, I've been friends with the same people since kindergarten. We tell the same stories, do the same fucking thing every weekend."

It sounds perfect to me—exactly what I want, actually. Friends, attachments, obligations. But I can understand longing for something different.

"Anyway, I mowed lawns and worked four different jobs during the summers to help pay for it. And they eventually decided that if it meant that much to me, I could go, even though they still needed my help at home. But now that I'm here . . ." He hesitates. "I'm not so sure. I don't know anyone here. I'm not used to that."

My mind immediately summons the image of those two girls at the party walking away from him. That would never have happened in high school. Plus, Tory's disdain for him as a freshman and wearing the wrong thing . . . yeah. Liam Fanshaw is not king of the castle here.

"It's hard being new," I confirm.

He looks at me with a new glimmer of respect. "I guess I never realized how hard." He takes a deep breath. "And the dumb thing is, now that I'm here, all I keep thinking about is home. I wonder what my friends are doing. Where Stella is," he says, with a shrug, as if trying to minimize it.

He's still in love with her. I try to swallow my disappointment, but it's a lump in my throat that won't go down.

"I mean, I used to go to basketball camp for a week and never think twice about home. But this . . ."

"It's because it feels more permanent. Because you're not going back in a week," I say.

"Yeah. I guess," he says. Then he takes a long sip of his coffee. "What about you?"

That catches me off guard. "What about me?" I ask, eyeing him warily.

"I told you my sad story; now you tell me yours," he says.

"What makes you think I have one?" I ask, folding a napkin carefully into fourths.

"I have never seen anyone more miserable at a party," he says. "You might as well have been reporting to detention or something. Why did you go, anyway? I didn't think that was your kind of scene."

I stiffen. "Maybe I want it to be my scene."

"Right."

"I'm serious!" I fold my arms across my chest. "What's so wrong with me that I couldn't belong there?"

"Whoa, Caroline!" he says. "I wasn't saying there was anything wrong with you, just that you didn't look like you were having fun."

I slump in my chair. He's right; I wasn't. "It's complicated."

"Come on, Caroline," he says, sitting back in his chair. "I showed you mine." He grins, and I blush in spite of myself.

The truth is that I already feel closer to him, like there's a bond forming between us, after what he shared. Maybe if I do the same, he'll feel it too. After all, I don't think Felicity and Ben would have ever figured out how to make it work without those first vulnerable talks, in the stairway (where she confesses that she followed him to New York) and on the rooftop (where they talk about seeing the city in the snow).

I can't—I *won't*—tell him everything, but a little bit probably won't affect my plan.

"After we moved, I never really found my place," I say slowly. "And my mom was worried about me. After she and my dad split up, she moved us to take a new job. I think she was freaking out that I wasn't fitting in in Arizona, and that it was her fault. One night she was crying about it, and I . . ." *Careful, Caroline.* "I felt like a total freak. I didn't end up making many friends, so high school sucked. I decided that I needed to start over, and here I am," I finish.

There. The vague shape of the truth, with the embarrassing details excised.

Except Liam is now leaning back in his chair, his stare pinning me to my seat. I start to squirm.

"Jesus, Caroline," he says with a laugh. It's not mean-sounding. Not exactly. "Why didn't you just go out? Talk to people?"

"It's not that easy," I argue. "How are you supposed to go out when you don't have friends?"

"Not even to Fetterman's party junior year?"

"I wasn't invited."

Liam looks at me in disbelief. "No one's ever invited to blowouts like that. If you hear about it, you show up. That's it."

"Really?" I ask.

"So now you're here and trying to start over," he says. "Trying to make friends."

"Yeah." I blush.

He gives a low whistle. "Caroline, it's not that hard to meet people—" he begins.

"Of course it's not hard for you," I say, frustrated. "You can talk to people. And everyone loves you."

Liam picks at the cardboard sleeve on his cup, avoiding my gaze. "Not everyone," he says, his jaw tight. "And definitely not here."

I don't know what to say. What I want to do is reach across the table and touch his arm. But I'm not sure if I should.

"So what's your plan?" he asks.

"My plan?"

"Oh, come on, you can't tell me you don't have a plan," he says. "I've known you for years."

"You have not," I say immediately, even though the idea brings a rush of pleasure. Is there anything better than someone saying that they know you? Especially when you thought you were invisible?

"Okay, I kind of knew you. You always had the answers in class, even if it was hard for you to say them," he points out.

I open my mouth to protest and then clamp it shut. "I *had* a plan," I admit. "To be a new version of me, to fit in and make friends." I leave out Phase II, the part about being *his* friend and where I hope that might, one day, lead.

He chews his lower lip in thought. "You have to double down and get out there. More parties. More social stuff. It's like that . . ." He pauses, snapping his fingers while he thinks. "What's it called when someone's afraid of spiders so they dump the person into a tank full of tarantulas?"

"A nightmare?"

He ignores me and then it clicks. He points at me. "Immersion!"

"Immersion therapy?" It sounds vaguely familiar.

"Yes, that," he says, looking pleased. "And I can help you. I'm not exactly busy these days."

I stare at him, stunned. This is exactly what I was hoping for. Sort of. I wanted our friendship to evolve more organically, but this could work.

Unless he's only doing it because he feels sorry for me.

I'm caught suddenly between the desire to say yes, to get more time with Liam, and the humiliation of needing his help. I mean, maybe it could work. Felicity tutored Ben, after all. It's just a bit of role reversal with us.

"What are you doing on Tuesday?" he asks.

"Why?"

"Just answer the question."

"Class, probably, depending on my schedule."

"PBTs are having another party to celebrate surviving the first day of classes."

I grimace, remembering the noise. The grabbing. The puke. "Why?"

"Rush doesn't officially start for freshmen until next semester, but the fraternities throw parties to get to know people. You should come."

"I think I've exhausted my supply of sexy librarian–wear," I say.

He laughs, even though I was being serious. "There's no theme this time," he adds. "So no . . . what did you call it? Sexy librarian–wear?"

I nod.

"No sexy librarian–wear needed," he says, his hand up like he's taking a solemn vow. "And we'll go together. Hang out. It'll be fun."

"And you're willing to . . . I mean, why would you do that?" I have to know. If he's pitying me . . .

"We're Merriman South Bulldogs. We have to stick together."

I just look at him.

"*And* you can help make me look better in front of the brothers," he adds. "I might want to join, and they need guys who can bring girls—*any* girls—to a party."

Um, ouch? I feel like "any girls" has the subtext of "even the non-hot ones" beneath it.

Are you seriously going to turn this down, Caroline? Come on! Maybe it's not the ideal scenario I was hoping for, but Liam and I would be spending time together, becoming friends. In a few weeks I'll have a new circle of friends with Liam and me at the core. And maybe, by that point, his pain over Stella will have faded and . . .

"Okay," I say.

He grins, and I can't stop myself from smiling back at him. "Good deal," he says, rapping his knuckles against the table, like a judge issuing a verdict. He pushes back his chair and stands. "It's going to be great. Being here, I mean," he says, with determination. "And this proves it." He gestures back and forth between the two of us. "What are the odds that we both ended up at Ashmore?"

"Yeah," I say. "What are the odds?"

Chapter Ten

The next morning, I ease out of bed as quietly as possible, slide into my robe, and then grab my shower bucket and flip-flops. But every noise I make—the shampoo bottle tipping over with a thunk and the thwack of my shoes against the linoleum—seems impossibly loud.

Lexi is a silent lump under her covers, facing away from me. The sound of her key in the door woke me up around two, and she came in on a wave of stale smoke. But she didn't say anything, and she didn't turn on the lights. I had trouble falling asleep again after that.

I don't want to wake her up and make everything worse.

I avoided our room all day yesterday. There was plenty to keep me busy and away. By the time Liam and I returned to campus, everyone was pouring out of Knutsen. Liam waved before disappearing into the crowd. I followed a clump of people to the Admissions Office for an official campus tour so I wouldn't get lost on the first day of classes. Then, after grabbing a sandwich at the union to eat on the way, I went to the open houses offered by the English Department and the Communications Department. And I dawdled at the library for a few hours, using one of the computers to make my course schedule with multiple backup options for registration today.

When I finally dared to go back to our room to grab my laptop, no one was there.

Still, I stayed away, just in case. I found an empty lounge on the main floor of Brekken so I could eat my take-out from the caf and watch *Felicity* without having to use my headphones. I went back to the room around midnight reluctantly, when I was falling asleep on the couch and the RAs were making rounds. One of them, definitely not in the mold of Noel Crane, Felicity's understanding and cute RA, snapped at me and told me I couldn't spend the night on the couch.

Now I open the door as little as possible, trying not to let the light in from the hallway, but when I glance back at Lexi, I'm convinced suddenly that she's only pretending to be asleep to avoid me. Something about the perfect evenness of her breathing and the tension in her body that's obvious even through her covers.

I slip out and close the door gently behind me. The hall is empty and quiet except for the distant rain sound of the showers and a toilet flushing in the communal bathroom.

Taking a breath, I replay my conversation with Liam in my head. This is going to be great. Liam-and-Caroline is going to be a thing. Who cares if Lexi doesn't like me? I don't need her.

I make my way to the bathroom, which is overly hot and smells like fake flowers, thanks to all the body wash and the obnoxiously pink soap in the dispensers.

There's a line for the showers. Well, one person, if that counts as a line. Sadie is standing by the counter in her robe, waiting patiently, white shower caddy in hand. She looks different with her hair loose and wavy around her shoulders instead of in its perpetual braid, the end in her mouth.

There are four shower stalls and three are occupied, but the far right one appears to be open.

"Um, sorry?"

She looks up at me.

"Are you waiting? Or do you mind if I . . ." I gesture to the empty stall. "I want to get to registration." There's a slight possibility that if all the normal 100-level Communications courses are filled, I could get stuck in something called Comm 107: Improv for Beginners.

She shakes her head, and I, taking that as permission, start to move around her.

But she catches the sleeve of my robe and pulls to stop me. "No." Her cheeks flush red.

"Oh . . . sorry."

"You don't want that stall," she says.

"Why not?"

"Did you look?" she asks.

I have no idea what she's talking about. It's a shower. What is there to . . . oh. Now that I'm paying attention, a small but rather obvious pool of vomit is puddled on the floor, right at the corner where the shower curtain is pulled back. There's clearly been no attempt to clean it up, either.

I step back quickly. "Gross."

She nods. "I called housekeeping."

I must look confused because she points to a sign on the wall with a phone number and instructions to call if the bathroom needs anything.

Lexi's words from yesterday float through my mind. *My dad's been cleaning up Ashmore shit my whole life.* I wonder if he'll be the one called in.

I still don't know what I did yesterday that was so wrong, but maybe it's not entirely me. I guess, if I were Lexi, I might hate Ashmore students in general, if this were what one of my parents was dealing with constantly.

"Thanks," I say to Sadie.

"Welcome," she says with a bob of her head.

We stand there for another moment or two of awkward silence, and then, thankfully, Anna emerges from one of the non-vomity stalls and Sadie takes her place.

I have to hurry to get through my shower, once another stall opens, and then get dressed and over to freshman registration, which is being held in the Morningstar Hall in the union.

I'm braced for a fight to get the classes I want. If I'd slept enough last night, I might have had nightmares about the huge bulletin boards with printouts that they studied on *Felicity*, trying to work out which classes were available.

But this is nothing like that. The hall is filled with rows of long tables, not unlike the ones I saw being used for beer pong last night, though these are tastefully draped in Ashmore's school colors of blue and gold. Each table holds two adults—like *adult* adults—with laptops, staff from the Administration Office, I guess. It's kind of like checking in at the airport. Students step up and hand over their paperwork, and the person behind the laptop starts tapping away.

I'm relieved not to be facing a giant wall of printouts. But I was right about the lines. Even though I'm only five minutes late, the line wraps around the room and nearly out the door.

It takes almost an hour to reach the front. I wish they had let us register online ahead of time, like the upperclassmen.

I step up and hand over my filled-out form when one of the laptop stations becomes available.

"Did you get your advisor's sign-off?" the woman asks in a bored voice, taking my sheet.

"Uh, no . . . I e-mailed him, but I haven't . . ." Dr. Hickey wasn't in his office yesterday when I went to the Communications Department open house.

She sighs. "He's always behind." She starts typing. "He'll have to sign off and then approve any changes you make," she warns.

"Okay." I wait with bated breath. *Please no Improv for Beginners. No Improv for . . .*

"You're set." She signs my form and hands it back to me.

I stare at her. "Wait. That's . . . that's it?"

"Yep, that's it. Your schedule will be in your Ashmore e-mail by this afternoon. But I would head over to the bookstore as soon as you can. The freshman courses are loaded, and they don't always order enough of the required texts."

"Thanks." I slide through the crowded room and out the doors to bolt across campus to the bookstore—thank you, campus tour yesterday!—where, as it turns out, unsurprisingly, another long line awaits me.

It takes me a few minutes to figure out how the system works—you find your class number on the shelf tag and then take the required books that are stacked above the tag.

My arms are breaking from the weight by the time I make it to the checkout counter, but I found everything I need. I nabbed the very last copy of *Jane Eyre* for my English 100 class.

Things are looking up.

After checking out, I drag my bags back to the union to get food. I skipped breakfast to hit registration first thing, and my stomach is now rumbling. The union is closer than going back to Brekken, and I figure my chances of running into Lexi there are way lower.

And if I'm honest, my chances of running into Liam are slightly higher. Our conversation yesterday still doesn't feel quite real. Maybe he's already thought better of it. I just . . . it would be nice to see him again.

I'm in line to pay, though, when I recognize a familiar profile two people ahead of me.

Lexi.

Her hair is down and still wet, and she's juggling a sheaf of paperwork along with her boxed salad. She must have come from registration.

I slip over to the next cashier line. Juggling my bags of books and my paper boat of food, I finish paying and turn to exit the cafeteria.

And almost bump into Lexi.

"Hey," she says.

"Hey." I avoid eye contact and head for the counter where they keep the straws and napkins.

"Wait. Caroline." She follows me.

"I didn't know you were here, okay?" I jerk napkins out

of the overfilled holder, tearing them in the process.

She makes an exasperated noise. "I know that. It's not . . ." She exhales. "Look, I'm sorry about yesterday."

I cautiously face her.

"It wasn't about you. I was frustrated, and you were in the wrong place at the right time." She rolls her eyes, but it seems directed more at herself than at me.

"Okay," I say.

"The thing is," she begins.

A shrill whistle cuts through the air, and we, along with half the cafeteria, turn to look. Erica, dressed in an unfamiliar yellow uniform, is at the entrance. Her magenta hair is pulled back into a tight ponytail, and a cigarette is tucked behind her left ear. She raises her hands in an exasperated *What are you doing?* gesture. "I have to get back to the diner. I only get forty-five minutes," she shouts to Lexi.

"I'll be right there," Lexi calls.

Erica rolls her eyes and leans against the doorway.

Lexi turns her attention to me. "Yesterday, what that guy said—"

"Derek?"

"Yeah. It pissed me off, because that is exactly the kind of entitled asshole Ashmore attracts."

"An Ash-hole." It pops out before I can stop it.

"Exactly," Lexi says. "I've been coming to campus and

dealing with their crap for forever. But that's the deal. My dad's job comes with free tuition for me. And it's a good school, you know? Better than I can afford."

Oh. I hadn't thought about that, and the fact that I hadn't makes me wince.

"But that makes it hard to feel like I belong here, like everyone else. I'm a townie to them." Lexi jerks her head toward the cafeteria in general. "I'll always be a townie. And sometimes it feels impossible to escape all the history." Her mouth tightens. "All my mistakes."

"Jordan?" I venture.

"It doesn't matter," she says.

Except it clearly does to her. Possibly to him, too.

"I wanted to say I'm sorry and I didn't mean what I said." She lifts her chin. "That was wrong, and I know you're not—"

"Caroline!"

I flinch automatically in surprise, and then turn to see who's yelling at me.

For me, actually. Because it's Liam, standing up at a table across the cafeteria. When he sees me notice him, he waves me over. "Come on!"

And literally, it's like a fantasy moment from high school coming true. *Liam* wants me to sit with him.

The burst of joy is so heady I'm almost dizzy from it.

I wave at him awkwardly, with a heavy plastic bag of books

around my wrist. "One second!" I must look like an idiot from the sheer magnitude of my grin.

I turn to Lexi. "That's my friend Liam." I can safely use that word now. Liam Fanshaw and I are *friends*! "The one I went to high school with. Do you want to come and sit—"

She's already shaking her head with a grim expression. "Don't worry about it," she says tightly. "I'm eating with Erica. I'll see you later."

"Oh, but wait, couldn't we—"

She turns on her heel and walks away.

I'm baffled until I glance back toward Liam, and this time I notice his tablemates. It's a mix of guys and girls, but I recognize some of the guys from the party the other night. Phi Beta Thetas. Including Jordan, right next to Liam.

Oh.

"Was that the roommate?" Liam asks as I approach. He pulls out the chair to his right for me and then takes one of my heavy bags and puts it on the floor.

I try not to grin even harder at the gesture—I might strain a muscle or something. "Yeah." I sit and drop my other bag. It lands with a loud thump.

"She seems like a bitch," Liam says.

I exchange an awkward glance with Jordan, who has paused in eating his pizza. "Yeah, uh, maybe. She's better today. How is yours?"

"We're up to two and a half piss bottles." Liam grimaces.

"You need to talk to your RA," Jordan says.

"His parents came and got him this morning. Maybe he won't come back," Liam says. Then he looks down at his tray. "Forgot ketchup. Back in a sec."

I pick awkwardly at my sandwich, feeling out of place with Liam gone.

"Is she okay?" Jordan asks, catching me off guard.

"I . . . Lexi?"

"Yeah."

"I think so?" I don't know her well enough to answer that, and even if I did, something tells me that she wouldn't want me talking to Jordan about it.

He doesn't respond.

"You guys were friends?" I ask carefully.

"No," he says after a slight hesitation.

"But there definitely seems to be—"

"Drop it, Caroline," he says.

My mouth snaps shut.

Liam comes back to his seat, his hand full of tiny paper cups of ketchup. "What did I miss?"

"Nothing," Jordan says, but his stare burns into me. *Don't say anything.*

So I smile, or try to, because I honestly don't know what to say anyway.

Chapter Eleven

It turns out that the first day of a class in college consists mostly of the professor reading the syllabus to you. Or making you read it aloud.

I had my laptop, fresh notebooks, and multiple pens at the ready, expecting some *Legally Blonde*–type moment where the professor calls on you to answer a question about a mysterious assignment you didn't even know you had.

But nope.

So far classes are the easiest part of being at Ashmore—no more strenuous than sitting on a train listening to them announce next stops. I am, however, slightly more freaked out about the amount of homework. I have a hundred and forty pages of reading for Thursday. As in the day after tomorrow. And three fifteen-page papers due by the end of the semester.

And I have two entirely different classes tomorrow. If it's the same level of work for those, I might as well give up on sleep now.

I don't know how I'm going to get it all done.

Which means it makes even less sense that I'm going to this party tonight, let alone stressing out about what to wear.

I should be finishing chapter 3 in Modern Communications. Instead I'm staring at a closet full of clothing that looked super cute when I bought it but now seems too fussy or uptight. People wore pajamas to class today. Actual pajamas, not yoga pants or whatever. No one did their hair or makeup. Just rolled out of bed and headed out the door. I . . . don't know what to do with that. Everything I own is too structured. Except, apparently, for theme parties, but tonight's party doesn't have a theme.

Tory's not here to ask, either. She's already out for the night. I saw her swaying drunkenly down the hallway earlier. When she noticed me watching, she whispered, way too loudly, "Pregaming in my room, darlin'! You should come next time."

Leggings, maybe? I pull a pair from my closet and put them over the back of my desk chair.

My phone buzzes somewhere, and I tear through the clothes on my bed to find it, half expecting that it's Liam texting to cancel, even though we talked about the party yesterday at lunch. When we exchanged numbers. (I have Liam's number!)

The thought of him canceling fills me with a confusing mix of disappointment and relief. I want to see him. I do not necessarily want to go to another party. Or talk to strangers. But maybe it'll be better with Liam at my side.

My phone keeps buzzing, so it's a call. And only one person calls me. I slide the bar to answer.

"Mom. Hi."

"Hi, Caroline. I wanted to check on you. See how the first day of class went." She sounds breathless, and I hear the nasal tones of the hospital intercom going off in the background. She must be checking on a VIP patient.

"It was fine, Mom."

"Do you think you'll like the classes you chose?"

"I don't know. They're all intro-level freshman requirements. I won't get to take anything interesting until next semester." The Sociology Department has a lecture series on fandom culture, which looked awesome. Probably better to keep that to myself, though.

I yank the blue shirt out of my closet and hold it up to myself in the mirror.

"And how is . . . everything else?" Mom asks carefully.

"I'm not making people up, if that's what you're wondering." I toss the shirt onto the pile on my bed.

"Caroline, I didn't say that you were," she says, sounding wounded.

No, that was just the entire purpose for the call. If I don't shut this down, she's going to be calling every other day until her visit.

So I let the silence hang. The black tee, perhaps? Keeping it simple, that works sometimes, right?

I pull it out and put it on top of my leggings. That's a lot of black.

My mom sighs. "All right, I'm sorry. It's just . . . I can't help but worry about you."

"I know, but—"

"You are scheduled to check in with Dr. Wegman this week?"

"I already did. On Sunday."

"And that's helping?"

"Mom!"

Lexi walks in, carrying her laptop. "I need my charger. Have you seen it?" she asks without even glancing in my direction.

"Mom, I have to go. I'm getting dressed for a party tonight, and Lexi needs me." Desperate times, desperate measures.

Lexi looks up sharply at me.

"You're going to a party tonight," my mom says.

"Yeah."

"You?"

"Mom."

"No, I meant by yourself or . . ."

"With a friend," I say. If I mention Liam, this whole thing will fall apart.

"Really?" She sounds both thrilled and skeptical.

"Yes, really." I turn away from Lexi. "It's great here. Meeting lots of new people. New friends all over the place." I have to clamp down against the long-ingrained urge to start throwing out names. People in my classes, on my wing, or ones that exist only in my head. But Lexi is listening.

"Well . . . good," Mom says. "Then I look forward to seeing them in a couple of weeks."

Is it me, or did she put an extra emphasis on the word "seeing"?

"Okay, I have to go. Love you, bye." I hang up before she can say more, and I flop back on my bed and the mound of clothing.

Lexi is frowning at me, not even bothering to search for her power cord. Instead she sits on the edge of her bed, her laptop folded in her arms.

"So PBTs again tonight?" Lexi jerks her chin at the leggings and shirt on the back of my chair.

"Yeah." I frown. "How did you—"

"Tory," she says with a shrug.

"Oh." Tory talks to everyone, apparently.

"Not the black. It's so close to your hair color and you're too pale. You'll look like you're going to a funeral." Lexi gets up and goes to her closet. "Here." She pulls a shirt with thin red and white stripes out of her closet.

"Thanks," I say, startled. I take the shirt. It's a simple, loose shirt, but with a deliberately uneven hem in a casual, effortless style. It's nothing like what she wears now. A remnant of that earlier wardrobe, maybe?

She shrugs it off. "Sure." But she seems sad. Or, rather, angry-sad, as everything about Lexi seems to be one shade of pissed off or another.

"You . . . you want to go?" I venture.

"Fuck no," she says, her mouth twisting into a sneer.

"Okay," I say, edging away. I cannot figure her out.

On my side of the room, I shed my shorts and T-shirt and pull on my leggings and Lexi's shirt. A quick glance in the mirror shows that she's right. The red brings color to my complexion, making me look less like a consumption victim from the 1800s.

"You're going out with that guy again, the one you went to high school with?" she asks, kicking the heel of her boot against the linoleum, creating black scuff marks.

I look at her in surprise.

"I saw you guys at lunch yesterday," she reminds me.

"You should have come over," I say. "Liam is amazing." Though he might not have been quite as amazing to Lexi.

She stares at me for a long moment; then she scooches farther onto her bed and opens her laptop. Assuming the conversation is done, I grab my makeup bag—so slight compared to Tory's box of miracles—and head for the door. The lighting is better in the bathroom.

"You were friends with him in high school?" she asks. "Good friends?"

I hesitate. "Not exactly. But our social circles overlapped." *In my imagination.* "But I think we're both kind of missing home." Well, he is, at least. And I'm happy to help.

"Mm-hmm."

Whatever. I grab the doorknob.

"Just . . . be careful, Caroline."

"What? Why?"

When she doesn't answer right away, I look back at her. She's fidgeting with the cracked plastic edge of her laptop cover. "Lexi?"

"Townie girls are always an easy mark for Ashmore guys," she says finally.

I frown. "What does that have to do with—"

"Especially when those girls are desperate to fit in. And when those guys are feeling less than the superheroes they used to be back home."

It takes me a second to put the pieces together. "Is that what . . . you and Jordan were . . ."

"I didn't say anything about me," she says sharply, not looking up from her laptop.

Except that has to be what she's talking about, given what I've seen and overheard between the two of them. But why would she bring that up now?

It clicks. "Wait. You think Liam is doing that? Using me to feel better about himself?"

"I don't know," she says. "I'm just saying, be careful."

"That's ridiculous," I say. "He's not like that." Is he? No, of course not! Yes, we talk about high school a lot, but that's because we have that in common. And we naturally talk more about him than me in those conversations because, hello, I didn't have a life in high school and he did.

"I'm not saying it's intentional . . . ," Lexi begins.

"He wouldn't do that," I say.

"Okay."

She's wrong. She has to be. Whatever happened between Jordan and Lexi is totally different and has nothing to do with Liam and me.

But now that Lexi's made the connection, I can't stop thinking about it, and it snaps something inside me. "You know, just because you're miserable here doesn't mean you have to try to make everyone else unhappy too."

She looks up, surprised. "Caroline, I wasn't trying to—"

"I'm finally getting the life I want," I say, my voice trembling. "You don't get to—"

"Because of him?" she asks, skepticism thick in her tone.

"You don't get to ruin it," I say. "You don't know him and you don't know me. We're not *friends*, remember?"

Her mouth tightens into a thin line, and she holds her hands up in surrender. "You're absolutely right," she says flatly. "Sorry to hold you up."

But I'm already pulling open the door and then slamming it shut on her words. On her.

Chapter Twelve

The Slug is a metal sculpture, donated by an artist alum and situated on a patch of central campus lawn on the way to Greek Row. According to the campus guide on the Ashmore website, it's supposed to represent a wriggling butterfly breaking free of its cocoon: new life, new opportunities, etc. However, because of the "wriggling" position, it looks more like a slug that has somehow managed to defy gravity and stand upright on its narrow end.

I hurry down the sidewalk toward it, and to my relief I spot Liam waiting, his head down while he checks his phone.

"Hey," I say, breathless from rushing.

"Hey." Liam doesn't look up from scrolling on his phone.

"Is everything okay?" I ask after a moment.

He glances up at me then, seeming to register my arrival for the first time. "Yeah. Stella started school today." He stares at his screen again, as if trying to divine some new information from what he's already scrolled through.

"Oh. Is she doing all right?" I can't imagine Stella struggling with new people and a new location. She's one of those people who moves through the world like she expects everyone else to step aside or fall in line behind her.

"I'm sure she is," he says. "She's with Braden and Tyler. And Martina, I guess."

In other words, most of his friends.

He tucks his phone into the front pocket of his jeans. "Ready?"

"No," I admit.

"Oh, come on, it's going to be fun," he says, nudging me with his elbow as we start walking toward Greek Row.

I force a smile. "Sure!" The thing is, though, I don't think I like parties. This is a revelation to me. I spent so much time in high school wishing I'd been invited; it never dawned on me to wonder whether I'd actually *enjoy* them.

I never knew how overwhelming they were, in reality, until the other night. Yet one more thing that looks and sounds—and probably smells—better on television and in movies. Not that I'm going to tell Liam that.

He seems to know anyway. "Keep an open mind," he says. "That's all. I think it'll help. You have to go out to meet people." He gestures in the direction of the party ahead. "You won't make friends staying in your dorm room by yourself like a loser, right?"

He says it with a smile, but the words still sting.

"Right," I manage.

The mannequin is no longer on the roof, but otherwise the Phi Beta Theta house looks the same as it did the last time we were here.

Liam leads the way up to the front door and gets us in even faster than Tory did.

Inside, the girls are wearing regular clothes this time, and I don't see any fedoras on the guys. But there's still the stale beer smell, and the music from below that makes my feet tingle with the vibrations through my flip-flops.

The party is apparently in the basement again.

Ducking between two very large guys fist-bumping over my head in the hallway, I follow Liam down the stairs.

It is less intimidating this time. Maybe because I know what to expect. I don't recognize anyone, but Liam is greeted with handshakes and backslapping.

Liam gestures to me, and probably says my name, each time, but I can't hear him or what anyone says in response. I wave hello at them and they wave back, but most of their attention is reserved for Liam, which is good.

The keg in the corner is not manned by anyone—I don't see Jordan anywhere—so Liam fills the cups and hands one to me.

I take it and shift out of the way, moving to stand behind him. He smells so good.

But he turns and pulls me forward. "No," he says, leaning to shout in my ear with a smile. "No hiding in the corner."

Reluctantly, I stand where he's placed me, trying hard not to fold my arms over my chest. I feel so much more exposed without him in front of me, even though no one seems to be paying the slightest bit of attention to us.

"So now what?" I ask, raising my voice to be heard and fighting the urge to inch closer to the wall.

He takes a swallow from his cup and contemplates me with a thoughtful expression. "Talk to someone," he says.

His words send a cold spike of fear through my middle. "Who?"

"Pick someone."

"But I'm talking to you."

He rolls his eyes, leaning closer to me, his hand on my shoulder pulling me in so his words will be audible. "It's not that hard," he begins. "You just . . ." Then he pauses, probably seeing the panic in my expression. "It's small talk at first, nothing big," he says, and takes another swallow of his beer. "Talk about how hot it is down here, or ask where you can get a beer."

"How many?" I ask.

"How many what?"

"How many small-talk things do I need to say?"

"Jesus, Caroline."

"I told you, I'm not good at this!" And it's even harder with him judging me and finding me lacking. This was a terrible idea.

Tears prick my eyes.

He sighs and steps closer, until my cup-holding hand is brushing his chest, and then he bends his head down toward mine, like he's going to whisper something to me.

But he doesn't.

I'm confronted with his face, inches from mine. The longer-than-they-should-reasonably-be eyelashes. The tiny scar along the bottom of his chin. The intense blue of his eyes. His mouth quirking upward in a smile.

Then his gaze drops, and for one horrible, wonderful, endless second, I think he's going to kiss me. *Oh God. Yes. Please.*

But instead he pushes my shoulder, not too hard, but enough that I'm forced to take a step back and bump into something—no, someone—behind me.

I spin around, mortified. The someone in question is a tall guy wearing the Phi Beta Theta letters. He's adorable in a kind of dorky way, with floppy dark hair and glasses. And he's shaking spilled beer off his hand onto the floor.

"I'm so sorry!" I blurt.

He waves my words away with a smile. “No harm done. It’s crowded down here.”

“Yes, but my friend—” I cut myself off before I can explain that Liam pushed me into this guy, because *how*, exactly, can I explain that without sounding like a crazy person or a loser or both? Behind me, I can feel Liam watching, as if his gaze has weight.

“Sorry,” I say again instead.

“I’m Del.” He holds his hand out.

I shake it automatically, realizing only belatedly that he’s looking expectantly at me for something.

Oh. My name.

“Caroline,” I manage after a second of throat-gargling awkwardness, which I hope he can’t hear over the music.

“Nice to meet you, Caroline. I’m one of the brothers here. Welcome. I hope you’re not partial to ever hearing again.” Del rolls his eyes.

I laugh; I can’t help it. But in spite of that, the horrible conversation gap is coming, I can feel it, and I don’t know how to stop it.

“So . . . ,” I begin, with no idea what word should come next. My mind flips through scenarios, growing more panicked with each one dismissed. I can’t ask him about getting a beer because I have one in my hand. We’ve already talked about how crowded it is. Well, he has. What else?

What else do I know about him? That he's in a fraternity, but I'm betting that he can't say much about that because secrets and rituals and whatever. *What's your major?* That's so lame.

"I should let you get back to your boyfriend," Del says after a beat of silence.

"Oh no!"

He looks startled by the force of my exclamation.

"He's not . . . we're not . . . I . . ." Only wish he were my boyfriend? "We went to high school together," I manage. Is this small talk? Or helpless babbling? It feels more like the latter.

"Oh. Okay." Del pauses. "Well, that's his loss." He gives me a shy smile.

My face goes hot, but not with embarrassment, at least not the same variety I'm used to experiencing. "Um, thanks."

"See you around, Caroline," Del says before walking away to call to someone across the room, perhaps one of the brothers.

When I turn around, I find Liam smiling at me.

"Told you," he says, tilting his cup at me.

"That was . . . that's just . . . ," I sputter.

"A success?"

"So that's your plan?" I ask. "To walk around forcing me to bump into other people unexpectedly?"

"It worked, didn't it?" Liam asks. "Sometimes you gotta break it down to the most basic element first. Like practicing free throws or running laps to build up endurance."

I narrow my eyes at him. "It's going to take a very long time if you intend to push me into everyone on campus," I say.

He laughs. "Fair enough. I won't do that again. I thought it might help you to have a win under your belt. To feel good and know that you can do it." He pauses. "He thought you were cute."

I have no idea what to say to that.

"He's right," Liam says with a wink.

That loud whooshing noise in my head? The rush of air flooding in to fill the space where my brain used to be. Before it exploded. Because Liam Fanshaw called me cute. And winked at me. *Again.*

"Come on. This way."

He leads me to a beer pong table in the corner, where a game is nearly finished. One side is completely clobbering the other. Only two cups are left for them, while the other still has all ten in place.

I wait, bracing myself, not sure what's coming next.

"We have next!" Liam calls, when there's a break in the action.

One of the guys on the winning team nods in

acknowledgment and then shouts, "Freshmen coming up!" His statement is greeted by a variety of derisive noises.

I gape at Liam, and then pull him back a step, away from the table. "Are you kidding me?"

"What? It's perfect for you," he says, leaning down. He's so close to me. "Gives you something to concentrate on. Plus, the alcohol takes the edge off."

"I've never played before!"

But before we can argue further, the team that's ahead sinks the last shot, and the people around us shout and jeer. The losing team, a guy and a girl, groans and starts protesting about something.

"Are you in?" Liam asks, walking backward toward the table, to "our" side. "If not, I have to do this by myself." People around him boo, giving the thumbs-down. Because we're freshmen or because I might make him do this alone? I don't know.

Who do I want to be? Okay, not necessarily someone who is a champion beer pong player, but definitely not someone who is afraid of it.

"Fine." I make myself move toward him, despite the leap of nerves in my stomach and my suddenly trembling hands. All these eyes watching me. "But we might lose."

"It won't be the first time I've lost at beer pong," Liam says. "You know Dante?"

Big guy. Football player. A senior when we were sophomores.

"Sort of."

"He and I played once at Tyler's house, and we lost so badly, they trolled us for the next two games."

He sees my blank look, and explains. "They make you sit under the table as a penalty." Again, his smile is fond, like this is a *good* memory.

One of our opponents, red-faced and sweaty, bounces the ball down to Liam as soon as the cups are set up.

"Wait!" The other guy, his teammate, shouts. "Back row!" Everyone around us stops, turning to look for . . . something.

I look with them, though I have no idea what it is I'm searching for.

"I should probably warn you," Liam says, distracting me. "They apparently play by the back-row rule here."

My eyes widen with alarm, and I shift my attention to him. "What does *that* mean?"

"If the other team clears their cups to the back row before we land a single shot, then there are consequences."

"What kind of consequences?"

He jerks his chin toward a door on the other side of the basement, and I turn in time to see it thrown open by two very naked people, who run, shrieking and laughing, into the room. The girl is trying to cover everything with her arms as she bolts past; the guy, however, seems to be focused on making it across the space as quickly as possible. He's skinny, so the muscles and tendons are standing out in his arms, which are pumping like he's in a race.

I feel a rush of embarrassment, and I look away swiftly, but not before I recognize the guy and the girl. It's the team from a few minutes ago. The one that lost at the table we're now playing.

"Streaking," Liam says.

I feel dizzy suddenly, like I might faint. "I . . . I can't do this."

"It's a good rule of thumb," Liam says, turning back to the table. "Always ask about the house rules before you agree to play."

"But I didn't . . . You're the one who . . ." I can't even find the words.

"Nothing like raising the stakes for motivation," he says. "Forces you to operate under pressure."

"No." I turn and start to walk away.

He catches my arm. "Caroline." He leans forward to whisper in my ear. "We're in this together." There's a faint wrinkle of worry on his forehead that makes me soften slightly. "Trust me?" he asks.

Looking up into his familiar face, one I studied for years

from across the cafeteria, various classrooms, even the basketball court, how can I say no?

I nod reluctantly.

"We'll be fine."

"All right, let's do this!" the loud guy from the other side shouts.

Liam takes the first shot. And misses.

"It always takes me a shot or two to warm up," he says.

Ignoring our audience—or trying to—I aim for the center cup, which seems to be the most logical shot with the best odds. But the ball skews inexplicably left, bouncing off the rim of the farthest cup on that side.

I feel like this is some horribly twisted game of strip poker—not that I've ever played that, either—where every missed shot gets us one step closer to nakedness.

I watch, in mute horror, as the other team makes shot after shot. The beer is poured into my cup and Liam's equally. And I drink as much of it as I can, grimacing at the yeasty, sour taste, trying to keep up. I have no idea what the penalty is for not finishing the beer, but I'm not about to find out.

Finally the red-faced guy misses, and it's our turn again.

Liam hands me the ball, and without letting myself think too much about it, I lob it toward the other end of the table. Better to get my shot out of the way so Liam, former basketball star, can try again.

But to my surprise, the Ping Pong ball catches on the rim of the center cup and rolls around for a heartbreaking second before dropping in.

The crowd explodes into cheers, and a few of them even pat me on the shoulder, while I stand still in shock. Some of the guys congratulate Liam on his choice of partner. Then Liam pulls my free hand up for a high five. "Nice job," he says with a wink.

Liam sinks his next shot, and every other one after that. I hit a couple more but not enough, so we lose, but we are still fully clothed.

"You did that intentionally," I say to him, after we've finished drinking and stepped back from the table. I'm feeling full from the beer and maybe a little tilty, but surprisingly good, like a weight has been lifted from me.

He shrugs, refusing to answer.

"I hit the shot," I say in amazement.

"Yeah, you did."

And for a second it feels real. Like I belong here.

Because of Liam. Just like I'd hoped, like I'd dreamed.

"Thank you," I say, staring at him in wonder.

He smiles at me in a way that makes my heart bump in a disconcertingly uneven rhythm. "Knew you could do it."

"Don't do it again," I add hastily. "But thank you."

He puts an arm around my shoulders and pulls me in

close against his side. He still smells good, like pine and soap and warm skin. How is that possible?

"You're welcome," he says, his gaze searching my face.

Acting on an instinct I didn't know I had, I tip my chip up.

He leans closer, and my heart pounds so hard I feel shaky from it. But when his mouth brushes over mine, everything else drops away.

Chapter Thirteen

The morning light through the open curtains is too bright. It takes me a second to figure out why it seems to be coming from below me.

Because I'm in Liam's lofted bed. With Liam. His back is pressed against mine. And a quick glance down shows me that, yep, I'm wearing his T-shirt from last night.

And nothing else.

After that first kiss, we played one more game of beer pong, which we lost. And then Liam suggested we go back to his room. His roommate was still out of town.

My whole body goes warm as I remember where he touched, where *I* touched, in vivid detail. We didn't have sex. Not in the most technical definition. But waking up next to him is intimate on a whole other level.

It feels surreal, like it happened to someone else in a

show I was watching. Except it didn't. It was me! It *is* me.

A giddy smile spreads across my face. I knew that a fresh start at Ashmore was what I needed. I never dreamed it would also give me everything I was too afraid to even hope for. In the first week, no less!

I roll over, careful to keep my mouth below the line of Liam's shoulder—no point in sending morning breath to greet him. "Hey," I whisper, resting my hand on his side.

I'm expecting him to roll over toward me, maybe touch my hair again. No kissing because, again, morning breath.

Instead Liam jolts beneath my touch. "Hey . . . Caroline." His voice is foggy and distant with sleep—and possibly a hangover.

"I didn't mean to wake you," I say. *Not exactly true.* I shift closer. "I was thinking we could go get something to eat." *Make out a little more.* "I don't have class until one." I have *two* new classes today, in fact. In addition to all of yesterday's homework, which I should be worrying about or at least making a plan for. But I can't seem to bring myself to care about either of those things with Liam next to me. "And maybe later we could go to the union? I think they're showing that new movie with the guy who played Magneto. Or we could try the bowling—"

Liam shifts away from me abruptly to sit up.

"Is everything okay?" I ask. "Are you feeling sick from the—"

"Listen, Caroline . . . ," he begins, without looking at me.

A distant alarm sounds in the back of my mind, like a siren growing closer and closer, and my heart is thumping like I'm being chased by a serial killer.

"This is awkward," he says with a forced laugh. "Last night was fun, but I think maybe you got the wrong idea. I just got out of a relationship, and I don't want to . . . you know, move too fast into something else."

I feel the blood draining away from my head. Is it even possible to pass out while you're lying down? I have no idea. "No," I say faintly. "I . . . understand." *No, I don't!* He *was the one who kissed* me*! He was the one who started this!*

I need to get out of here, but I can't seem to make myself move.

"You were, um, great," he says, reaching out to pat my leg. "But I think maybe we should just be friends, you know?"

Get up, Caroline. Move. Or he's going to keep talking, and it's going to get worse.

I lurch upright, scrambling away from him and down to the floor.

"Caroline, are you okay?" he asks.

I can't speak. The words are locked in my throat. I'm standing, pantsless, in Liam's room. In front of Liam, who is telling me how much he does not like me "that way."

I make my chin jerk up and down in the semblance of

a nod, so he won't ask me again if I'm okay. Then I find my clothes and get dressed under the cover of his shirt.

"We're still friends, Caroline," he says.

"I'll . . . your shirt . . ." I can't get the words out. The thought of being exposed in front of him again, even for the few seconds to switch tops, makes my throat lock up.

"You can give it back to me later," he says with a careless wave of his hand. He sounds relieved. Relieved that I'm leaving. I can feel the embarrassed heat scorching through me.

Tucking my/Lexi's shirt under my arm, I start for the door.

"I'll text you later," he says. "We can meet for dinner."

Mute, I bob my head at him without looking back.

I can't get out of his room, off his floor, and out of Granland fast enough.

No one is out and about on campus. It's still too early. So I am the sole witness to my heart-crushing humiliation. Other than Liam, of course.

I hurry the short distance to Brekken, the grass damp on my feet through my flip-flops. *Maybe it's not that bad. Maybe it'll just be awkward for a few days, and then it'll be like it never happened. It's not like I ever really expected that Liam and I would . . .*

Except after last night I kind of did, and suddenly it feels like I'm losing something. Even if I never actually had it. Or only had it for a few hours.

Tears slide down my cheeks to drip off my chin. *It's not fair.* I had everything for a brief shining moment, only for it to vanish?

Breathe, Caroline. What would Felicity do?

I don't know. Because this never would have happened to her!

That only makes me cry harder.

At the Brekken entrance, I fumble in my pocket for my ID card to unlock the door.

"Hey," a voice says out of nowhere

I jump. But it's only Tory, sitting against the wall, half hidden by the bike rack. Actually, "sitting" might be a generous term. She's slumped against the wall, waving lazily at me. She's wearing . . . I'm not sure *what* she's wearing. It might be an Alice in Wonderland costume. If Alice were prone to teased hair, body glitter, and deep cleavage. Also, Tory's dress has what appears to be vomit stains down the front.

"What are you doing out here?" I ask, swiping at the tears.

"Forgot my ID," she says. Her accent is heavier when she's been drinking. *Ah-Dee.* "Couldn't get in."

"Have you been out here all night?" I ask, hurrying over to help her up. Yep, definitely vomit.

She pats my cheek. "Bless your heart, no. Only about . . ." She squints at me. "What time is it?"

"I don't know," I admit. "Early."

"See?" She points at me with a laugh as we stumble toward the door. "You were a bad girl too."

I help Tory to our floor and then to her room, where she collapses on her bed. I shove piles of discarded clothes out of the way until I find a trash can and set it next to her.

I let myself out, closing the door behind me, and then, dread curling in my stomach, I head to my room.

After slipping into the darkened room as quietly as possible, I shut the door and tiptoe toward my bed, pausing only long enough to put Lexi's shirt in my laundry basket.

Lexi stirs. "You okay?" she mumbles.

I go still. "I'm . . . great!" I say, forcing my voice up into near-apocalyptic levels of peppiness. "Thanks for the loan. I'll wash it and get it back to you."

"Mm" is all she says.

I ignore it—and her—to yank back the covers on my bed, climb in, and then pull the sheet and comforter over my head.

But I can't cry, not with Lexi in the room. So I lie there, my brain circling through everything that happened, trying to find the place where I messed up.

It can still work out. It will still be okay.

I keep telling myself that over and over, trying to believe it.

Eventually I must fall asleep, because when I open my eyes again, the room is brighter, the light managing to penetrate my bedcover cocoon.

I peel back the covers to find that Lexi is up and gone. Checking my phone, I see that it's almost noon.

And I don't have any new texts. About meeting for dinner or otherwise.

But then again, it's not like he doesn't know where to find me at the last minute. Maybe he's not thinking about dinner yet. It is just lunchtime.

Or maybe he's never going to text me again.

Against my better judgment, I pull up our last text conversation. An ugly desperation moves me to type. Sorry about last night. Still on for dinner? How about the union caf? In the mood for pizza. I add the cross-eyed, tongue-sticking-out emoji for good measure. A perfectly normal "we're still friends" text if I ever saw one. Which, frankly, I haven't, but I think I'm on point.

I hold my breath and hit send.

The "delivered" notification pops up. A moment later the gray typing dots appear, and I exhale in a loud rush; the relief is so intense it feels like I'm falling.

But then the dots stutter, pause, and vanish.

And even though I wait, they don't come back.

Chapter Fourteen

Wednesday passes in a slow blur. I try to focus on classes—*you're overreacting, Caroline; he's just busy*—but it's hard to concentrate. The silence from Liam is so loud.

In my room at the end of the day—after eating pizza in my room by myself—I pull up my favorite episodes of *Felicity*—my never-fail for comfort—but here and now all they do is remind me of everything I don't have. By the time the theme music comes up, I'm crying, and I have to switch over to *House Hunters*.

I think about calling Dr. Wegman, but that would involve leaving out a lot of pertinent details. And he'd probably only remind me (again) that it's a process and that not everything will go the way I want it to. Obviously.

When Lexi comes back to the room at the end of the

day and settles in with her laptop on her bed, I catch her watching me from time to time. She wants to say something, clearly, but she refrains.

Which is good. Because everything is going to be okay. It's not like she was right about Liam. Yes, things got out of hand last night, but it happens. It's a bump in the road.

Come tomorrow, once we've had a little time and distance, everything will be fine. He and I will be back to eating together and going to parties, as *friends*. Ashmore is still the place for me. When Liam and I are seniors—and probably dating other people, a thought that hurts my heart—this will be an experience that we'll look back on and laugh about.

Except that when tomorrow does come, still no texts. *He's avoiding me. He has to be.*

I want to believe that's just paranoia talking, but it's starting to seem like the most likely explanation, especially when I see Jordan and the other PBTs at the lunch table in the union cafeteria on Thursday, like before, but no Liam.

By Friday morning, my rationalizing is growing thin. I've been at Ashmore less than a week and somehow managed to ruin everything.

Life around me is going on like normal; people are laughing and talking like they don't have a care in the world, which only makes me feel worse. Like I'm isolated again, trapped in a bubble that separates me from everyone else.

I drag myself to classes, but only because Lexi will notice if I don't go, and I refuse to have *that* conversation. The minutes tick by excruciatingly slowly. I look for Liam everywhere, until I realize that he might catch me doing so, and I can't decide if being caught is worse than missing a glimpse of him and the small possibility that he might wave me over and say hello, like nothing happened.

Distantly, I'm aware that it's a perfect day outside. The sky is that deep shade of blue that means autumn is coming, and the leaves on the trees are starting to change to lighter shades of green and yellow. Groups of people are out on the quad, studying on blankets, playing Frisbee, or standing and chatting. Students in brightly colored armbands are chasing one another across and up and down the sidewalk, with flags on little metal wires.

Scavenger Flag. That must start today. It's a weeklong Ashmore tradition, a unique combination of a scavenger hunt and capture the flag. Liam mentioned it at lunch, told me we should sign up as a team.

Guess that won't be happening. Sadness and regret cut through me.

On my way home from my last class on Friday afternoon, my phone buzzes in my pocket, and I immediately grab for it, nearly dropping it in my eagerness.

It's a text, but not from Liam.

It's from Sophie: Hi Caroline! Your mom asked me to send her flight info. Details below. Two weeks from tomorrow! :)

Two weeks. I stop on the sidewalk leading to Brekken, my feet frozen in place, even as people are forced to flow around me.

My plan is in pieces, and I don't have anything to replace it. My mom is going to show up here and find that everything is exactly the way it was in high school. I'm alone. Not fitting in. Only it's worse this time, because I chose to be here, I had a chance, and somehow I messed it up. She'll take me home for sure.

But does that even matter anymore? What's the point of being here if . . . if Liam is not my Ben? My breath catches in my chest, and despair feels like a knife digging deep into my lung.

How did it all go so wrong so quickly?

The Scavenger Flag players nearby give a cry of triumph, making me jolt and drawing my attention.

There are four or five of them in green armbands, high-fiving one another, and then one of them, a guy, picks up a girl teammate and spins her around until she shrieks with laughter and pushes at him to let her down.

Envy and anguish are twin pulses in me. That might have been me. That could have been Liam, picking me up.

Wait. *Wait.* That guy . . . his blond hair, the way he throws his head back to laugh.

I'm not close enough to see his dimples or the scar on his chin. But it's Liam.

My stomach churns and then falls. He's here.

He's not too busy. His phone didn't die. He's not trapped in his room with a broken leg, waiting to be discovered. Or any of the other increasingly ridiculous scenarios I've conjured for why he wasn't returning my texts.

Not that I really thought any of those were true, but—based on the horrible sinking feeling in my stomach—I guess some part of me was still hoping against hope that they might be.

But no. Liam is hugging a pretty redhead who is not me.

And then, suddenly, I'm moving, feet no longer stuck to the ground. Instead they're carrying me easily, mechanically, across the sidewalk and the grass, to the Scavenger Flag players.

To Liam.

"Caroline. Hey." Liam gives me an uncomfortable smile when he sees me coming. And I want to die.

But anger rises up hot and fierce, burning away some of the humiliation.

"Can we . . ." I jerk my head, indicating a spot a few feet away.

His pause is infinitesimal, but I sense it anyway. "Sure. Give me a minute, guys," he says to his teammates.

"What's up, Caroline?" he asks, when we're out of earshot. "Are you okay?" I hear more than a hint of wariness in his voice.

"I thought . . . I thought we were going to . . ." I tip my chin toward the armband tied around his bicep.

He glances down at it. "Oh. Yeah. I was talking to some guys, and it turns out that Granland had a couple teams already going, so I thought I would just join them." His forehead furrows. "That's what you wanted to talk about?"

"You didn't text me back."

His cheeks flush, and he looks away from me, staring at some point in the distance. "Yeah, I'm sorry. I've been busy."

The lie hangs in the air between us.

I fold my arms across my chest, hugging myself. "*You* kissed *me*," I say. "*You* invited me back to *your* room."

He makes an exasperated sound. "I know that," he says. The muscles at the back of his jaw are tight, standing out beneath his skin. "But I didn't know you were going to be all . . ."

Don't say it. Don't say it. Don't say it.

". . . weird about it."

He said it. Tears flood my eyes and roll down my cheeks.

"Are you serious right now?" I try to ask, but my voice only comes out as a whisper.

"It was one night," he continues, avoiding my eyes. "We were both lonely and missing home. It was no big deal. You're acting like I owe you something, and I don't."

The one person who made me feel important, who made me feel *seen*, is now pretending like I don't exist.

"I don't understand," I say, my voice clogged and congested. "This isn't . . . this isn't like you."

He scuffs his shoe against the grass. "Caroline, we don't even know each other."

"That's not what you said the other day," I say, scrubbing the back of my hand against my cheeks, trying to wipe away tears.

"Look, I'm sorry, okay? I didn't mean . . . This is college—I didn't think you'd take it so seriously. We were keeping each other company for a few days, making it feel less scary, that's all."

Past tense: We *were*.

"But I came here for you." The words are out before I can stop them, before I even realize that I was thinking them.

His eyes go wide, and he takes a step back. "Caroline . . ."

"You were always nice to me," I say quickly, trying to explain. "I figured any place where you went would be the same, and that we could be friends once we got the stupid high school baggage out of the way. You were my Ben, you know? Like on *Felicity*? You showed me that I could have more than . . ." I trail off, seeing that my words are only making it worse. I wish that the ground beneath me would tear itself open and swallow me whole.

But it wouldn't help. Because Liam's teammates, who are now close enough to hear at least some of what we've been saying, are whispering and exchanging significant looks. It won't be long before some version of this is all over campus.

Oh God. "I have to go." I turn away.

"Caroline," he says with a mix of impatience and apology, lifting his hand in a half-hearted attempt to stop me.

But he doesn't succeed, nor does he put any more effort into it.

And *he* doesn't follow *me*.

Chapter Fifteen

On Sunday afternoon, Lexi drops a plastic takeout container of food—half a turkey sandwich, pre-packaged apple slices, and a cookie—on my bed when she comes back from her study group at the library.

I haven't left our room since Friday except for the bathroom. I even canceled my appointment with Wegman, claiming a migraine, though I'm sure that made him suspicious. But what's the point of trying to keep him on my side? It's not like I have any reason to stay here now.

Lexi doesn't say anything about the food, doesn't wait for thanks. Just goes to her side of the room and begins emptying her backpack.

For some reason, though, this gift out of nowhere makes me equal parts angry and grateful. And then even more angry at the thought that Lexi has taken pity on me. "I'll be out of here soon," I say. "So you don't have to worry about it." I can't quite bring myself to call my mom and confess, but she'll be here in a couple of weeks anyway and she'll pull me out, no question, once she sees how I've failed.

I reach for my earbuds again. I've been hiding beneath my covers with Netflix and the mind-numbing comfort of *Beachfront Bargain Hunt*.

"Did you sleep with him?" she asks without turning around.

"Close enough." My eyes begin to well. "I don't need you to say I told you so."

"Did he tell you he loved you and then make fun of you to his friends? The way you dress, the way you talk? How hickish your family seems?" Her voice is taut with anger and pain. "Did he lie to you repeatedly when you confronted him about the rumors?"

I freeze.

"Did he beg you to take him back, but only in private because he couldn't stand up to his fraternity brothers?"

I drop my earbuds. "Did that . . . was that you and Jordan?"

She takes a deep breath, her shoulders rising and falling with it. "The summer before my senior year in high school, I was lifeguarding at the pool on campus. They open it up to the community once school is out. Swimming lessons, aquarobics, all that shit. Jordan stayed on campus after his freshman year to take summer classes. But he used to come in early in the morning to swim laps. We started talking. A lot. He's from Baltimore, never felt like he fit in here in Iowa. Because, you know, it's Iowa. Nothing like the East Coast. Plus, his mom is white and his dad is black, and he . . . I guess he never felt like he fit in anywhere." She shakes her head. "It's not the same, but I understood. I'm tied to Ashmore, the town *and* the college. In town, my dad's job sets us apart. Tuition costs more than most people in Ashmore make in years. I'll get a degree, have a chance to leave, unlike most of my friends. But I'll never belong to the college, either, not completely. Not the way the real students do, the ones who can afford to be here."

I resist the urge to point out that she is a real student too. She's taking classes, like everyone else, and that's all that should matter.

"But with Jordan it was like we belonged . . . together. Like we just fit because we didn't fit anywhere else. If that makes sense. It did at the time. Anyway, I don't know, things progressed. And suddenly we were spending every second together. And I . . ." Lexi's voice breaks.

"You love him," I whisper, drawing my knees up to my chest.

"I did," she allows. "I thought I did."

"What happened?"

"School started. He decided to rush PBTs." She shrugs. "You know the rest. He was pretending to be someone he wasn't. Either to me or his brothers, I'm not sure which. It ended . . . badly."

He betrayed her—that's the word I would use. Taking the parts she felt most vulnerable about and handing them over to people who wouldn't hesitate to use them against her. Then he lied about it.

Suddenly the change in her appearance—from the black sweater and pearls in her senior photo to who she is now—makes sense. It's an aggressive fuck-you to Jordan and anyone else who thinks she's lesser.

In spite of myself, I'm impressed. That takes guts.

"But why would he do that?" I ask.

"Because he's a fucking coward who desperately needs approval from a bunch of jerks to feel better about himself?" She drops onto her bed across from me.

"I . . . maybe. He still cares about you, though. I've seen it." I sit up.

To my surprise, she nods. "Maybe."

"So . . . ," I prompt. In spite of my own difficulties, I feel the flicker of investment in their love, in her story.

"It doesn't matter," Lexi says, reaching for her laptop and a notebook. "He doesn't love me enough. And I might only be the hick townie daughter of the school janitor, but I deserve better than that."

My mouth falls open.

Lexi straightens her shoulders, her chin going up in challenge. "You think I don't?" she asks, like she's daring me to say yes.

"No! I think that you absolutely do. I just . . . I don't know how you do it. How you don't care about fitting in."

She looks tired as she opens her notebook and uncaps a bright pink highlighter. "Who says I don't? Every damn day. I want to belong here like everyone else. I want someone who loves me because of who I am, not in spite of it. Is that so much to ask?"

"No," I say.

"The mistake, I think," she says, "is believing that once someone else checks the 'yes' box on you, then you'll have what you need. Then you'll be happy, then you'll be okay with yourself. I don't think it works like that." She glances at me pointedly.

I fidget with the edge of my comforter. "My situation is more complicated than that."

"I've heard," she says.

The blood drains away from my head, making my face go numb. I knew it was a possibility, a strong possibility, that rumors would start after my conversation with Liam in front of his Scavenger Flag teammates. But having it confirmed . . . I swallow hard. "So I'm the psycho creeper who followed a guy to college." I'm hoping, praying, that no one has made the *Felicity* connection yet, even though I was stupid enough to reference it when I talked to Liam. That will only make it more humiliating.

"I don't think I've heard it described quite that way," Lexi says. "But something like that, yeah."

I drop back onto my bed and pull the covers over my head. "Oh my God."

"It's not that bad, Caroline. And even if it was, who cares?" Lexi asks.

"I do!"

"Why?" she demands, getting up and yanking my covers back. "What makes him so perfect and wonderful? Why does he get to ruin everything?"

"He didn't ruin anything. I did."

"Because you believed him when he flirted with you. Thought it might mean more?"

I nod miserably.

She sits on the edge of her bed. "Caroline, if every person who made that mistake left campus, it would be a ghost town around here."

"But I followed him. I—"

"So? I'm sure people have done stupider things for

stupider reasons. You liked him, right? You guys were friends and you thought he was picking a good place?"

I hesitate, then dodge that part of the question. "He seemed to have it . . . *life* figured out," I admit in a whisper. "I wanted part of that for myself."

Lexi snorts. "No one has it figured out. Some people are just better at faking it than others."

An automatic denial is on the tip of my tongue before I remember Liam's confession that he thought coming to Ashmore might have been a mistake.

It hurts thinking about that memory, a time when it seemed Liam and I were on the same level, but I can't deny that it's also evidence that Lexi might be right. "I don't know," I mumble. "And it doesn't matter anyway, because I'm not going back out there."

Lexi gives me an exasperated look. "Do you not know how this works? The more you hide, the more you act like the rumors are true, the more people are going to—"

I jerk upright. "But they are true!"

"As far as you and a few others know. But that's it."

"So far," I say.

"Caroline, it's not like everyone on campus is talking about you," Lexi says as she picks up her highlighter again. "Most of them don't even know who you are. And anyway, even if they did, acting like a kicked puppy and cowering up here is only going to confirm their suspicions."

My shoulders stiffen. "Hey!"

"I'm sorry, is that *not* what you were doing?" she asks, opening her eyes wide with faux innocence.

"Whatever."

"You haven't even tried," she says, shaking her head.

That pisses me off.

I sit up, nearly toppling my computer. "You have no idea how much I've tried, how hard I've tried!" I say, my voice shaking.

"To be what you thought he'd like, to do what he wanted?" she asks with a sneer.

I shut my mouth. Her words are too close to the truth to deny.

She puts her highlighter down on the notebook next to her. "What about you? What's here for *you*, Caroline? Did you even try to make Ashmore yours? Instead of lying to your mom about all the friends you're making, why don't you actually go out and try to make some?"

I *knew* she was listening that day.

I feel the burn of humiliation spreading across my skin, and I can't resist snapping back at her. "Great advice from someone who actively hates it here. I don't see *you* trying."

Lexi slaps her notebook closed and shoves it, along with her laptop, into her backpack and heads for the door.

"Just because some advice is easier to give than it is to take, Caroline, doesn't mean it's wrong," she says. Then she leaves, letting the door bang shut after her.

I flop back on the bed, fuming. What difference does all this make to her anyway? She's made it very clear that we're not friends.

And I don't *need* her help. If I want to hide in here and give up, what business is it of hers? Maybe she'll even get to keep the room as a single next semester. Everybody wins.

I try to return to Netflix, but Lexi's words continue to eat at me. I'm not cowering. I'm . . . removing myself from a bad situation, that's all. And I did try here. Maybe not exactly in the way she described, making it *mine*. But what are the odds that Ashmore would end up being the one place where I fit in as myself?

After about another twenty minutes I get up. I can't stand lying there, listening to the Lexi in my head. Even Chip from *Fixer Upper* can't drown her out.

I'm beginning to suspect it's because some part of me thinks she might be right.

After peering cautiously into the empty hallway—I'm not sure what I'm expecting, a crowd whispering and pointing fingers?—I head for the bathroom, scurrying with my clean clothes and shower bucket in hand.

Maybe a shower will help. It has been a while.

Out of habit I avoid the puke shower, and then I feel a surprising wave of nostalgia when I realize I won't have to deal with that issue anymore once I'm home.

Why, though? Not having to deal with that should be one of the awesome things about going home, not something to miss.

It's just that . . . going home, as tempting as it is right now, also feels like failure. All the challenges, the things I have managed to do successfully here—not as many as I'd like—will be gone. I'll be starting over somewhere else, with new pitfalls. Assuming my mom ever lets me out of her sight again. If I give up on Ashmore after pushing so hard to go here, that's only going to panic her further, make her feel even more guilty for moving us to Arizona and somehow permanently screwing me up.

Yet, at the same time, the thought of leaving my room to go to classes tomorrow makes me shudder beneath the weak spray of the shower. People will stare; they'll whisper. And it'll feel like it's all about me, even though logic says there have to be other disasters-in-the-making on campus besides me.

Of course, Lexi's point is that they're doing that already. But if I'm out there and acting like I don't care, that at least suggests a different side to the story.

But it also means the possibility of running into Liam somewhere on campus, and I . . . I am not ready for that.

After I've finished showering, I brush my teeth and put fresh yoga pants on; then I gather up my stuff and head for my room.

But the familiar smell of fresh popcorn—hot, salty, and buttery—greets me as soon as I pull open the door, and my mouth waters, out of both habit and need. I should have eaten that sandwich Lexi brought me.

I hear voices, giggling and talking over one another, in the distance. The lounge, maybe?

Curiosity—and hunger—pulls me toward the source. The voices get louder as I edge closer, and I detect the sound of a familiar theme song: *Gilmore Girls*.

"No, I'm telling you it's the same guy! The one from *Supernatural*."

I peek around the corner and find the twins, Sadie, and a couple of girls I don't know spread out on the couch and the floor with blankets, pillows, and snacks.

Instinctively I pull back. I don't want them to see me. But I can't quite make myself retreat, either.

Gilmore Girls is a good show. Not as good as *Felicity*, but nothing is.

The idea of going to my room makes me feel restless and vaguely claustrophobic. But that's what I should do. Because they've probably heard the rumors already. I'll feel awkward and stupid and friendless if I go in there.

And how is that different from how you'll feel if you go back to our room? Lexi in my head asks.

Damn her.

All right. Fine. If I do this, at least Lexi—the figurative and literal versions—can't accuse me of not trying again. There is nothing more *me* than binging on a show with bags of microwave popcorn. If there's a place I might belong, it's in this room.

And this is my lounge, my floor. I have the *right* to be here. It's not like I'm begging them not to turn me away.

It only feels like it.

I tighten my sweaty grip on the handle of my shower bucket, dirty clothes stuffed on top, and start forward. Probably should have taken the extra minute to drop the bucket and clothes off in my room, but if I did that, I'm pretty sure I wouldn't come back.

The twins look up as I walk in. "Hey," they say in unison, but only after giving each other a knowing look. It's almost enough to drive me out.

But the other girls, the ones I don't know, say hello.

"We're watching *Gilmore Girls*," one of them says with a friendly wave. She's wearing a Packers jersey and sleep shorts. "You want to join us?"

"We're taking a mental vacation for a few hours," the other girl says, twisting her hair, all done in tiny intricate braids, into a knot on the top of her head. "No homework, no classes, no drama." She wrinkles her nose.

"No, no more Jess!" Cara snatches the remote from Lara. "Dean only."

Sadie silently offers up the bowl of popcorn to me.

And that's it. My choice to stay or go.

Cautiously, I take the bowl and sit on the floor at the edge of the blanket, staying close to the door . . . just in case.

We watch three episodes, debating the merits of Rory's various love interests, and I'm able to help by confirming that Dean on *Gilmore Girls* is Sam from *Supernatural*, and that his brother on *Supernatural* is named Dean. (To be honest, it is confusing.)

"See? Thank you," Ina says, mock glaring at Lauren, the one who invited me to come in. Lauren and Ina are roommates, from Four North. "I told you."

Lauren holds her hands up in surrender. "You win." She stands. "Ladies, I'm afraid mental-vacation time is over for me. I have problem sets calling my name."

"Boo," Sadie says softly, surprising me.

"Then *you* talk Professor Dunlevy into accepting papers on the mother-daughter dynamic of Rory and Lorelai instead," Lauren says, chucking a handful of popcorn at her.

Sadie ducks, then nods thoughtfully, as if seriously considering this idea. They must have class together.

Cara and Lara begin gathering up blankets, and Ina helps them. "Same time next week?" Ina asks. "I think I'm going to need it to survive accounting on Mondays without my brain exploding."

Cara and Lara look at each other. "Sure." Sadie bobs her head in agreement.

Then Ina glances at me. "You in too?"

I expect the twins to smirk and nudge each other, but they're just looking at me, like everyone else, waiting for an answer.

"Um, yeah," I manage eventually. "I can . . . I'll bring the popcorn."

"Sounds good," Ina says.

And with that they finish gathering up their stuff and leave, still talking as they head toward their rooms.

I stand in the now-empty lounge, staring after them. Okay, it wasn't exactly the kind of social success I pictured when I first got here, but it was *something*, and far more comfortable than anything else I've tried.

And I survived it. Actually, aside from that one awkward moment with the twins at the beginning, it was . . . almost normal.

Huh.

Maybe going to classes tomorrow wouldn't be so bad. If I decided to try.

Chapter Sixteen

"What a freak."

About halfway through Professor Wheeler's lecture on the two-party system, the whispered words drift down from the row behind and above me, followed by a fit of high-pitched giggles.

I stiffen, humiliation setting my skin aflame. I have to fight the impulse to turn around. They're not talking about me. They can't be.

I held my breath during my first class, but nothing happened. Other than a few people staring at me, but that might have been my imagination.

I started to think Lexi was right and I was blowing this way out of proportion. Then came political science, my biggest lecture, full of my fellow freshmen.

"No, I'm telling you, Liam said she followed him here,

like a complete psycho. Because of some old show."

Oh God. Definitely me.

My shoulders begin to ache from holding myself still. I'm not going to react. I can't. But coming to class was a mistake. I should never have let my minor success last night in the lounge guide any decision on venturing out onto campus.

And to make things worse, I'm trapped. To leave the auditorium, I'd have to descend ten rows and cross the main floor to the exit or climb five rows to the door on the second level. Either way, the girl who is talking shit about me would notice.

I keep scribbling in my notebook, pretending to take notes, but I turn my head slightly to the left, using the corner of my eye to look behind me. I catch a flash of long red hair.

Liam's pretty teammate. The one he was hugging. Are they . . . together now?

I face front again, and a tear rolls off my chin, landing with a splat on my notebook.

So fucking stupid, Caroline.

"Are you okay?" my seat neighbor—Darlene Samuels—whispers.

I wipe my cheek, disguising the motion by pretending to have an itch, and nod. This is so much worse than I even imagined. What am I doing here?

"And then she, like, chased him down in front of everyone,

demanding to know why he hadn't texted her," the redhead continues. "I saw it happen. I was right there. I mean, oh my God. Shoot me if I'm ever that pathetic."

It dawns on me belatedly that this monologue is loud enough that I'm *supposed* to hear it and react. This is not a random gossip session. She wants to see me bolt from the room.

It's a very Stella move. A very *high school* move.

For some reason, that pisses me off. This is college. Or it's supposed to be. Yeah, I messed up, but I *can't* be the only one.

Please don't let me be the only one.

Either way, I refuse to let this *bitch* win. She's not going to drive me out of class and then get the chance to go around campus gloating about it.

Lexi would probably have the guts to turn around and glare at her or even tell her to shut up. But if I tried that, my expression would give away my true emotions. So instead I plant my feet on the floor and force myself to keep my eyes on Professor Wheeler. Staying—tense, sweating, and miserable—is my rebellion.

The pseudo whispering continues through the rest of class, but less and less frequently once I don't react.

Still, the urge to flee as soon as Professor Wheeler dismisses us is nearly impossible to resist. But I make myself stand there, packing and repacking my backpack until students for the next class filter in. I tell myself I'm making a point, and I am. But it's also because I don't want to give that girl a chance to ambush me in the hall outside.

I won't be able to hold it together if she says that stuff to my face. The thought of Liam laughing at me with her makes the hole in my heart ache until it feels like it's going to turn me inside out.

Eventually, though, the professor for the next lecture arrives and starts making class-beginning noises. I have to leave.

With a firm grip on my backpack straps, I take the steps down to the main floor and then out into the hall, muscles aching with tension and bracing myself for that shout. *"Hey, aren't you the girl who . . ."*

But it doesn't come.

I lunge for the doors to the outside and then bolt for Brekken. People run on campus all the time, though it's usually to class, not away from it. But this time I don't care.

I arrive at Brekken, out of breath and sweating. I climb the stairs, enter our room, drop my backpack on the floor, and crawl into bed. That's it. I tried. I'm done.

But when Lexi bangs in that evening, she tosses a handful of brightly colored flyers at me. "Come on," she says. "We're going to be late."

I shove the flyers off me and burrow deeper under my covers. "I'm not going anywhere. I went to class today. That was more than enough."

"Not according to you."

It takes me a second to track back to our conversation yesterday, when I accused her of not trying.

I groan and pull a pillow over my head. "I don't care. Do whatever you want. Try, don't try. I'm done. Today was awful." I tell her about the girl in my political science class.

"The first day is always the worst," Lexi says, her voice sounding muffled. "But this will be different."

"How?" I ask, through the pillow.

"I guarantee that bitch and her friends will not be at this event." She sounds so pleased with herself, so confident.

I sit up, letting the pillow fall aside, intrigued in spite of myself. "Where did you get these anyway?" I ask, reaching for the flyers.

"Our mailbox." She's stuffing her books back onto the shelf and reloading her backpack with materials for her night class.

I pick up the flyer closest to me. "You want to eat pizza with Young Republicans?" I ask.

"What? No." She puts her backpack down and stalks over to my bed, scooping up the flyers, sorting through them and tossing aside the ones she doesn't want. A bright yellow one drifts down to land in my lap:

Are you a marathoner . . . of movies?

Are you addicted to binge . . . watching?

Join the Film Board, Wednesdays at 7 in the Chargers Room in the Union. We set the schedule for the movies and TV events on campus. Want a *Star Wars* finals week? How about Theme Thursdays? (Last year's *Parks and Rec* showing was a huge hit!)

Plus, your roommate will be happy you left the room for once. And we promise, no spoilers of any kind.

"Here. This one." Lexi thrusts a pale pink flyer at me, with a sketch of a cat curled up on a rug.

"Knittin' Kittens?" I ask, wrinkling my nose.

"No," Lexi says impatiently. "Knittin' *for* Kittens? See?" She points at the number between the words.

Knittin' *4* Kittens. Oh.

"It's a fundraising group for the Angels of Ashmore, the no-kill shelter in town. It's where we got our cat, President Fillmore."

"You have a cat named President Fillmore," I say in disbelief.

"It's a long story," she says.

"Lexi, do you even know how to knit?" I ask. "I don't."

"Do you think the cats are going to care if you knit instead of purl or whatever?" she asks. "We're making blankets for *homeless* animals. Plus, it's sponsored by the Gammas."

"Who?" I ask warily.

"A sorority. They're a little intense sometimes, but they're nice."

"Uh-huh."

"Trust me, Caroline," she says. Then she adds, "Every year they get a group together to help my dad and his guys rake the leaves, all right? I know them. Some of them, anyway. They're okay." She sounds grumpy about this fact.

"This is a bad idea," I say.

"Okay, Caroline. Let the poor kittens shiver in the cold, after being dumped in a box outside."

I glare at her. "It's like seventy degrees." I had no idea she could be this manipulative.

"Sure. *Today*." She sweeps her hair up into a sloppy bun and ties it off.

"Why do you even care?" I ask.

Lexi drops her hands to her sides, rolling her eyes at me. "I don't know. Because maybe it occurred to me that you *might* be right."

"Don't go overboard now," I mutter.

"And if I'm miserable for the next four years while I'm here, then that's the same as letting them win."

"Who?"

"The people who make me feel like I shouldn't be here because I didn't pay for it. The people who think I'm not *Ashmore material.*" She affects a snobbish voice. "So I'm going. Fuck them." She hoists her backpack over her shoulder, then grabs her keys and phone off her desk.

She starts for the door. "Are you coming?" she asks, over her shoulder. Her voice is softer than normal. And it occurs to me that she might be nervous, though that's hard for me to imagine. Lexi doesn't seem like she's ever been nervous about anything. Angry, yes. A lot. Always.

"All right, all right." I shove back my covers. "Will they have kittens there?" Because I think I could make that work. If I have a pile of purring kittens in my lap, I won't care if people are staring at me. I was never allowed to have a pet. No space or time for it when we lived in New York, and my mom was too stressed once we moved.

"Uh. Sure, Caroline," Lexi says.

I can't see her face, but I think she's rolling her eyes at me again.

Whatever. For even the possibility of kittens, I'm in.

There are no kittens immediately visible when we walk into the designated classroom on the lower level of Gellerson Hall. But there is a lot of knitting. A few small groups of people—

mostly girls, but a couple of guys, too—are gathered at a mismatched collection of tables spread throughout the room, with brightly colored skeins of yarn in front of them. The soft clacking of needles punctuates the quiet sounds of conversation.

I don't recognize a single person in here. But Lexi is right: I have a hard time seeing any of them caring about me and Liam or rumors about why I came to Ashmore.

"Welcome!" A girl hustles up to us as soon as we cross the threshold. "I'm Dena! How are you?"

Lexi shifts uneasily. "Great. We're great," she says with a grim smile.

"Great!" Dena beams at us. "Well, come on in. We have several stations set up with patterns and materials. Afghans, if you're super ambitious, but we also have washcloths, cup cozies, and scarves—"

"Wait," I say. "You're making scarves? For . . . cats?"

Dena stares at me blankly for a minute, then laughs. "Oh, no," she says. "We're not making things *for* the animals. We knit the scarves and washcloths and stuff to sell on campus to raise money for the shelter."

I elbow Lexi hard in the ribs, and she emits a small grunt in response.

"Oh, that's too funny!" Dena says. "You thought we were knitting for . . . oh, no." She smiles at us expectantly, waiting for us to join in.

And I wait for Lexi to explain, but she doesn't say anything. Her neck has flushed red, though.

"Uh, see, the thing is," I say, scrambling to find the words. "We don't know how to knit. Either of us. And we thought if it was for the animals, they wouldn't care if it was . . . you know, janky."

Dena is watching me as though I'm spouting complicated calculations that she's being forced to solve and then translate into English. And now others in the nearest group are putting down their knitting to listen in.

God, this is humiliating. And why isn't Lexi jumping in to help me? This was her idea!

"But if you're selling them . . . ," I continue, doggedly.

"We should go," Lexi says, turning abruptly.

"Wait, wait." Dena grabs hold of her arm. "We welcome everyone. Including beginners." Then she cocks her head to the side, eyes narrowing in recognition. "Wait. You're Mr. Chandler's daughter, right?" she asks Lexi.

Lexi stiffens visibly. "Yes."

Dena squeals and then loops her arm through Lexi's, drawing her deeper into the room, and I follow. "Oh, he's so wonderful! Do you know he helped us find a space for our geraniums?" Dena asks. "It's our sorority flower, but we're not supposed to plant anything 'without official university permission.'" Dena makes a exasperated noise. "As if the

Deltas asked anyone before they put in *their* hideous plants."

Lexi shoots a look at me over her shoulder, something between amusement and desperation.

"So, uh, where do we start?" I ask loudly, to redirect. For once I get to be the conversational rescuer instead of the perpetual rescuee.

Dena sets us up at the scarf table, supposedly because "it's so easy, even for beginners!"

A TA named Matt, who is cute in a tall, skinny, Michael Cera kind of way, gets both of us started with something called "casting on."

"My mom owns the yarn shop here in town," he says, blushing. He can't quite meet Lexi's eyes. "Stitch and Bitch. But with an asterisk where the *i* should go," he says. "So she doesn't get fined by city council, I guess . . ." His voice trails off. Then he clears his throat. "Let me know if you have any trouble."

"I didn't know," Lexi mutters as soon as he walks away. "We can go. This is dumb."

"It's okay. We're here." I scowl at the needles Matt gave me and the pale blue yarn trailing off them. "I don't think I have enough hands to do this right."

Lexi leans over to look at my stitches, which resemble a tangle of necklaces in a jewelry box—the strands twisted up and impossible to separate. "Is it supposed to look like that?"

"I . . . have no idea," I admit.

She snickers.

"Shut up." I elbow her arm. "Like yours is so much better!"

"It's not a giant knot," she says, holding her knitting up.

"I don't think it's supposed to have that many gaps," I say.

"It's a scarf," she insists. "Maybe it keeps you so warm, you need ventilation . . . holes."

"Ventilation holes?" For some reason, this cracks me up, and then I'm laughing until tears leak out of the side of my eyes. It's nice to be crying out of happiness for a change.

Lexi shakes her head at me, but she's smiling. "You're ridiculous, Caroline."

She's probably right about that. But for the first time, I don't mind it—I'm having too much fun.

Chapter Seventeen

I pull the yellow flyer from the back pocket of my jeans to look at it one more time, even though I know I'm in the right place. The Chargers Room at the union. From the outside, it's another nondescript meeting room in the basement of the union, one of at least a dozen reserved for groups and committees.

But I hear people inside, talking.

This is a gathering for the Film Board. The first official activity that has appealed to me—the real me—since my arrival on campus.

But right now I'm almost as scared as I was that first night with Tory at Phi Beta Theta. My heart pounds like I'm running for my life.

The chance to have a say, though, in what movies are shown on campus, and helping people discover awesome new/old shows? It might as well have said CAROLINE SANDS, THIS IS FOR YOU across the top of the flyer.

And I guess, maybe, that's why I'm nervous. Because if Film Board doesn't work out, then the chances of finding a place on campus where I fit in are fairly slim. Yarn Club—which is what I've started calling Knittin' 4 Kittens, much to Lexi's annoyance—was fun, and I'll keep going to support her and the kittens, but it's not really my thing. Lexi's right: My knitting is mostly knots, and not the good kind.

I fold up the Film Board flyer again and jam it into my pocket.

Okay, so I'll just go in. And if it's awful, I don't have to come back. Besides, it's not like I'll be the only person checking it out.

That sounds good. But as soon as I walk through the door, heads turn in my direction. Six people are gathered as a group around one of the ubiquitous-on-campus gray plastic tables, three on each side. None of them *look* like new students, with the slightly uncomfortable and/or panicked expression that I imagine is on my face currently. A pizza box sits in the middle, alongside a paper bag of bread sticks, both of which are filling the room with powerful wafts of garlic, even with their respective containers unopened. The white board on the opposite wall is wiped clean except for the words "Why me?" written in a blue-inked and beautiful cursive.

Yeah. Yeah, I'm feeling that right now.

This many eyes on me at once is almost enough to make me back out and leave. Especially when one set of those eyes—a whole face, actually—belongs to someone familiar. It takes me a moment to place him. Dark, floppy hair, glasses, Phi Beta Theta letters on his shirt.

Oh no.

Del.

He's the one I met the night I played beer pong with Liam, the night it all went wrong.

Liam mentioned he might rush the PBTs, and I'm sure people saw us kissing that night, so I can't imagine that the brothers, including Del, haven't heard *something* about what happened between us.

I can't move. Can't breathe. I'm frozen in the doorway, like a horribly awkward statue.

It's probably only a few seconds, but it feels like years. Then Del smiles and waves. "Hey! Caroline, right? I'm Del."

I nod. "I remember."

"Haven't seen you around much lately. You're here for Film Board?" he asks, and then, without waiting for an answer, he gets up and drags a yellow swivel chair from the corner to the end of the table. "Come on in; have a seat. We haven't even started yet." He turns the chair to face me.

I examine his expression; he doesn't *seem* to be mocking me.

The studious-looking girl on the other side of the table waves me in. "I'm Lissa. This is my committee."

"*Our* committee," the guy next to her mutters, brushing off the front of his crisp and spotless button-down shirt. His dark curls are cropped close to his head, the notebook in front of him is open to a blank page, and his pen is precisely parallel. Everything about him screams sharp angles and straight lines.

Lissa rolls her eyes. "This is Martin. He's cochair and our official pain in the ass."

"I thought that was Brett's job," the girl with the thin silver ring in her eyebrow says with a snicker, from the other side of Del.

"Hey!" The blond guy drumming his hands impatiently against the table stops. "I just asked if we could eat first, that's all."

So. I *am* the only new person.

But I can't leave now, and it's getting weird standing here, so I dart forward and take refuge in the chair Del has provided, turning toward the table.

"And you know Maisy and John," Del says, gesturing to the pierced-eyebrow girl and the guy rocking back on the legs of his chair. Maisy waves and John shoots a two-finger salute with a sly grin that makes me immediately uncomfortable.

No, I don't. But they do look familiar; I'm not sure from where.

"Right. Okay, I call this meeting to order," Lissa says.

"Are we seriously going to be this formal?" Brett asks with a longing look at the pizza box.

"It's not *that* formal," Martin says. "She's not even following Robert's Rules of Order, and—"

"Guys, can we not have a repeat of last year?" Del asks, pushing his hair off his forehead. "Especially in front of the new people." He jerks his head toward me.

And once again, all eyes are on me. I try to smile, but it feels more like a grimace. *Thanks, Del.*

"Let's get through the fall semester and then we can eat, okay?" Lissa pulls her laptop closer to her, while Brett moans.

After about twenty minutes, I can see why Brett was concerned. Martin keeps arguing with everyone else, and we're not even past Halloween on the calendar.

"You can't just play *Rocky Horror Picture Show* every weekend in October," Martin says.

"Actually," Lissa says, scanning her laptop screen. "I have a note from physical plant asking us not to show *Rocky Horror* at all because of the mess it causes. There was toast and rice everywhere last year."

Wait. What? Toast and rice are not usual movie snacks as far as I know.

Del sees my confusion. "You haven't been before?"

"Virgin!" John says.

"Oh. Well, no . . . I mean . . . I don't know what that has . . . I . . . ," I stammer the words tripping over my teeth and tongue.

"It's part of the movie," Del says, shooting John an irritated look. "That's what they call anyone who is new to the audience-participation part. You throw props, shout lines back at the movie."

"'Castles don't have phones, asshole,'" Lissa offers.

"Okay," I say slowly.

Del laughs and bumps my arm with his. "It's fun, I promise. We'll show you what to do." He smiles at me, and I reflexively smile back. The idea of being included in their circle makes me feel for the first time like I *might* belong here. The real me, I mean.

"Again, assuming that we get permission," Martin reminds us.

Brett lays his head down on his arms. "But it's a classic," he whispers.

Is he always like this, or is it the low blood sugar making him so dramatic?

"What if we offer to clean up?" Maisy asks. "I bet I can get some of the drama majors to help out. They love the audience-participation part."

"We could post a sign-up sheet on the community board online," Del says. "If we don't get enough volunteers for cleanup, we won't do it. That should be enough of a threat."

"Okay, but that's still only one weekend in October, and I'm not running slasher movies again," Martin said, clicking his pen on and off. "They're ridiculous, and last year we had that idiot running around on campus afterward in a hockey mask, scaring everyone."

"Martin's right," Lissa says grudgingly. "We had the city police and campus police involved because of the 911 calls. Better not to risk it."

"I'm so hungry," Brett moans.

That gives me an idea. "What about zombies?" I say before my fear can get the better of me.

Martin's mouth pinches in annoyance. "What, like *Zombieland*? *World War Z*? So overplayed."

I try not to feel the sting of his dismissal. "No," I say. "More . . . more like a retrospective. You could pair movies based on similarities or differences."

"Slow zombies versus fast," Del says after a moment.

"Right," I say, relieved that someone understands.

"And classic zombies, like *Night of the Living Dead*," Martin adds, looking thoughtful.

"With *Pride and Prejudice and Zombies*," Maisy says. "Another form of 'classic.'"

"We could even show the *Walking Dead* pilot," Del says. "They have a black-and-white version. Assuming we can get the rights. Run it with *Twenty-Eight Days Later*, maybe."

"I like it," Lissa says, typing on her laptop. "Familiar but different. We'll have to see what we can afford."

It's a small thing, but the feeling of having contributed creates a warm feeling in my chest.

"Speaking of TV shows, we should talk Marathon Mondays," Lissa says. "We need to kick that off next week or the week after."

Brett groans.

"Oh, here, for God's sake." Maisy flips open the pizza box and shoves it in his direction. "We're never going to get anything done unless we feed him," she says to Lissa.

The second Brett has pizza in his hand, he perks up.

Del hands out paper towels to everyone, while Maisy distributes cans of soda and bottles of water.

"Okay," Lissa says. "But let's keep talking or we're going to be here all night."

As the pizza box and bread sticks make their way around the table, Del leans over and explains. "For Marathon Mondays, we pick a couple of shows per semester. It's more of an informal thing. We show two or three episodes in a row—"

"Which is why comedies are better," Martin interjects. "Shorter episodes and broader appeal."

"—and we have food and discussion afterward," Del says, ignoring him. "It's like recreating the whole 'water cooler' effect. Making TV social again. Some people when they first get here tend to hole up in their rooms. I know I did." Del shrugs, showing no sign of embarrassment. "It's a way to make them comfortable and draw them out."

Brett holds his hand up. *"Better Off Ted,"* he says through a mouthful of pizza.

"*Parks and Rec* was a workplace comedy," Lissa says. "Not sure if we want to repeat ourselves." But she writes it down.

Other options are tossed out, rapid-fire.

"Broad City."

"Sex and the City."

"Brooklyn Nine-Nine."

"Friends." Which is met with groaning from half the table.

"Fine." Maisy glares at everyone. "*Seinfeld*, then. They're classics."

"They're also expensive," Lissa says. "Think older and cheaper. If we do it officially, the right way, we have to pay for the rights to—"

"Wait. I know." John sets his chair on the floor with a sharp thump and waits for silence. "What about *Felicity*?" he asks, smirking right at me.

A chunk of pizza crust catches in my throat, and I can't breathe.

The uncomfortable quiet that follows tells me that

everyone knows exactly what John is referring to. Even if they didn't know that *I* was the person at the center of that rumor, they do now.

Suddenly those feelings of belonging and contributing are washed away, and I feel horribly exposed, like in one of those dreams where you go to class naked and don't realize it until you're there, standing in front of everyone.

I try to swallow, but the pizza crust is firmly lodged. Coughing, I reach for my water bottle and knock it over instead, sending it rolling away.

Del catches it, twists off the cap, and hands it to me.

I take it and swallow half of it at once, trying to clear my throat. At least the choking provides an alternate excuse for the tears blurring my vision.

"Are you okay?" Del asks, his forehead furrowed with concern.

I nod, avoiding his gaze. I want to shrink to the point of invisibility, disappear into my chair.

"Asshole." Maisy glares at John and throws a hunk of bread stick at him. It bounces off his shoulder and lands on the table.

He picks it up and pops it into his mouth with a smug smile.

"A disgusting asshole," Maisy adds.

"What? Five-second rule," John says, his mouth full.

Lissa clears her throat. "All right, let's stay focused. I don't think we—"

"Actually, I think it's a good idea," Del says suddenly.

Betrayal and hurt slice through me. It's not like we're friends, but he was being *friendly*, at least. I keep my gaze fixed on the table in front of me, tucking my shaking hands beneath my legs. I'm not going to run. I can't. That will only give more life to the gossip.

"Kind of like what Caroline was suggesting with the retrospective," Del continues. "We could do a CW/WB pilot review. All the first episodes of their most famous series. Including *Felicity*." His voice is calm, nonjudgmental, not even a hint of laughter.

Relief crashes over me.

"*Dawson's Creek,*" Maisy says.

"*Buffy,*" Brett adds. "*Supernatural.*"

"Right, anything that's streaming now that people might be familiar with," Del says, shifting forward in his seat. "And then we could set it up like *The Voice* or whatever. Have people vote on which shows they want to continue with. It'll draw out fans of all the shows if we make it a competition."

"I like that," Martin says. "We can use that idea for the posters. Vote for your favorites."

"Because some people are *really* into their favorite shows," John says, rocking back in his chair.

"Shut up, John." Maisy kicks the legs of his chair, forcing him to lurch forward and grab for the table to keep from falling over.

He glares at her.

"Can we keep going, please, children?" Lissa asks.

And just like that, the conversation returns to the movie schedule.

I stay alert, waiting for John to open his mouth again. But the rest of the meeting passes without another reference to me or *Felicity*. It's almost like it didn't happen.

Except for the quiver of tension still running through me, the lingering damp stickiness of panic sweat on my skin, and the soreness in my throat from choking.

At the end, when everyone is standing and gathering up their stuff, John leaves first.

"See you back at the house," he says to Del with a head bob.

Maisy rolls her eyes at John's back. "Bye, John!" Then she looks at Del. "I have no idea what I saw in him."

"John is . . . John. Unfortunately," Del says, his mouth flattening into a thin line.

"Thank you," I blurt before I can stop myself. "For saying something. It's complicated, and I . . ."

"He likes to stir up trouble," Del says, a faint hint of pink coloring his cheeks beneath the dark rims of his glasses.

"Even when we were pledges together, he always made things worse."

Maisy glances back and forth between us and then steps toward the door. "I'll be right out here," she says, seemingly to the room. But her smile is directed at us.

I don't know what else to say to Del. "Well," I say finally, "I just . . . appreciate it."

He waves a hand dismissively, almost knocking over his empty water bottle on the table. "It's not a big deal. Some people are dumb when it comes to rumors. I prefer to make up my own mind."

Even though I know the rumors are, in fact, true in this case, I can't bring myself to say that.

"So, we're having a game night in my room tomorrow." He pushes up his glasses, his gaze flitting around the room. "You should come over. We're playing Last Night on Earth. It's a board game. Zombies versus humans. I think you would . . . It'll be fun." The color in his cheeks grows deeper.

He's nervous. He's nervous talking to *me*, Caroline Sands. The thought almost makes me giddy. Del is cute. And very sweet. But . . .

He shoves his hair back with one hand. "You should join me on Team Zombie. I keep losing. Statistically, the odds should be on our side, but . . . humans with chain saws, what are you going to do?"

"It's definitely a dilemma," I agree.

"It's super nerdy, but fun," Maisy adds, sticking her head in the doorway, where she's obviously been eavesdropping. "And crushing Del every single time we play makes it even better."

"Thanks, Mais," Del calls with a grimace.

Their exchange startles me into a laugh.

Del shoves his hands in his pockets. "So, what do you think?" He bites his lower lip, waiting for my answer, and it's adorable.

But . . . he lives in the PBT house. Where, if John is any example, the brothers may have lots to say if I show up there. *Liam* may be there.

"I don't know . . . ," I hedge.

"Maisy is coming."

"Opting out of the beer pong tournament. As if everyone hasn't seen me naked already," Maisy says with a wince, rolling her eyes.

This causes Lissa and Martin to look up from their quiet discussion on the other side of the room, but I barely notice as everything finally clicks for me: Maisy is one of the streakers from the party. *That's* why she looks familiar. John, too. Ew.

"Oh, and your friend, Tory. She's coming too," Del says.

"You know Tory?" I ask, surprised.

"Everyone knows Tory," Maisy says dryly, folding her arms across her chest.

A part of me is envious. We've been here a week and a half, and Tory is on a first-name basis with most of the campus, it seems.

But wait . . .

"Tory is coming to play a board game?" I ask.

Maisy snorts.

"She said she was when I talked to her about it the other day after class, but I suspect she'll end up in the pong tournament downstairs instead," Del admits.

Yeah, I suspect that too.

"Just, uh, think about it, okay?" Del gives me an uncertain smile, as he turns to head for the door. "Tomorrow at eight."

Maisy winks at me. "You'll be among friends. Some friendlier than others," she says, tipping her head toward Del.

"Maisy," he mutters.

"Okay, I will," I say, still stunned, my face warm but in a pleasant, non-humiliating way for a change.

In fact, I'm not sure I'll be able to *stop* thinking about it.

Chapter Eighteen

By the next morning, I've made up my mind. And then, for the rest of the day, I keep changing it.

I *should* go. I want to go. It doesn't have to be a big deal. I like Maisy. And Del. And, to Lexi's point, making actual friends would help my mom's visit next week go more smoothly. Mom has checked in with me a couple of times this week in advance of her trip to campus, and it's a relief, to an unexpected degree, to have stuff to tell her that's not a lie, or even an exaggeration.

But going down to PBTs again, after everything that happened, when Liam might be there . . . I'm not even sure how I'd feel about that. Potentially seeing him again. That could be . . . I don't know.

I should definitely *not* go. I need more time and distance. Maybe the next time Del and the others have a game night.

Assuming they invite you next time.

When classes are finally over on Thursday, my brain has become spiralized mush from going in circles. I walk into our room and flop on my mattress, not even bothering to take off my backpack.

"Goddamn it," Lexi mutters under her breath, from her bed.

I turn my head to look at her. She's scowling down at her laptop, which is balanced on her crossed legs.

"What's wrong?" I ask.

"I think I was supposed to yarn over instead."

I sit up. "What are you doing over there?"

In response she holds up knitting needles and her mangled, holey attempt at a scarf.

"Is it supposed to be . . . triangle-shaped?" I ask.

She glares at me, but there's no real heat behind it. "I don't know what I'm doing wrong," she says.

"Why are you doing *anything* with it right now?" I ask. "I thought Yarn Club wasn't meeting again until next week." I'd stuffed my needles and sad attempt in my desk drawer.

"I bumped into Matt at the Union today," Lexi says.

"Hot TA from Yarn Club Matt?" His full name, as far as I'm concerned.

She ignores me. "He asked me how I was doing with it, offered to meet up with me later to help."

I grin at her.

"Shut up, Caroline. It's not like that," Lexi says, but her cheeks and ears are turning pink.

"I didn't say anything," I protest.

"He seems nice, okay?"

"He does," I say.

"It's just a scarf," Lexi mutters, scowling at the clump of yarn attached to her needles.

It dawns on me that this conversation is more about Lexi talking herself into going, into *trying*. So I agree. "Just a scarf."

"How about you?" she asks. "How goes the whole friend quest?"

I wince. Trust Lexi to bring up a sensitive subject with her typical bluntness.

"I noticed you weren't home when I got back from class last night," she adds.

"I went to Film Board. They're the ones who—"

"Set up the movies and stuff," she says. "Yeah, I know. How was it?"

I hesitate, kicking the toe of my shoe against at a mark on the linoleum floor. "Fun. Mostly."

Lexi puts down her needles on the keyboard of her laptop with a clack. "Spit it out, Caroline," she says.

"Del," I say. "He's on the Film Board. I met him last week when I was at that . . . party. He invited me and Tory,

I guess, and a couple of other people over to play a game. Something with zombies versus humans. A board game," I add. "It sounds like fun."

Lexi seems unimpressed by this, but then again, she was never an only child, desperately attempting to play Sorry! with herself as the only opponent. For me, board games have not lost their appeal. Plus, you know, *zombies*.

"And you like him," Lexi says, cutting straight to the heart of the matter.

I squirm. "I . . . don't know him." And I've recently learned the hard way that that can be a big problem.

"But what you do know about him, you like," she says. "So what's the problem? Go play the game."

"He's a PBT. He lives in the Phi Beta Theta house."

"Del," Lexi says with a frown; then her expression clears. "Oh. Delfino. His first name is Marc, I think, but nobody calls him that. He was okay, as far as I know. He's a sophomore."

"Yeah." I was figuring that, if not older.

She looks at me. "But Caroline . . . ," she begins.

"I know, I know!" I hold my hands up to stop her words. "Believe me, I've already thought about it, okay?"

"They're going to give you shit, guaranteed. Maybe not Delfino, but someone will."

"Yeah." I hesitate. "One of the other guys at Film Board, John something? He's PBT and—"

Her mouth twists in distaste. "Yeah, I'm familiar with John."

"He's already said some stuff, but Del and Maisy—they're friends—they made him shut up."

Lexi shrugs. "I mean, if you want to go . . ." There's something she's not saying. But before I can decide if I want to ask her about it, she continues.

"I think you have to be honest with yourself about why you want to go, Caroline," she says, setting aside her knitting to type on her laptop.

I stiffen. "What does that mean?"

"It means if you're only going because you're hoping Liam will see you and suddenly realize he made a mistake and there'll be some grand reunion, *Felicity*-style or whatever"—she gestures to the poster on the wall behind me—"you gotta know the odds of that aren't good."

I blink at her. Once, that would have been my first and only thought: Will going to the PBT house—or anywhere, really—bring me into proximity with Liam and give me the chance to reconnect with him?

But this time, it didn't even dawn on me, a realization that startles me.

However, now that Lexi mentions it . . .

I take a breath against the sudden ache in my chest. I probably won't see him. I'm not even sure if I want to. Okay, that's a lie—I want to, but it's like when you're starving and you want to take that first bite of pizza before it's cooled enough to eat. You know it's a bad idea and it'll hurt, but that's not quite enough to make the urge go away.

As for the *Felicity* aspect, it's definitely true that Ben was always more interested in Felicity when she was seemingly happy with someone else. So going to game night with Del might work to my advantage in that regard. But honestly, I haven't had a whole lot of time to compare my life to Felicity's fictional one in the last week or so. Keeping up with my own reality has been enough.

"Liam's not a magic bullet," Lexi adds. "Being with him won't fix anything."

"I never said it would!" I just thought it, a lot. Before, though. Not now. I don't think.

"It's up to you," Lexi says, still managing to convey exactly what she thinks is the right/only choice. Which is infuriating. Just because she wants nothing to do with that fraternity because of Jordan doesn't mean that's the right choice for me, too.

"But what about that stuff you said about doing what *I* want? Not letting the rumors stop me?" I demand. "Making Ashmore mine? That's what I'm trying to do!"

"So then go, Caroline," Lexi says. "But know what you're getting yourself into."

That, I want to tell her, is exactly the problem: I have no idea.

Tory is on board when I track her down in the cafeteria after dinner to ask if she's going for game night. "Of course, darlin', let me get my face on!" she says, patting me on the shoulder and heading for her room.

Then, to my complete non-surprise, as soon as we arrive at the Phi Beta Theta house, she takes off for the basement, drawn toward the barks of male laughter like a mosquito to freshly exposed skin.

Which leaves me standing alone in the hallway, near the stairs. It's much quieter here on this random Thursday than it was the first weekend or on the first night after classes. There's no one to ask where Del's room is, something I should have thought about before now.

I hesitate, tempted to follow Tory downstairs to where the beer pong tournament is probably underway. At least that's familiar, even if it's not something I enjoy, and I can probably find someone to tell me where Del's room is.

Someone like Liam? a voice in my head that sounds suspiciously like Lexi's asks with scorn.

No. I push that thought aside and make myself start up the stairs, though I'm half expecting a group of brothers to come charging down and accuse me of venturing into their personal space, uninvited. Like when I tried to use the "wrong staircase."

But I *am* invited this time. So that's exactly what I'll say if someone questions me.

But no one does.

At the top of the stairs, a long hallway stretches the entire width of the house, with doors on either side. Most of them are closed.

But one is open, casting a triangle of light into the hall. Familiar voices drift toward me.

"You can't do that! Just because I got the lighter and the dynamite last time—"

"Because you cheated!" Del sounds exasperated.

Maisy laughs. "How did I cheat? I drew a card, Del. If anything, it's on you for not shuffling thoroughly enough."

I can't hear Del's exact response, but the grumbling tone of it gives me a pretty good idea of what his thought is on *that* idea.

I head toward the open door and then pause cautiously, poking my head in before entering.

Del and Maisy are kneeling, facing off over a game board set up on an oversized glass-and-metal coffee table that looks like a reject from the eighties. It doesn't seem like it belongs in a fraternity house. Or with anything else in the room, which includes an ancient couch and love seat in a shocking red-and-orange floral pattern with stuffing poking out of the holes where upholstery buttons used to be, a cheap press-board entertainment center that's tilting severely to the left, and an aquarium bubbling atop a stack of plastic milk crates. Behind the entertainment center, a deep purple curtain divides the room, giving the back half, presumably where the bed or beds are, some privacy.

The living area is messy, in the sense of shoes piled in the corner, an overflowing recycle bin, and a pizza box on the floor with a giant shoe print on it, which I hope is supposed to be garbage. But it's not as gross as the basement would have led me to expect.

Del glances up suddenly. "Hey, you made it!" he says, standing.

"Sorry. I . . . I wasn't sure which room, so I . . ."

He gives me a chagrined look. "I didn't say, did I?"

I shake my head.

"Sorry. But you found us anyway—that's awesome!" He seems genuinely pleased that I'm here. "Come on in." He waves me forward, and I step over the threshold. "Welcome to the palace."

The palace? Um . . . okay.

Maisy reads my expression and laughs. "Right? It's only because his roommate's last name is King. There is nothing palatial about this shit hole."

"Hey," Del says, with faux hurt. "I'll have you know we vacuumed today. In preparation for company." His gaze skips back to me, a shy smile pulling at the corners of his mouth.

"I'll send out the royal decree," Maisy says, taking a sip from the red cup at her elbow.

"We're getting set up," Del says to me. "Zombies on this side." He indicates the space next to him.

"Unless you want to be on the winning team," Maisy interjects.

Del scowls at her.

"No, I . . . zombies are fine," I say.

Maisy winks at me. "I bet they are."

I try not to squirm from embarrassment.

Del valiantly ignores Maisy and gestures toward the couch. "You can sit here. Do you want something to drink?"

He steps around me as I perch on the edge of the couch and heads for a mini fridge by the entertainment center.

"I'll get the others," Maisy says, getting to her feet. "Be right back."

"We have beer and some seriously questionable milk," Del says. "And this might be orange juice, but . . ."

"Beer is good," I say.

He hands me a cold can of Miller Lite as Maisy returns with three others in tow, two guys and a girl.

"Lachlan," Maisy says, pointing to the blond guy with hair

down to his chin and an impressive goatee. "His girlfriend, Gina." She nods to the curvy girl with long dark hair pulled up in a sloppy bun. "They're on Team Human with me. You get Mayer," she says with a dismissive wave to the last member of the trio. He's a good foot taller than Del and broad through the shoulders. He's wearing a White Sox hat, and ASHMORE SWIMMING AND DIVING is printed across his blue sweatshirt in flaking white letters.

"Fuck you, Maisy," Mayer says pleasantly. He's clearly joking, but the heat in the way he looks at her makes it seem like he might not be opposed to such an idea.

"You wish, Mayer," she says, blowing him a kiss, her gaze lingering too long.

Oooh. Definitely something there. I wonder why they're not together. But no one else mentions it or even seems to notice their flirting.

As awkward as it feels to be the only new person in a group where everyone else has history, listening and watching them interact fills me with both a tiny sense of being part of what they have and envy that it's not more.

"This is Caroline," Del says, slipping past me to sit on my left. "She's joining us on our brave attempt to save the world from humanity."

"I think it's supposed to be the other way around," Gina says, as she sits on the floor across from me.

"Not on this side of the table," Mayer says, taking a seat on the couch to my right.

"Zombies bite back," I say.

Del laughs, which sends a wave of warmth through me. "Exactly."

The game, as it turns out, is more complicated than I thought at first glance. Dice and cards and weapons and regeneration spots. Kind of like *Clue* on crack. Zombie crack.

But sadly for us on the brain-devouring side, the zombies are eradicated in just over an hour of playing, leaving Maisy, Gina, and Lachlan triumphant.

"We might need to rethink our strategy," Mayer says, cracking his knuckles.

"Chain saws," Del says glumly.

"And dynamite," Maisy says with glee. "Don't forget the dynamite."

As Del and Lachlan reset the board for their respective sides, I catch Maisy's eye. *Bathroom?* I mouth.

"The bathroom?" she asks loudly, making me cringe. "Oh, sure. The guest bathroom is downstairs, directly across from the front door. And believe me, that's the only one you want to use." She wrinkles up her nose.

"Okay, thanks." I stand and start to edge past Mayer, who shifts his legs out of the way.

"Del," Maisy says. "Your guest, your *female* guest, is going to the bathroom."

"Oh!" He lurches to his feet. "Sorry, Caroline."

Oh God. Can this be over? I just wanted to pee. "I . . . really, it's okay. I don't need an escort," I say, which makes Gina laugh.

"No, it's not that," he says, moving past the table and disappearing behind the room-divider curtain. He returns with a bottle of hand soap, a handful of paper towels, and a roll of toilet paper, all of which he gives to me.

"It's sort of BYO . . . everything," he says with a sheepish look. "If we leave stuff down there, it disappears."

"Including the knob on the door once," Maisy offers.

"But it's back now," Gina adds, when she sees my expression.

"Boys," Maisy says with a shrug.

"Okay, um, thanks?" I say to Del.

"Sure." He beams at me.

And I leave then, juggling my supplies, before he decides he needs to walk me down, too.

I find the bathroom exactly where Maisy said it would be, doorknob and lock firmly in place, which is even better. Aside from a layer of grime on the beige tile floor that appears to be permanently ground in, it's relatively clean.

I'm washing my hands when I feel my phone buzz in my

back pocket. After drying my hands with the thoughtfully provided paper towels—Del is right; there is nothing in here, not even a holder for the toilet paper; only holes in the wall where it should be—I pull my phone out to find a couple of missed calls and a voice mail from my mom.

Checking up on me again, no doubt. Even though she'll be here a week from tomorrow.

After balancing the soap and toilet paper in the crook of my arm, I open the door and then start texting a response, telling her I'm out with friends (TRUE!) and I'll call her tomorrow.

But with my head bent over my phone, I only make it a few steps into the hall before I sense a presence right in front of me and jerk back to avoid a collision, tripping over my own feet.

"Caroline!" Hands land on my shoulders to steady me.

I know that voice, those hands. I freeze, my thumb stuck on the space bar. *Liam.*

My heart can't decide whether it wants to flutter with anticipation or sink like a rock. So instead it's a nauseating rise and fall, like someone has set up a roller-coaster track in my chest.

I glance up to see him frowning at me. His eyes are *so* blue, though they're bloodshot at the moment. Once again, just seeing him sends that years-old wave of longing through me.

But this close to him, I can also smell the yeasty scent of beer coming off him, and he's swaying slightly. He's clearly been here for a while.

He releases my shoulders. "You're here for . . ." He pauses.

For me? That's what he was going to say. The humiliation makes me want to curl up in the first non-nasty corner I can find.

"The beer pong tournament?" he finishes finally.

"No!" I say at the same time.

He looks startled at my volume.

"No," I say again, my voice high and squeaky. "I'm upstairs. With friends. We're playing Last Night on Earth. Zombies against humans." The words escape in a rush, making it all sound like a lie. "It's a board game. We lost." *Stop talking, Caroline.*

"Oh. Del?" he asks.

"Yeah."

"Told you he thought you were cute." Liam's smile looks sad, and it makes me want to reassure him, to tell him that I still care about him.

But I keep my mouth shut.

A loud cheer rises from somewhere below, and then music kicks on, the floor vibrating with the bass.

"Listen, I wanted to say . . . I'm sorry for how everything

played out last week. I just . . . it was a lot of new stuff happening all at once," he says with a grimace. "And I thought we were on the same page, but we weren't, and then you kind of . . ."

"Freaked you out," I say, softening toward him in spite of myself. *He was talking about you behind your back to other people. Do you remember the bitchy girl in political science? Do you remember how hard it was to leave your room?* But my anger with him can't get a solid foothold in the face of him apologizing. He's my Ben; he's the one who first made me believe I could have more.

"I didn't know what to do with that," he admits.

Not making me feel like shit would have been a good start, the voice in my head insists.

I shift my weight uncomfortably. "It's okay," I say, putting my phone away and readjusting my grip on the toilet-paper roll.

"Everything is changing so fast," he says, rubbing the heel of his hand against his eye. "Stella texted me yesterday—she's with some guy now. From her zoology class." He gives a bark of disbelieving laughter, but I can't tell whether it's because of the guy or the timing or the fact that it was zoology.

"I'm sorry," I whisper. The urge to reach out and soothe him, to touch his arm reassuringly, is overwhelming. But the sharp and bitter memory of him pulling away from me in bed that morning keeps me in check.

"Yeah. It sucks," he says.

Another cheer comes from the basement along with a muted cry of dismay.

"I . . . I should go. We're setting up a rematch." I step around him.

"Wait, Caroline," he calls after me.

My feet drag to a stop on the industrial-grade carpet, and then I face him.

He rakes a hand through his hair, mussing the blond waves. "I was hoping we could still be friends," he says. "Maybe start over?"

I don't know what to say.

"Come with me," he urges. "Be my beer pong partner."

Despite everything, the offer makes my insides light up with joy. *Stupid, stupid joy.*

"What about the redhead?" I ask instead of answering.

"Who?" he asks, confused.

"Scavenger Flag. Your teammate?"

"Oh." His expression clears. "Kaity. No . . . it's not like that. Not like us." He gives me a hopeful look.

My heart jumps. "We would lose," I remind him, trying to catch my breath.

His gaze searching mine, he steps closer, reaching out to tuck a strand of hair behind my ear. "It's okay. I could use more beer." Then Liam jerks his thumb back toward the bathroom. "Give me a sec."

Before I can respond, he disappears inside the guest bathroom and shuts the door.

No one gave him supplies. I clutch mine tighter. Del and Maisy, they're waiting for me upstairs. Team Zombie is waiting. I like them all, even the people I just met tonight. Gina, Lachlan, and Mayer. I could see myself being a regular part of their game night, if they'd have me.

But Liam is asking for me, asking to start over. How am I supposed to say no to that?

The toilet flushes behind the closed door.

Except . . . I can see how it will go tonight. If I abandon Del and the others and go with Liam, we'll play—and lose—at beer pong. And at some point, there might be kissing. Again. He's drinking and lonely, like last time.

And that means there's a better than decent chance the events of last week will replay in the same fashion. I can't do that again. I don't *want* to do that again. And how much worse will the humiliation be the second time around? I can live without finding out.

Besides, I'm doing okay. I have Lexi and Yarn Club and Film Board and Team Zombie. And that's after one week of trying.

I'm all right. I don't need him. The revelation rocks me back on my heels. What Lexi said was right—he's not a magic bullet.

The door opens and Liam emerges with a frown. "They don't have any soap."

Obligingly, I step forward and give him a pump from the bottle Del gave me.

"Thanks, Caro," he says with a wink, returning to the sink to wash his hands. "Knew you'd have my back."

Caro?

"I . . . I'm going to go," I blurt loudly over the sound of the water. I feel like I'm jumping off the edge of a cliff.

"What?" Liam turns the faucet off.

"I have to go," I say, backing up. "But . . . I'll see you around."

"Caroline," he says. I can hear the hurt in his voice, and I squeeze my eyes shut against it.

It's enough to make me stop, but I open my eyes and keep going anyway. I don't want to go through that pain again, not after the effort it took me to get to this point. Maybe it's weak or cowardly, but I don't think it is. Sometimes strength is knowing your limits and defending them.

"Did you fall in?" Maisy asks as I rush into Del's room.

"Almost," I say.

She snorts with laughter.

Gina pegs Lachlan in the chest with one of our zombie figures. "You guys need to put the seat down, I told you."

"No, it's fine. I'm fine," I say with wonder. Now that I'm

away from Liam, away from the temptation of changing my mind, it's true. Maybe this isn't how I pictured college and finding friends, but it's working, and that's what matters.

I smile at Del as I hand him back the soap and toilet paper. He seems taken aback at first, then he grins at me.

"Ready to try again?" he asks as we settle on the couch.

I look at him and the rest of them gathered around the table. Gina and Lachlan are playing footsie, literally, while Maisy sets up a new playlist on her phone. "We need victory music," she claims, while Mayer rolls his eyes.

"Yeah," I say. "I am."

Chapter Nineteen

My phone buzzes angrily on the desk behind me.

It can't be morning yet. But opening my eyes a bare slit reveals light filtering in through our closed curtains. With a nine o'clock class this morning, I shouldn't have stayed out so late last night. The zombies finally won in round four, which meant by the time I helped Del clean up and tracked down Tory, who was not ready to leave and sent me on without her, I didn't get home until nearly three.

Lexi groans. "Shut it off, Caroline!" A pillow hits my shoulder before falling to the floor.

I reach my hand up and back to fumble for my phone and pull it down, expecting to see my alarm flashing at me. But it's a call. My mom.

I forgot to finish texting her last night. I didn't even listen to her message.

Answering the call with one hand, I rub the sleep out of my eyes with the other. "Mom, hey."

"Caroline, I'm surprised you answered." She sounds pissed.

I wince. "I'm sorry I didn't call you back last night. I was out with friends, and I lost track of time—"

She's quiet for a long moment; then she says, "Friends like Liam Fanshaw?"

Fear shoots through me like I've put a penny in a live outlet. "What?"

"Caroline, I know."

I jerk upright, shoving the covers back. Lexi mouths *Is everything okay?* but I can't answer right now, the whole of my focus on my mother.

"What are you talking about, Mom?" My voice sounds weak and shaky, because I'm afraid I know exactly what she's talking about.

"Caroline . . ." She sighs. "Fine, if you insist on doing it this way." I scramble out of bed and head for the door. This is not a conversation I can have in front of Lexi.

"I ran into Dr. Fanshaw in the hospital cafeteria yesterday evening," my mom says as I step out into the hall. "I was working late. We got to talking while we were waiting in line to pay. And she mentioned that she thought Liam might be having some trouble adjusting to his new environment at college."

Shit. I can already see where this is going.

"And when I mentioned I thought you might be having similar issues—"

I squeeze my eyes shut.

"—she asked where you were attending school. Imagine my surprise when, in an amazing coincidence, my daughter and her son go to the same small college in the middle of Iowa." Fury vibrates in her voice.

"Mom," I say quickly, opening my eyes. "It's not like how it sounds. I—"

"Really, Caroline? Because it sounds like, after making up stories for years about this young man whom you don't even know, you decided to *follow him across the country*."

I've never heard her this angry.

"Okay, parts of that are true, but you're making it into something worse than it is. I'm not, like, a stalker." I hug myself, shivering in the cooler air of the hall, and double-check to make sure my door is closed behind me.

Silence is her only response.

"I'm not!" I insist. "You have to understand the context and—"

"No, Caroline, I don't. That's my prerogative as your parent. My job is to protect you, even if it's from yourself."

"Mom—"

"I admit, I made some mistakes. Disrupting your life at

such a critical time with a move, and then not being . . . as present as you obviously needed me to be, afterward." She swallows audibly, and guilt rises up to throat-punch me.

"It's not your fault, Mom," I say. "I—"

"But you lied to me, Caroline. Not just once, but hundreds of times over the years, and then you continued lying to me even after you swore to me that we were done with this. That you were better."

"I am better! This is not the same, not at all!"

The door across the hall opens, and Cara sticks her head out into the hall. She holds her finger up against her lips.

I mouth, *Sorry*, and she retreats to her room.

"Tell me, then, that he's not why you chose Ashmore. That you're not continuing to live in some bizarre fantasy world where—"

"Mom, it wasn't . . ." I take a deep breath. "Look, you're right, in the beginning I came here for him. I thought if I started over in a new place, if I made myself into a different version of me, one he would like better, then—"

She makes a soft sound of dismay.

"—I would have everything I ever wanted. Friends, a place to belong. All the things that Liam seemed to have. But I was wrong. It's not about him. It's about me. And I'm finally figuring it out, okay? I actually was out with friends last night. Real friends. Not Liam."

"But how am I supposed to believe that?" she asks, sounding defeated and tired. "How am I supposed to believe anything you say, Caroline?"

Panic rises up in me, and I do my best to stomp it down. "Well, when you come here next week, you can see—"

"That's why I called this morning. I've changed my flight."

"What? Why?"

"I'm coming in Sunday afternoon, and Caroline, when I get there, I want you packed and ready to go," she says.

My mouth falls open. "Mom! You can't . . . Everything is . . . I have friends . . . Yarn Club . . . zombies . . . ," I stammer, unable to find my words.

"I can't let you do this," she says. "I won't let you ruin your life."

"But Wegman—"

"Wegman agrees with me," she says.

Oh. Fuck.

"He was very disappointed to hear that you've been lying to him from the beginning."

Shame washes over me.

"I'll see you the day after tomorrow," she says. Then she adds, in a softer voice, "I know this must feel like I'm punishing you, but your judgment isn't . . . clear right now. You'll understand when you're older, I promise. I love you."

The phone goes silent.

I press my back against the cold cinder-block wall and slide to the floor.

She's coming to get me. She wants me to pack. She wants me to leave!

Lexi opens our door and steps outside, yawning. She's thrown on a sweatshirt and pulled her hair up into a sloppy bun. "That didn't sound good," she comments. "Are you okay?"

I can't answer. I feel numb everywhere.

"Come on," she says, extending her hand.

I take it, and she pulls me up from the floor and leads me back into our room.

"So," she says, settling cross-legged on her bed. "Your mom is pissed about something."

I pull my knees up to my chest. "It's . . . yeah. She wants me to leave Ashmore." My voice breaks on the last word, and tears blur my vision.

Her eyes go wide. "Why? Did something happen at home?"

I shake my head.

"Okay, then what?"

I shake my head again. I can't tell her. She'll think I'm a huge freak. Not that it matters, because I'm not going to be here anymore after Sunday anyway.

"Caroline," she says over a huge yawn. "It's too early and

I'm too tired for this shit. Just tell me so we can figure out what to do."

We. She means it. The tiniest bit of hope flutters in my chest.

"It's . . . complicated," I say, swallowing the lump in my throat. "My dad took off a few years ago with a woman from his work. They're both doctors, so they're . . . saving the world or whatever."

Lexi wrinkles her nose.

"Right? He left me and my mom in New York, and I haven't heard much from him since."

"I'm sorry, Caroline. That sucks." Her mouth tightens in anger, on my behalf.

"It doesn't . . . it's fine. Well, it's not fine, but that's not the real . . ." I clear my throat. "I never felt like I fit in, even in New York, but it was so much worse when we moved to Arizona. I was a sophomore, and I didn't know anyone, and my mom was freaking out, blaming herself because I wasn't 'adjusting well' or whatever." I took a deep breath. "So I started making up stories, things I'd done during the day, places I'd gone, people I'd talked to."

Lexi's forehead creases.

"Friends, essentially. I wanted to make her feel better at first, but then I figured out I liked my fake life better than my real one. It got out of hand, and she ended up throwing me a surprise graduation party that no one showed up for. Because most of the friends I'd told her about weren't real. I borrowed the characters from my favorite show."

Lexi's gaze darts to the *Felicity* poster above my head. She's putting the pieces together, and I can't bear to see her reaction.

I focus my attention on a loose thread in the hem of my pajama pants, wrapping it around my finger until the tip goes purple. "I went to therapy and everything and got her to trust me enough to let me go away to school. Here at Ashmore. I wanted a fresh start—a new me, you know? And I thought I needed Liam for that." I hesitate. "But I didn't really know him. Not even as little as I told you."

I dare to look up and Lexi is watching me, expressionless.

"He was basically a stranger to me—that part of the rumor was true. I just had this idea of him in my head . . ." I rest my forehead on my bent knees. "But I was wrong, of course." My voice is muffled. "My mom found out about it. That I came here for him, even though that doesn't matter anymore. *He* doesn't matter anymore. She's freaking out because—"

"You lied." Lexi's tone is preternaturally calm.

"Yeah." I wait for her to say more, but when she doesn't, I look up, expecting disgust and/or irritation, same as I saw on Joanna's face on the night of my ill-fated graduation party.

But it's neither; it's fury, instead. "You lied," she says again through clenched teeth. "From the beginning."

Confused, I'm not sure what to say. "Yeah, I did, but I was only trying to—"

"I shared stuff with you I've never talked about with anyone, and you were lying this whole time?" She's practically yelling. Cara is going to be knocking on our door soon.

"Only at the beginning," I say desperately, not sure why she's reacting this way. "And then when we were talking about Liam, I didn't want you to think I was . . . it wasn't about you. It was about me."

"Isn't it always? So you were pretending to be someone you're not," she says. "A little bit here and there, no big deal."

Now, too late, I get it. It's not just that I pretended to have friends at home in a few chat messages months ago, or even that I lied about how well I knew Liam; it's that I did the same thing Jordan had done, in a way. I kept my real self hidden and lied, while she told the truth and was vulnerable. Even after she told me she didn't want to be friends.

Shit. "Lexi, I'm—"

"Don't." She stands up and grabs her backpack from the floor and starts jamming books and notebooks inside.

I try again. "You know what it's like, to want to fit in and—"

She spins to face me. "Don't you dare. This is not the same. Not at all. I was screwed over by someone I cared about. *You* lied. To everyone. You brought this on yourself."

Her words sting like a slap. But she's not wrong.

"I can't believe I thought we were actually friends." She scoops up her laptop, her keys, and her phone.

"Where are you going?" I whisper.

"I can't do this with you right now, Caroline." Lexi slings her bag over her shoulder and stalks toward the door, yanking it open. "Maybe one of your fake friends can help you."

I flinch. "But wait, are you coming back or . . ."

The door slams shut on my words.

Chapter Twenty

Lexi doesn't come back before the start of her first class or after it's over. I should be up, doing homework. Or, packing my stuff, per my mom's instructions.

Instead I'm lying on my bed, staring at the ceiling, listening to the sounds of my floormates getting ready for the day. Shower buckets clattering down the hallway; someone running with a backpack, keys clinking inside; a shriek of laughter, followed by another voice giggling and shushing.

Out of the corner of my eye I see Felicity on my poster. Her soft, enigmatic smile, the one that used to promise friendship, true love, and that everything will work out, now seems to be mocking me. Amused at my suffering.

Maybe it worked out for me, but it's sure as hell not working out for you, Caroline.

Furious, I shove myself up to stand on my mattress and

reach for the top edge of the poster, tearing it down the middle with the satisfying rasp of ripping paper. Felicity's head divides unevenly, leaving her chin on the right side but most of her face—and that smile—intact on the left side.

I yank that side down, struggling at first with the adhesive tabs holding the poster to the wall, and crumple it up into the smallest ball I can manage before chucking it toward our garbage can.

Lexi's garbage can, come Monday.

My rage-fueled energy depletes suddenly, and I drop back to my bed, curling up in a ball on my side, knees tight to my chest. Tears drip onto the comforter beneath me.

I should never have come here. I should never have *tried*. It was pointless. Even when I succeeded, I failed. At home I would have been miserable, yeah, but that kind of pain was a dull ache of unhappiness, not this sharp knife of despair.

I lie there for a long while, the thought of going to the storage room in the dorm basement and pulling my suitcases out filling me with a depressive lethargy that keeps me pinned to the bed and crying.

Eventually, though, I can't ignore the need for the bathroom any longer.

I drag myself off the bed and shuffle out into the now-deserted hall. It's that eerily quiet gap in activity that I've noticed a few times before. Everyone who has to be up for a morning class is already gone, and those who don't have class are still sleeping.

All the better. I don't want to see anyone. Once I'm gone, they'll probably assume it's because of Liam and the rumors.

I hate that. I don't *want* to leave. But I'm not sure there's any good in staying. I just can't figure out what everyone else seems to have mastered—knowing who they are and being comfortable with it.

Damn it. My eyes are burning with tears again.

I push open the door to the bathroom, and the creak of the hinges echoes inside. The abandoned feeling continues in here. No one is at the sinks, and all the toilet-stall doors hang open, but I can still hear water running. At the far end of the room, a single white flip-flop lies, discarded and seemingly forgotten, at the entrance to the shower area.

Creepy.

I start toward a toilet stall midway down the row—this one is decorated with magazine clippings that have chirpy headlines, like "Ten Conversation Starters He Can't Forget" and "How to Be the One Everyone Wants."

But as I reach for the door, my foot slides in water. I glance down to see a thin stream trailing out from the shower area, rolling toward the sinks and the floor drain out here. I walk farther to the back of the room.

"Hello? The water is overflowing," I call, raising my voice to be heard over the shower.

I pause, waiting for a response. "If you're in the one on the far side, the drain doesn't work right in there." It's the vomit stall, and it's been screwed up since that first day.

There's no answer, not even the clunk of a shampoo bottle against the floor, or the clatter of a razor dropping into a shower caddy. My gaze falls on the single flip-flop.

It's weird that someone left it there.

My imagination kicks into high gear, and I take a couple of steps to cautiously peer into the shower area, half expecting to see two people locked in a naked embrace or blood smeared on the wall in a serial-killer-type message.

Instead I see, poking out from the vomit stall, tanned, slim, bare legs on the floor, toes pointing toward me. The nails are a pale shade of lavender.

Moving faster than I imagined possible, I step forward and yank back the curtain.

Naked, Tory lies at an awkward angle in the cramped area, her head pressed against the wall, a pile of vomit to the side of the shower spray.

She's not moving. Her eyes are shut. Her long dark hair is wet and sticking to her like seaweed. How long has she been in here?

"Tory." My voice comes out as a whisper instead of the shout I intend.

I move into the stall, fumbling to shut off the water before bending down to her. "Tory!" I shake her shoulder. But she doesn't respond. I can't tell if she's breathing.

"Help!" The word escapes as a panicked bleat. "Help!" Should I go get someone? I don't feel like I should leave Tory by herself. I try to pull her up off the floor, but her skin is too slippery from the water. I grab for the towel on the hook behind us. *"Help!"* I want to shout for Lexi. She was a lifeguard—she probably knows CPR. But she's gone.

The main bathroom door bangs open.

"Help! In here!" I shout. I always thought I would be good in an emergency, but right now all I want is for someone else to come in and take over.

When I look back, there's Sadie, pinching the end of her braid in one hand. "What's wro—" She stops as soon as she sees me kneeling over Tory.

"I don't know, I . . . I think maybe she passed out. Hit her head. I don't know. She's been throwing up."

Sadie, to her credit, nods calmly and turns as she pulls her phone from her pocket. "I need an ambulance. Ashmore campus, Brekken Hall, fourth floor," she says as she hurries out of the bathroom door. "I can show you where."

"Come on, Tory, get up," I whisper. I wrap the towel around her shoulders as best as I can.

Lexi bursts into the bathroom at a run, her boots clomping on the floor in a reassuring clatter. "What's going on? I was in the lounge and I heard shouting . . ."

When she sees me, anger and confusion flash across her face. But they vanish as soon as she takes in the scene.

Tears that I hadn't known were lying in wait immediately pour forth. "She needs help. I don't know." I tug at Tory's covered arm. "I can't lift—"

"Wait," Lexi says, dropping to her knees, not caring about the water or the puke, and I move to the side. She presses her fingers against the side of Tory's neck and then leans over to watch her chest. "She has a pulse and she's breathing. But she might have hurt her head or her neck when she fell. We shouldn't move her."

"But—" I sob.

"Caroline," Lexi says in a surprisingly gentle tone, "shut up."

So I kneel on the other side of Tory and hold her hand.

The wait for the ambulance feels excruciatingly long.

One minute the bathroom is quiet and still, except for me trying to stop crying and the occasional drip and echo from the showers or sinks.

Then the next minute I hear Sadie out in the hall. "In there!" Lexi gets up and out of the way, taking me with her a mere second before the room explodes in activity. Two EMTs in dark uniforms run in, carrying a stretcher board with them.

"What happened?" one of them asks as they set to work, tearing open plastic coverings on syringes, removing equipment from their bags.

Lexi looks to me, and I find the words, push them out. "I don't know. I found her like this. She's . . . she's been drinking a lot. I think. I tried to wake her up, but . . ."

"Got it," the EMT says without looking in my direction.

After a few minutes they have Tory in a neck brace and on the stretcher, a white sheet covering her body but not her face, thankfully. According to television, at least, that means she's still alive.

And then they carry her out.

But Tory doesn't wake up, not even a little, during all of that.

Chapter Twenty-One

Lexi, Sadie, and I follow the ambulance to Mercy General in Lexi's dented red truck. I didn't think to ask which hospital, but Lexi seems to know without question.

The waiting room at the hospital is horrible. It's green vinyl chairs, scuffed linoleum, and *Seinfeld* reruns on the television. At least it's empty, which helps.

Now I'm curled up in one of the chairs, arms wrapped around my legs. We've been here for the better part of two hours already and no one has told us anything. Sadie is studying something on her phone, while Lexi sits in her chair, seemingly unruffled except for her trembling hands.

"Is she going to be all right?" I ask, clenching my teeth against chattering. It is so cold in here.

"I don't know," Lexi says, locking her hands together in her lap. "It depends on her head and neck injuries."

"And whether she aspirated any of the vomit," Sadie adds.

"Right," Lexi says.

I stare at them. I don't understand how they're so calm when Tory could be paralyzed or dying for all we know. But then I remember: nursing for Lexi and premed for Sadie. This is what they will deal with every day in their future.

A nurse in scrubs appears in the doorway. "You're here for Tory St. James?"

"Yes," Lexi says when I can't speak.

"She's awake now, but a little out of it. We're treating her for alcohol poisoning." The nurse gives us a censorious look as if we were the ones who poured it down her throat. "Her lungs are clear and her CT scan and X-rays came back fine. We're going to keep her overnight for observation, but she should be ready to go home sometime tomorrow afternoon."

"She's all right?" I ask, barely able to believe it.

"Can we see her?" Lexi asks.

The nurse leads us down a hallway to a room divided by blue curtains.

Tory is on the left side with her eyes shut. She has a white bandage on the right side of her head, probably from where she hit the shower wall. Her hair is damp and frizzy where it's drying, and she's wearing a hospital gown. She looks smaller than I expected. And young and vulnerable, despite—or perhaps because of—the smeared makeup beneath her eyes and on her cheeks.

She opens her eyes when she hears us approaching.

"Hey." Tory waves weakly with her non-IV hand, as we hover near the side of her bed.

"Not too long, girls," the nurse warns us before leaving.

"You're okay," I say, my voice coming out choked.

"You found me?" Tory asks, her gaze skating over the three of us, unfocused and dazed-looking.

"Caroline did," Lexi confirms. "I'm not sure if any of us would have thought to check the shower. Not that fast, anyway." She gives a little nod in my direction.

I told them on the way over, babbled actually, about the flip-flop and the water and the bad feeling I'd had.

"Sadie called 911 and Lexi came to see if you needed CPR. She kept me from moving you in case you had a head injury." The memory of the moment makes a lump rise in my throat.

"Thanks, darlin'," she says, reaching to pat my hand. "All of you."

"What do you remember?" Lexi asks. "We don't know how long you were in there."

"I don't . . . I . . ." Tory frowns. Her gaze snaps to me. "You helped me inside."

"That was last week," I say quietly.

"Oh." She blinks. Her dark eyes grow shiny with tears. "Oh."

"You'll remember more when you have a chance to rest and get rehydrated," Sadie says with confidence. I'm not sure if that's true or if she's simply attempting to reassure Tory. Either way, it's a gesture that I would not necessarily have expected from Sadie, based on my first impression of the awkward girl with her braid in her mouth at our meeting.

Then again, that's the same girl who kept her cool and called for an ambulance while I was freaking out. The same one who offered me popcorn and the silent invitation to join the *Gilmore Girls* marathon. So, yeah. First impressions are bullshit.

"Okay," Tory says with a sniffle. But then she shakes her head. "I'm going to have to call my parents. The hospital is already asking about insurance. And I . . . They're going to find out anyway. . . ." She's crying in earnest now. "I'll have to tell them that I messed up. Again."

I don't know how she messed up before, but clearly, she's upset about her parents finding out about this. I would have pegged Tory as having everything figured out. But maybe Lexi was right—no one knows what they're doing; it's just that some people are better at hiding it than others.

"It's going to be okay. *You're* going to be okay," Lexi says.

I squeeze Tory's hand, careful of the needle.

• • •

We stay with Tory for a few hours, keeping her distracted with stories about classes or, in Sadie's case, the herd of pygmy fainting goats her family has in their backyard at home somewhere in downstate Illinois.

From the pictures on Sadie's phone, the goats look super cute, and I want a black-and-white one by the time she's done talking about them.

The nurse comes back in to change Tory's IV and take her blood pressure, and she kicks us out shortly after four so Tory can rest.

Tory watches us go, and even though she smiles wearily and waves at us, I'm positive she's going to cry again as soon as we're out of sight. Part of me wants to hide somewhere and sneak back into her room and stay so she's not alone.

Lexi, Sadie, and I are quiet on the way out of the hospital and into the visitors' parking lot. Birds are chirping in the trees, and someone is laughing nearby, like it's a normal Friday. But with us, it's just the sound of our flip-flops and Lexi's boots on the pavement, punctuated by the jingle of the keys in her hand. "I realize this may be inappropriate, given everything that's transpired today," Sadie says as we approach the truck. "And with Tory still in the hospital."

Lexi and I look at her.

"But I'm hungry," she says, pushing up her glasses.

"Vending machine M&M's and coffee are not cutting it."

My stomach growls loudly in response, as if answering Sadie's statement with a *ME TOO*.

"I know a place," Lexi says.

None of us mentions the fact that the union cafeteria is open all day. I don't know about Lexi and Sadie, but I'm not ready to go back to campus yet. People will have seen the ambulance and us running out after it. There will be questions.

So we pile into Lexi's battered pickup truck and go.

Over the Moon is one of those real greasy-spoon-type diners, off the side of the highway on the way into the town of Ashmore. Bright pink neon sign outside. Red pleather booths inside with matching bar stools at the counter, which holds several glass stands of pies, cakes, and cookies.

The cab my mom and I took probably drove us right past it on our way to school, and I never noticed.

The sign at the entrance tells us to seat ourselves, so Lexi leads the way to a booth at the back on the right, in an otherwise empty section. I'm not sure why, until Erica emerges from the back, in that yellow uniform that clashes with both her hair and her nose-ring stone.

Her automatic professional smile, plastered on, grows wary as she recognizes us. From our first meeting, I got the distinct impression that Erica doesn't care for Ashmore or its college students any more than Lexi does.

"What are you doing here?" she asks Lexi, ignoring Sadie and me.

Lexi takes a breath. "It's been a long day and I think we need pie. A lot of it."

Erica's expression softens as she hears everything that's happened.

"So basically, you saved the day because you all were being antisocial," Erica says.

"I was studying after class," Lexi says. And avoiding our room and me, but she doesn't mention that.

"I was being antisocial," I admit.

"I'm lactose intolerant," Sadie says, studying her menu.

When we look at her, she glances up. "That's why I wasn't in class," she explains. "Too much milk at breakfast."

And for some reason, that strikes all of us, including Erica, as hysterically funny.

"What?" Sadie asks with a shy smile. "It's true."

"That makes it even better," Lexi says between gasps for air.

Eventually we manage to give our order to Erica, including pie.

And once it arrives, Lexi drowns everything with ketchup from a communal bottle, which prompts Sadie to quote a study about the number of germs found on such bottles. And then Erica, overhearing as she passes by with a tray full of dirty dishes, pauses long enough to tell a story about the time someone—*not* her, of course—served a relentlessly complaining customer a hamburger that had been spit on by every member of the kitchen staff.

It's almost seven by the time we leave, but it feels closer to midnight after everything that's happened. The sun is low in the sky, painting everything in a warm orange-gold glow. Sadie actually falls asleep in the truck, as soon as we're in motion. Her weight is warm against my side, with the three of us jammed in the front seat, me in the middle.

Despite the horrible events of this morning, I feel content. This is not a *Felicity* moment. Over the Moon is not Dean & DeLuca coffee shop. Lexi and Sadie are not Julie and Elena. I'm not Felicity. Liam is definitely not Ben.

But that's okay. For the first time in my life, I want the real thing and not the imagined version in my head.

"I'm sorry," I say to Lexi as she drives us to campus. "I shouldn't have lied to you in the first place. Or kept lying to you."

She lifts one shoulder in a weary shrug. Her window is down so she can blow out the smoke from her after-dinner cigarette. "You weren't happy with who you were, Caroline. I understand that better than most, if not the lying part of it. And to be fair, I didn't give you a whole lot of reasons to trust me enough to tell the truth."

"But I should have tried to—"

"Yeah, you should have. But it's not all on you. I should have remembered that people fuck up sometimes. Doesn't always mean they're horrible." She exhales a stream of smoke toward her window, and I wonder if she's thinking about Jordan.

The silence that follows is companionable, the tension between us eased, if not quite gone.

"I don't want to leave Ashmore," I say.

"Then don't," she says.

"It's not up to me anymore. My mom is coming on Sunday. She told me to be packed and ready when she gets here."

"Ouch."

"Yeah."

The evening air rushes past, filling the truck cab with a dull roar.

"So what are you going to do about it?" Lexi asks, startling me.

"I . . . don't know." I hadn't thought of there being anything to do, I guess. Mom is upset, and she's decided I'm leaving, so I'm leaving. Right?

"Caroline, do we have to have this conversation again?" Lexi sighs, but she doesn't sound angry. Not anymore.

I frown, confused. "What are you—"

"Look," she says, flicking her cigarette butt out the window. "It's the same thing."

"I have no idea what you're talking about."

She makes an impatient noise. "You're always thinking about what everyone else wants for you or from you. How to be someone Liam will like, what stories to tell so your mother will feel good."

I bite my lip. She's not wrong.

"You said you started lying because you didn't want your mom to worry. Okay. But you're done with that now. So what do *you* want?"

"I want to stay, but—"

"So what do you need to do to make that happen?" she presses as she makes the turn onto campus.

"I don't know," I say, surprised by the revelation. "I don't know if it's even possible."

Lexi rolls up her window. "Then I guess you have to decide if you're going to *try*," she says dryly, giving me a look.

I roll my eyes. I never should have said that to her (even though I was right). She's going to hold it over my head for the rest of my time at Ashmore.

Even if that's only the next forty-eight hours or so.

Chapter Twenty-Two

My stomach makes a gurgling noise as the yellow cab pulls into the turnaround in front of Brekken. I should have made index cards. I'm always better with index cards.

But index cards aren't normal. And "normal" is the watchword of the day.

Yesterday, after the hospital discharged Tory, we picked her up and got her settled in her room. Lexi checked in with Ayana, giving her an update on Tory, and then went to her study group. I tried to figure out exactly what to do, how to convince my mom that Ashmore was the right place for me. That I was happy here.

Of all the things I considered and discarded—dozens of crumpled balls of notebook paper now littering our floor—the only thing that seemed to make sense was the one thing

I'd never tried before: Tell the truth and stand up for myself, even if it makes my mom unhappy.

I don't want her to feel guilty for the move to Arizona; I never did. She was only doing what she had to do. But I also don't want to be responsible for her feelings forever.

The problem is, ever since my dad left, I've had this precarious, tilting feeling inside, like I'm standing on the edge of an endless drop. It feels like if I say or do the wrong thing, something bad might happen and Mom will be gone too. Or maybe she'll leave, like he did.

So now, being honest and making her unhappy feels way scarier than lying and keeping the peace. This is probably part of what Dr. Wegman has been trying to get me to realize about being myself versus being someone else that I think others will like better, including my mom.

I watch now as my mom gets out of the back of the cab. She's frowning, her forehead creased with lines. When she walks into Brekken, she stops as soon as she sees me.

"Caroline." Mom sounds surprised to find me waiting. She looks me up and down, searching, it seems, for obvious mental or physical infirmities before folding me into a tight hug.

"Hi, Mom," I say against her shoulder. She releases me, smoothing my hair back. Dark circles shadow the area beneath her eyes.

"Are you ready?" she asks. "I asked the cab to wait." She looks around. "Where are your things?"

I take a deep breath. "They're in my room. Where they're supposed to be."

Her expectant expression collapses in disappointment. "Oh, Caroline. We don't have time for this today. You know how long it takes to get to the—"

"I'm not going."

She goes still, radiating disapproval.

"I know you think this is about Liam," I say. "But it's not. It's about me. Yes, I came here for the wrong reasons, but I want to stay for the right ones."

She shakes her head. "Honey—"

"I've made a home here, friends. For the first time in *years*."

Mom winces.

"Arizona was not your fault," I say quickly. "It would have been hard for me no matter where we went. I didn't know how to be comfortable with myself. I still don't, but I'm working on it."

"Which is exactly why I want to bring you home—" she begins.

"It's exactly why I need to *stay*," I say. "You can't fix this for me, Mom. I need to do this for myself."

"But you're not off to a very good start. All the lying, Caroline, even after you promised me—"

I grimace. "I know, I messed up, but I—"

"Caroline!" Lexi calls from behind me.

I turn.

"I thought you were meeting us in the cafeteria," she says as she approaches, giving me a look, silently communicating . . . something.

Meeting? Us? Who? "I, um . . ."

"Hi, Mrs. Sands. Nice to see you again." Lexi extends a hand to my mother.

My mom glances from Lexi to me, in question. *Is this the same girl?*

"Nice to see you, too, Lexi," Mom says, shaking her hand.

"I found her," Lexi shouts over her shoulder in the direction of the cafeteria. Sadie and Tory, still looking a bit pale, emerge from the doors. Followed by Del and Maisy and Matt the Hot TA from Yarn Club.

"Oh, um, hey, guys." I wave lamely and then yank Lexi off to the side of the lobby, away from my mom and everyone else.

"What is this?" I hiss.

"I told them your mom was buying lunch," she says.

"What?"

"Relax—the cafeteria was the best place to watch to see if you needed us. I told them she was worried you weren't settling in and was thinking about pulling you out. They did the rest themselves."

I watch as Del introduces himself to my mom, saying something with expansive gestures while Maisy watches with equal parts amusement and fondness. Mom, looking confused but also charmed, shakes his hand. The fact that he's here must mean Lexi overcame her PBT distaste to reach out to him, and that's . . . that's huge.

My eyes start to water.

"Seeing is believing, Caroline," Lexi says. "If you're trying to prove you belong here, what better way than showing her that? And I thought you could use the help."

"Thank you," I say, my voice cracking.

She steps back warily. "Do not get mushy on me, Sands. This is just . . . what friends do."

I laugh through my tears and wipe under my eyes. "I thought we weren't friends."

"We're roommates," she says, dismissing my words with a wave. "That's even better."

Tory and Sadie are talking to my mom now, with Tory carefully pulling the lid off a see-through container marked PRALINES to offer Mom one.

They are pulling out all the stops.

Which is the kindest, best thing that could possibly happen. But it won't be enough. I know what I have to do.

"I need to finish talking to my mom," I say to Lexi.

"I figured," Lexi says, folding her arms across her chest.

"But at least she now knows you're not alone."

Before I can thank her again, she spins on her heels and charges back toward everyone else. "Come on, guys. Caroline is going to catch up with us in the cafeteria *later*." The emphasis on the last word, in combination with the serious side-eye she gives my mom, is a challenge—or quite possibly a threat.

Then she waves them in the direction of the Brekken cafeteria and leads the way. Matt is a hurried step or two behind her.

"We'll see you in there, darlin'," Tory says with a faint smile, clutching the praline container to her chest as she follows Lexi, and Sadie nods.

Maisy surprises me by wrapping her arm around my shoulders. "I'll save you a seat. Or"—she pauses with a faux-reflective look toward the ceiling—"maybe Del will."

"Maisy," Del mutters in protest, and then Maisy pinches my cheek and lets me go.

Once they're gone, Mom clears her throat. "They're lovely, Caroline . . ."

I feel the "but" coming and rush to cut it off. "And they're real. No Felicity, not a fictional character among them. One hundred percent friends of mine. Well, except maybe Matt. The tall one?" The words spill out faster and faster. "I think he was here because he has a crush on Lexi and would probably do anything she asked, including stabbing himself in a non-vital area with the size thirteens."

Mom frowns at me.

"Those are the big knitting needles," I mumble.

"Be that as it may, Caroline," she says. "It doesn't change anything."

My heart plummets. But instead of a surge of panic closing off my throat and stealing my words, I feel anger urging me to speak.

"It does, actually," I say as calmly as I can. "It proves that I can do it, that I'm okay."

"Of course you're okay, honey; that's not what—"

"No, you don't understand. Part of the problem in Arizona was that I was afraid. I was too scared to be myself and try to find people who might like me, because what if they didn't? What would that say about me? My own father didn't even want to stay in touch after—"

"I told you, it's more complicated than that."

"It's not that hard to make a phone call, Mom. He doesn't want to."

She starts to speak, but I cut her off again. "I'm not finished. It's my fault for lying, my fault for letting that fear beat me. But worrying that I was disappointing you made it worse. I kept thinking that I was letting you down by not being who you wanted and expected me to be. All those stories about the friends you made in high school, the activities—"

Her lips are pressed into a thin, pale line. "I was trying to help."

"I know. You were worried about me. But it felt more like pressure to hurry up and make things okay." I rub my palms down the sides of my jeans. "It felt like if I didn't live up to what you needed me to be, that I wouldn't be good enough for you, either. And I . . . couldn't. I couldn't lose you, too."

Her mouth opens in a small, shocked O and she rocks back a step as if I've slapped her. "I didn't . . . Caroline, I—"

"I didn't want you to be upset anymore." My voice breaks, and I wipe at the sudden rush of tears filling my eyes. "And I didn't want you to be stuck with a freak of a daughter, on top of everything else. So yeah, I lied. I made shit up. But I did it because I was scared. Scared of being alone, of being a disappointment, of being rejected again. And lying made me feel safer."

Mom reaches out and pulls me into a hug, one so tight I can barely breathe. "I would never walk away from you. Ever. Do you hear me? No matter what is happening, I love you."

"I love you, too," I say against her shoulder, hiccuping. Beneath the familiar scent of the Dove soap she uses to wash her face, I also catch a hint of the Japanese Cherry Blossom hand sanitizer and lotion she keeps on her desk at the hospital. Both are very much my mom.

She takes a step back but grasps my hands to maintain the connection. "Caroline, what are we going to do?" she asks wearily, but it seems a genuine question rather than a rhetorical one.

"I don't know," I admit. "I understand why you don't trust me and why you want me to come home. But that won't fix anything. Nobody has it all figured out, and—"

"Believe me, I know that, honey." She lets one of my hands go to dab a finger under her eye.

"But I didn't. I thought everyone else had the answers, and I was the one falling behind. But now that I'm here . . . I want to stay. I want to do what I couldn't do before. Please." I squeeze her hand. "Please."

She wants to say no. I can see it written in the lines on her forehead. "Everyone makes mistakes, Caroline," she says eventually. "The hard part is not knowing ahead of time which decisions will be the ones you regret."

I want to push, to tell her she won't regret letting me stay, but with effort I manage to keep my mouth shut.

"So," Mom says, "sometimes you have to choose what kind of regret you can live with."

I understand that, more than she probably realizes. I'm just not sure that the regret she can live with is one I'll be able to survive as well.

As soon as I walk into the cafeteria, six faces turn toward me expectantly. Lexi, Matt, and Sadie are on one side of the table, and Del, Maisy, and Tory are on the other. There's an empty chair at the end, between Del and Lexi, waiting for me.

It strikes me, then, how different my life is now from three months ago at my graduation party, an event marked by uneaten food, unoccupied tables.

Here there's only one empty spot, and it's *for* me. It makes me want to pinch myself to see if this is reality.

"Caroline?" Tory asks, crossing her arms over her chest, like she's hugging herself. The back of her left hand bears a bruise from her IV, now in stunning shades of yellow and green.

"What did she say?" Lexi asks, putting her fork down.

"Trial basis, until the end of the semester," I say. I'll have to check in with her and Wegman more frequently and possibly look into finding someone on campus to talk to about anything that comes up. "But I'm staying."

Tory cheers quietly. "That's great news!"

"Well, it's something, at least," Lexi says, sounding annoyed.

"It's everything," I correct her, my smile so wide I feel foolish, but I don't care. "And it's way more than I would have gotten on my own. Thank you." I turn to the rest of the table. "Thank you, all of you guys. For showing up. I know it's weird and you didn't have to—"

"My parents used to send care packages twice a week," Del says. "I'm the first kid in our family to go to college. I think they would have moved here if they could have."

"It's true," Maisy affirms. "He had so many packets of ramen, we used them to build forts during the water-gun war. Until Mayer ate a bunch of them."

"The ramen," Del adds. "Not the water guns."

He pulls out the chair next to him, and I drop into it gratefully.

Then the conversation shifts back to whatever they were talking about before. Maisy and Matt are arguing about some cartoon—or anime, possibly—that I've never heard of before, with Del dropping in comments occasionally. Sadie is urging Tory to drink more water, while Tory rolls her eyes.

It is both spectacularly normal and totally new: this place, these people gathered around me. And by no means perfect. But I kind of want a picture to commemorate the moment.

It's the start of the life I was searching for, even though it's nothing like what I expected. Liam didn't change my life—I did. And that's so much better.

"You okay?" Lexi asks, stabbing a forkful of lettuce as if it has personally offended her.

"Yeah," I say. "Just happy to finally be here."

ACKNOWLEDGMENTS

I wrote this book because I kept hearing from kids who were like me: introverted, a bit shy, maybe not great at joining in activities or reaching out to others. One of them told me he was looking forward to college because he'd have a chance to catch up on his Netflix queue. And I heard *myself* in those words.

I went to college determined to reinvent myself, just like Caroline. And I, too, took great comfort in fictional characters and their worlds. Luckily for me, I was "adopted" by an extrovert pretty early on and, through her, found people I could be myself with. I'd never before had friendships that lasted more than a few years or withstood a change in location, but these friends have been with me now for more than twenty years. I wanted to show the start of that same thing happening for Caroline. I wanted to give hope to the others who are/were like me.

I'm so grateful to Christian Trimmer, my editor, friend, and fellow *Felicity* fanatic for giving me a chance to tell this story and working with me so closely as I flailed through a couple of drafts. A huge thank-you to Catherine Laudone for guiding me through the final draft and being awesome.

Thank you to my amazing agent, Suzie Townsend, for not

batting an eye when I said I wanted to write a college-set YA about a girl who's obsessed with a twenty-year-old TV show. You are the best! My thanks also to Sara Stricker for all her help, and to everyone at New Leaf Literary & Media.

To Amy V. Bland and Kimberly Damitz, for dinners, drinks, and dough nuggets.

Thank you to Lydia Kang, my friend and fellow author, for helping me figure out a profession for Caroline's mother. (Any mistakes in the description of such are mine. I took liberties.)

Thank you to Linnea Sinclair for being my critique partner, sounding board, and sanity-check person. To my parents, Stephen and Judy Barnes, who live through every book with me: tears, frustrations, and joys—thank you for always picking up when I call! To my sister and fellow Valpo grad, Susan, who listens patiently and makes me laugh. To my brother, Michael, and his family—Jess, Grace, and Josh—for all their support. And to Age, Dana, and Quinn, for introducing me to Last Night on Earth (#teamzombie) and for so many conversations about this book!

Turn the page for a special excerpt from Stacey Kade's

For This Life Only.

ACCORDING TO MY DAD, Christmastime is family time. But after eleven straight days at home, I can tell you, it starts to feel a little more like prison time. I love my family, but there's only so much togetherness any sane person can stand.

And now, postdinner on a Saturday night, staring down the barrel of day twelve, I was ready to crawl out of my skin to see someone I wasn't related to.

"You have to let me take the Jeep tonight," I said, pushing open Eli's door without bothering to knock.

"What?" Perched on the edge of the bed, Eli slammed his nightstand drawer shut, a fleeting look of guilt on his face. Our face, technically, since we were identical. Blond hair, blue eyes, and ears that stuck out a little too far—that was us.

"What are you doing?" I asked, frowning at him.

"Nothing." Eli stood and pushed past me, heading toward the bathroom. "And forget it. I have stuff to do tonight."

"Right." I snorted, following him. "Like Leah?"

He paused to look over his shoulder at me, his mouth a tight line.

"Oh, come on, I was kidding!" I protested.

Okay, so maybe antagonizing Eli about his perfectly perfect girlfriend wasn't the best way to go about getting a favor, tempting as it was. The two of them were made for each other: the pastor's good son and the church council president's daughter who wanted to be a missionary. But they were also both rule-followers to the extreme and annoyingly exacting on themselves and everyone else.

Hey, whatever worked for them. I wasn't the one not-sleeping with her.

"Why don't you—" Eli began, as he flipped on the bathroom light.

"I can't ask Zach. Everybody's already over there." I leaned in the doorway, while Eli rummaged in the medicine cabinet. "I can drop you off at Leah's on the way," I offered.

The dusty pine smell of the drying-out Christmas tree downstairs mixed with the cinnamon candles my mom insisted on burning for "holiday ambience" was starting to get to me. Made me feel like the walls were closing in. I needed to be somewhere where I could breathe and be myself, even if it was only for a few hours.

"I said no."

I raised my eyebrows. "Seriously?"

He pulled drawers open and slammed them shut, looking for something.

"Fine," I said. "Then ask Leah to come get you. She has a car, right?"

He shook his head. "It's not fair to ask her to do that—"

"At the last minute, I know. But it's also not fair that we have to share a car when she could be using hers to get you," I pressed. "Division of resources or whatever."

"Not everything is about you, Jace," Eli said. Then he scowled. "Sarah!" he bellowed. "You left the toothpaste cap off." He pulled the capless and nearly flat toothpaste tube from Sarah's drawer. "Again!"

I stared at him. "What's wrong with you?" This was not my normally-even-tempered-to-the-extreme brother.

"It makes a mess, and it's gross. I hate that," he muttered.

"Jesus says not to hate." Sarah arrived in the doorway in time to make the pronouncement in her best Sunday-school-student voice. Her reddish-blond hair was sticking up in all directions, with a Disney Princess hair-thingy clinging for dear life on the side. She'd probably been pretending to be a pony again, which usually involved placing a blanket over her head as a mane.

"Yeah, well, I'm pretty sure Jesus would have been a proponent of putting the cap back on." Eli loaded toothpaste on his brush with a grimace.

"Actually, I'm pretty sure clumpy toothpaste wouldn't have been an issue. Son of God, water into wine and all," I pointed out quickly, in the name of keeping the peace and getting back to the main point. Me, taking the Jeep.

"See?" Sarah stuck her tongue out at Eli, and he rolled his eyes at her.

"E, please," I said. "I'm begging you. Mom is talking about another round of family Scrabble, and Sarah cheats more than I do. I can't take it."

"I do not cheat!" Sarah folded her arms across her chest, her lower lip jutting out. "I'm six. I don't know as many words as you do."

"You know better than to spell 'cat' with a 'q,'" I said. She'd gotten away with it because my parents thought it was adorable.

She gave me a sly grin. "Maybe."

"See? Cheater." I ruffled her hair further, and she squealed in mock protest.

Eli paused in brushing his teeth. "Won't Kylie be there?" he asked me quietly, around a mouthful of foam.

In spite of myself, I stiffened. "Probably."

He spat in the sink and rinsed his brush. "If you just talked to her—"

I grabbed the hand towel off the ring on the wall and chucked it at the side of his head.

"You missed a spot," I said, gesturing to the glob of toothpaste at the corner of his mouth. He'd go out like that if I didn't stop him. And it was bad enough that he was wearing his church camp T-shirt out in public. I could see the big block letters of last year's theme and Bible verse on the back through his button-down.

SEE YOU ON THE OTHER SIDE

For God so loved the world, that he gave his only Son, that whoever believes in him should not perish but have eternal life.

John 3:16

"Kylie doesn't come over anymore," Sarah said. "Why not? I liked her."

"Aren't you supposed to be getting your pajamas on?" Eli asked Sarah as he wiped his mouth. He took his role as the oldest—three minutes ahead of me—a little too seriously sometimes. Though in this case, I appreciated the diversion.

"You're not Mom or Dad," Sarah said. "You can't tell me what to do." Then she turned her attention back to me. "Did Kylie die?" she asked with a curiosity that bordered on weird and/or inappropriate. "Did God kill her?"

I groaned. A couple of weeks ago, my mom had taken Sarah to the funeral and graveside service of a longtime church member, Mrs. Gallagher. Normally we didn't get dragged to funerals, even the ones my dad presided over, but because my mom had to be there and Eli and I were in school, Sarah had to go. It was her first one.

Apparently, my dad had used the standard language about God calling a church member home, and that somehow got twisted in Sarah's brain. Since then, she kept popping up with these really bizarre questions about death and dying.

"Sarah, death is nothing to fear," Eli said. "If you listen to the scriptures, you'll see that Jesus talks about going ahead of us—"

I made an impatient noise. "When you die, you go toward the bright light, and Jesus and the rest of us will be there, waiting for you. Then everyone is in heaven and it's all good. End of story."

Eli sighed. "That's not really doctrinally—"

I rolled my eyes. "Kylie is fine," I said to Sarah. "She decided she liked the guys better at St. Luke's is all."

Sarah frowned. "Why?"

"I don't know, Sares." And right now, I didn't care. At least, not as much. I'd rather take the risk of running into my ex-girlfriend at a party than stay in one more night.

"That's not nice," Sarah said after a moment of contemplation.

"Gotta agree with you there," I said, and she tackled my leg in a sideways hug.

With another heavy sigh, Eli regarded both of us, his expression relenting. "Okay," he said, hanging the hand towel in the ring on the wall.

I straightened up. "I can have the—"

"I'll drop you off," he said. "But you have to tell Mom and Dad and find your own way home."

"Got it, not a problem," I said, relieved. Though I might have been overestimating the ease with which I'd accomplish both of those things. But one obstacle at a time.

"Jace, you should stay home," Sarah whined, clinging to my leg. "It's Christmas."

"Nope," I said. "Not anymore." Thank God.

My parents had a ritual for the Saturday evenings that weren't filled with wedding receptions, fund-raiser potlucks, or emergency calls. One glass of wine apiece, a big bowl of popcorn to share, and an old movie that would end by ten so my dad could be up and at the church by six a.m.

"Everything's ready for tomorrow?" my dad asked from

the couch, lowering the remote to focus his attention on Eli as soon as we rounded the corner into the family room.

Technically, we were both working at the church as interns this year, but everyone knew Eli was more into it than I was. Scratch that; he was into it and I wanted out of it. He would be the one to join my dad at the church as soon as he was done with college and seminary. Good for him, not for me.

"Yes. Did a mic check and replaced the batteries in your pack. Delores said Carey Daniels called in sick for acolyting, so I called down the sub list until I got someone. And the staple cartridge was replaced this afternoon, so the bulletins for all three services are done."

Dad nodded. "Good."

"Jacob?" my mom asked from her corner of the couch, taking in my jacket with a frown.

"Eli's going to drop me off at Zach's," I said.

"I thought we were going to do a final round of Scrabble." She gestured to the game set up on the coffee table. "We've already got the first Indiana Jones queued up. Sarah will be in bed before the face-melting part." The last was said in a pseudo-whisper.

"I heard that," Sarah shouted from upstairs. "I want to see!" Yep, that was my sister.

"Maybe tomorrow after church?" I offered to my mom, resisting the urge to shift my weight from foot to foot.

My dad sighed and sat up, moving to the edge of the couch.

I braced myself for the coming lecture.

"Jacob, if you're going out, don't give me a reason to hear bad reports. No drinking, no carousing, no breaking town curfew. Appearances are important. Because no matter how well you think you know everyone there . . ."

"Someone is always watching," Eli and I recited obediently, though my teeth were clenched.

"Exactly. And we have an obligation to be good examples." Theoretically, my dad was speaking to both of us, but his gaze was focused on me.

Because I was the one trying to have a life outside the church, to be someone other than just the pastor's less-good son.

It was something outsiders never understood. We didn't get to be individuals. We were Pastor Micah's family, a portfolio of my dad's work, shining examples of his leadership, his discipline, his faith at work in his own home. Our successes were his. Our mistakes—from a wrinkled shirt to a failing grade—were potential watch signs of trouble within the ministry.

God, as my dad's vague omnipresent "boss," might be forgiving, but the members of Riverwoods Bible Church weren't always so open-minded.

I was the "troubled one," by virtue of breaking curfew

a few times, getting busted at *one* party my freshman year, achieving lower grades than my twin, and generally being less involved in Riverwoods than Eli. (If there was a Bible study, he was a part of it.)

In other words, normal crap, stuff that would probably earn a week or two of grounding or maybe only a raised eyebrow and a scolding in a regular family.

But we weren't regular, unfortunately.

For the grades, my parents got me a tutor, and for the lack of involvement, they stuck me in the joint internship with Eli. But for the curfew violations and the party, my dad had enlisted me in community service at the Riverwoods food pantry for months. Part of that whole "being a good example" thing. I'd just finished paying for my last infraction. And with baseball practice starting up again in a couple of months, I did not want another session.

In a year and a half, I'd be done, out of here. On a baseball scholarship, I hoped, to somewhere else, where I wouldn't have to worry about anybody but me.

"Jace will be fine," Eli said with a confident nod at my dad, and I felt a rush of gratitude toward my brother, for extending his good credit over me. Whatever had been bugging him earlier seemed to be gone now. "Don't worry."

As always, Eli's casual word was more convincing than

my most earnest promises. Not that I bothered to make them very often anymore.

"Home by ten thirty," my dad said, pointing the remote at me. "Not a second later. You need to be at early service at least fifteen minutes before the prelude."

"Of course," I said quickly. Although at that point, I would have agreed to anything to get out.

Leap into summer with these

Swoon-worthy

reads by *New York Times* bestselling author Morgan Matson.

PRINT AND EBOOK EDITIONS AVAILABLE

From SIMON & SCHUSTER BFYR

simonandschuster.com/teen